ADVANCE PRAISE

CHOCOLATE BURNOUT

"A high point of the novel is Chantel and Astrid's friendship. Their rapport—and love of chocolate—has genuine warmth and humor."

— Valerie Kalfrin, award-winning journalist and contributor to The Hollywood Reporter

Chocolate Burnout, an African American Literature Book Club Top Ten Seller, is a charming and nuanced look into interracial relationships with a message as crucial today as it was in the 90s, when Emunah La-Paz's Chocolate Burnout project first came to be.

— Meriah Murphey, Simon & Schuster

"Chocolate Burnout is a humorous novel dealing with the aspects of interracial relationships."

— Sophisticate's Black Hair Care Guide Magazine

Chocolate Burnout recognized in the <u>Mavin</u> Foundation database of books by authors who touch on interracial relationships.

HUBBBARD SMALL PRESS
2487 Gilbert,
AZ 85295

ISBN: **9780578994857**
Library of Congress Control Number: 2019952943

Printed in the United States of America.

Cover art by Sonia Abril Medina, "Samzdesignz
Interiors designed by Harini Rajagopalan
Editors: Valerie Kalfrin, Judy Vorfled, Aleks Montijah

This book is not intended as a substitute for the physiological advice of physicians.
The reader should regularly consult a physician in matters relating to his/her mental
health and particularly with respect to any symptoms that may require diagnosis or
medical attention.

The information and views set out in this publication do not necessarily reflect the
official opinion of Hubbard Small Press Publications and the author. Neither
Hubbard Small Press Publications, the author and bodies, nor any person acting on
their behalf may be held responsible for the use that may be made of the
information contained therein.

"Everyone has inside them a piece of good news. The good news is you don't know how great you can be! How much you can love! What you can accomplish! And what your potential is."

— Anne Frank

CHOCOLATE BURNOUT
PART ONE

EMUNAH LA-PAZ

To: Faith

Acknowledgements

Special thanks go to my husband, Daniel Hubbard for his patience, understanding, faith, and most of all the encouragement he has given me.

CHOCOLATE BURNOUT

PART: ONE

CHAPTER 1

Chantel

Who would have thought I'd be here at peace within the tenable core of my own intricate being? At one point, I strived to have it all: a loving husband, two adorable children, and the Tuscan-style house of my dreams centered within the scope of one of Seattle's beautiful master-planned communities, surrounded by greenbelts and picket fences set amid gently rolling hills. What a life! And at the time, pride whispered, "You deserve it!"

Yet, in all honesty, I reaped exactly what I deserved, a life of complete and utter chaos. I must admit, I was self-centered back then, unable to define the other side of the story in life due to the hindering fact that I could not escape the only point of view in life that mattered, which was my point of view. My addictions brought forth sins that transcended into buried regret, weighing me down like an aimless ship, unable to keep afloat within my dark sea of existence, masked in taunting waves of compulsion and recapitulating storms. I've come to realize that some people actually enjoy a life of pandemonium. I'm ashamed to admit that I used to be one of those people who enjoyed a good storm every now and then; however, I am also one of those people who honestly believe that everyone has a promising, valiant novel within, a unique story that has yet to be unveiled and that ends with the most sought-after gem, the asset of peace.

My novel had been deterred, so to speak, due to the fact that I was too caught up inside of my own memoir, centered on my private, addictive, captivity of the mind. In spite of my egoistical ways, I had beneficial friends who cared about me, devoted aides who tried to free me from my own self-destructive behavior, and in the midst of it all, I failed to perceive that these compassionate people within my close-knit circle also suffered through their own insecurities and addictions in life. And yet I chose to focus on who I was trained up to be in the eyes of an overambitious older sister, whom I looked up to as my own mother. A Successful businesswoman out of Seattle, Washington. I prefer to call this juncture in my life stage one, a period in time when no one is being honest with anyone, a time of life in which I was not being honest with myself. I was simply going through the motions, trying to reach a level of "completeness" or "purpose." Yet deep down inside, there was a void, a restless addiction inside that led to my betrayal as I treaded through my daily routine. At times, I could feel the discomfort of existence, but I chose to write it off as if it were comparable to a mincing, misfit sock trapped inside the toe of my shoe. No one knew my inner discomfort that I'd often hope was analogous to an ill-fitting sock, that I could discard at any time; however, no one could remove the disquieting pain within the corners of my mind and soul, not even time.

I had trusted that stage one of my life would lead me effortlessly through the hospitable doors of stage two, and from there, my novel would emerge into fullness, defining my purpose and goodwill in life. Yet needless to say, stage one of my life was a complete and utter train wreck in which I had now found myself in limbo, somewhat imprisoned in stage two, lost in quandary, unable to move forward, deliberating, trying to pinpoint exactly what went wrong. Eventually, the daunting realization became the reflection of my own demise, and in order to uncover the exact root of the problem, I had to honestly reminisce to genuinely reveal my insecurities and my selfish motives. Positioning these inadequate feelings directly where they   once stood was imperative in order to find the kind of peace strong enough to calm the raging storm from within.

It was up to me to be authentic without fail. I had to acknowledge those who were willing to put their lives on the line in order to help me move past my private dependencies. This task would not be easy because this kind of straightforward mission challenged my prideful heart, pressing me to make room inside my closed heart in order to define how others perceived my character. Allowing   constructive   criticism   to   speak into my life was a bitter and humbling pill to swallow. Not many people are willing to look at their past intentions, relationships, or friendships in hopes of mending the past in order to move forward with peace of mind; then again, not many people live long enough to seize the opportunity.

In stage one of my life, according to close friends, the ones who knew me the best, I had a weak heart for men who lacked heart and soul. And yes, back then, in the 1990's men and unadulterated chocolate!

My boyfriend at the time was Cameron, whom I allowed to control my heart and bank account. I built Cameron up to be more than who he really was. I wanted desperately to mold him into the man I thought he was capable of becoming. Yet the more I tried to build Cameron up, the more he succeeded in tearing me down, emotionally. Cameron went back and forth between construction jobs and women, yet he enjoyed photography as a hobby; however, to make him sound more appealing to family and friends, I shared that he was an up-and-coming photographer. I knew full well that his best job title yet was professional heartbreaker. I had allowed this man to lie, cheat, and steal his way into my heart, and I had no one to blame except myself.

In a new, exciting world where women were molded and proud to do for themselves without the support of a man, I had a hard time grasping this concept. On the outside, I appeared to be one of those independent women who could take care of business at work and relax at home without the need for a companion. However, deep down inside, I severely lacked that self-determining quality. Being single got old quick! Deep down inside, I was the complete opposite of the independent woman. I was needy, and my existence felt undefined without someone to love. A dog or a cat did not fill that thrusting void. I desired to be wanted and valued by the opposite sex. Call me crazy, but I loved cuddling on the couch and renting Blockbuster videos back in the day. I loved fussing over men. Making the male counterparts in my life feel special, I thought, was my strong suit. The simplicity of kicking back with my significant other gave me purpose. This new breed of independent woman found comfort by lying next to the fireplace with a warm cup of hot chocolate and a book. As for me, snuggling next to a warm, strong body on a rainy Seattle night was my definition of contentment. The women I knew were OK with being by themselves until they could land Mr. Right, and I was the kind of woman who settled for Mr. Good Enough, just in case my Mr. Right got distracted and disoriented, lost deep within a jungle of uncommitted men.

Deep down inside, I knew that I had to let go of my uncommitted man; however, my hopeful side kept holding on for an illusion of what could be. The way I saw it back then was that Cameron could've have been the perfect guy if he hadn't been a lying, cheating, immoral human being. But in spite of my hopeful side, my best friend, Astrid, thought I was one of those desperate, mentally beaten down women showcased on one of those midday talk shows. As far as she was concerned, Cameron was a huge waste of time. Astrid thought I was delusional for holding on to Cameron, but back then, I viewed my relationship quite differently. I was not delusional; I was dedicated! I considered myself to be a patient princess who was allowing my wayward frog time to change into the perfect prince that I knew he could become.

Yes, committed and successful till the end was how I perceived myself back then. I felt that I was destined to do greater things in life careerwise, as well, besides sitting behind an office desk and attending seemingly pointless meetings all day long. I wanted to travel more, take time out to see the world with someone who meant the world to me and I to him. Yet every morning, my dreams of what could be transcended into a reality show of what was. My happy visions of Cameron actually holding down a permanent job and contributing to the household and luxurious vacations abroad while popping chocolate-covered cherry bon-bons into my mouth as I soaked in the sun's rays upon our private yacht disintegrated into thin air, destroyed by the sound of Cameron's snores caused by sleep apnea. Cameron's snores were louder than my faint alarm clock, yet the unsettling noise forced me out of bed, giving me enough time to take a refreshing shower. I spent countless times in that steamy shower, mulling over my thoughts, trying to actually figure out ways to make my dreams a reality, yet the only reality close to my desired vision was the chocolate-covered cherry bon-bons that lay stashed away inside my desk at work. My mind wandered so much that I found myself racing against time on my way to work, trying to pull my outfit together. Even though I did not feel like a high-profile corporate woman, I desperately tried to look the part, yet lately my clothes weren't fitting over my curves in a flattering manner, and my hair had a mind of its own as I struggled to maintain the thick, fluffy auburn locks as one ginormous ponytail.

Once that task was out of the way, I'd scarf down a piece of cold toast, saved by the savory taste of chocolate cream. I yearned to smother brittle bread in an orange and chocolate marmalade, followed by strong black coffee mixed with chocolate creamer. Yes, chocolate was the answer to all of my inadequacies. It would have been nice if Cameron were to greet me in the morning with an affectionate kiss and have my breakfast waiting for me, being that I was the breadwinner of the relationship, but Cameron was not that kind of guy. So to fill that morning lack of warmth, I turned to the only instantly fulfilling warm-heartedness love in the present time, chocolate love.

In those days, I rode the Metro to work and let dear Cameron drive my car to his sporadic job sites. I worked extra hard for every comfort I had in life, and one of my prized possessions at the time was a BMW. That car was like my well-kept child. The interior was sleek and inviting; it was like driving a comfortable lounge to work. The day that I allowed Cameron to start driving my most prized possession, I should have gotten my head examined. However I was determined to turn Cameron into marriage material, and in a marriage, mine becomes ours. Even though Cameron had nothing to offer at the time, I had hoped that one day, all of my generosity would pay off, and I would have reaped the harvest of being a devoted girlfriend turned fiancée turned wife. There was no doubt about it; back then I sure was dedicated! The Metro dropped me off right in Kent at the entrance of Litton Technologies, where I worked to support the dreams that I had in place. I was the manager of human resources, a prestigious title with overwhelming responsibilities. On this day, I was feeling overworked and undervalued, not to mention my hair—ugh! Little did I know that this day would be a turning point in my life. As I entered my office, I spotted a dozen red roses artfully arranged in a cut-glass vase sitting in the middle of my desk. I was shocked. Cameron had finally realized the value of my love for me, or so I thought.

Instead I discovered that card came from a less-desirable acquaintance: Eugene. Now, Eugene was a nice guy; however, he was not soft on the eyes. I can remember all the hot men in my life whom I referred to as a *tall drink of water*, but when referring to Eugene, a different substance entered my mind. Eugene was not in that category. Eugene was more like a short shot of castor oil...not my type! However, it did not stop the poor man from trying.

Eugene and Cameron used to be roommates; however, Cameron could not keep up with the rent. Eugene was always talking about how he could not wait to kick Cameron out. One day, Cameron showed up at Kent, furious with Eugene for throwing his stuff out and changing the locks. As for me, the first time I laid eyes on Cameron, I had never seen such a work of art in the flesh. Even though Cameron was highly upset with Eugene, there was a masculinity about the man that seemed to override the sensible side of my moral values, and before I knew it, I found myself offering Cameron and his shortcomings a place to stay—out of the goodness of my heart, of course.

Eugene was very upset with my decision, and the only other person equally upset with my poor judgment was my good friend Astrid, who was supposed to move in with me. However, I felt that I was doing a good deed by letting a man who had fallen on hard times move in. Sure, some may argue that I did not know Cameron. He was a stranger who had been proven to be unreliable through a reliable coworker, Eugene. Nonetheless, I felt that everyone deserved a second chance. I felt that I was being a Good Samaritan. Of course, Cameron was not all beat up and down on his luck, unlike the stranger in the Good Samaritan parable. I'm sure he had a friend who could have taken him in, but I felt the powerful need to step up, and so that's what I did. Nonetheless, Eugene and my friend Astrid were furious with me. All the while, Eugene kept trying to explain that I had made a big mistake by taking Cameron in, and my friend Astrid called me a desperate jackass who lacked direction. I could understand why Astrid was so upset with my choice. After all, Cameron had swept in on her roommate opportunity that had been promised to her first, and I should have honored her position. Not only was she trustworthy and reliable; she was one of my best friends. But at the time, Astrid's opinion did not matter. The only opinion that counted was mine. I was in search of the perfect male mate, a possible husband whom I could start a family with, and Astrid was one of those independent women who had become content with being single. Astrid was ready to move in and start her stray cat collection, and I, on the other hand, had found hope in Cameron, and from there, his beautiful body and bad habits moved in with me.

The fact that Cameron was now my live-in boyfriend did not stop Eugene from pursuing me relentlessly, and I must admit that I admired Eugene's persistent attempts to win me over. The beautiful flowers, his thoughtful measures, such as when he insisted on driving me home when Cameron could not commit to picking me up after work on time, showed his compassion for me. Without a doubt, Eugene was thoughtful and accessible toward my every need. Eugene had all of his ducks in a row, he was able to travel anywhere, he had planned to have a house built in a well-respected community, and I'm pretty sure he would be open to feeding me chocolate-covered cherry bon-bons on a private yacht. The only problem was that Eugene was not Cameron. Nonetheless, Eugene tried incessantly to step up as the man in my life. One particular day stands out constantly. On this day, I was feeling unfulfilled and doubtful, and on this odd day, Eugene's attempt to win me over with his array of flowers annoyed me to the brink of insanity.

"Miss Reed, Eugene Howard is here to see you. May I send him in?"

Oh well, there's no better time than the present, I thought. "Send him in, please, Yvonne."

The door flew open, and Eugene waddled in. Giving him an uneasy smile, I stood up. "Thanks for the roses, Eugene."

"They're beautiful, aren't they?" he exclaimed. "But not as beautiful as your smile."

This was not going to be easy. "Eugene, your gesture is sweet; however, I can't accept them."

"And why not?"

"You know why not, Eugene. I'm involved with—"

"A lunatic," he interrupted. "When was the last time you received roses or had someone take you out for a fine meal at an exclusive restaurant? When was the last time someone drew a nice hot bubble bath for you? Come on, Chantel. *Tell me.* Obviously, none of this has ever happened with Cameron because not only is he always broke, but frankly, he's not interested in *your* quality of life! If he was, then he would take care of his manly duties by hooking you up with a hairdresser. Chantel, you are a businesswoman! What kind of man lets his woman walk around with her hair pulled back in an out-of-control ponytail?"

I held my hand up. "That's enough, Eugene. Hold it right there. My social life, Cameron's financial affairs, and our relationship have nothing to do with you. Please try to understand. You and I work in the same facility. I find it very unprofessional for anyone to try to spark a romantic relationship with a fellow employee!"

"We work in two different facilities, Chantel. I'm a technician, and you work in the office," he said with a sulk.

"I don't care. People will talk, and it could end up costing both of us our jobs! I'm warning you, Eugene. No more roses. If this happens again, I will consider it harassment...and we don't want that, do we?"

Eugene resembled a little puppy that had just been slapped in the face with a newspaper for wetting the floor.

The intercom interrupted our conversation.

"Miss Reed, Janeva Blake is on line one, and Astrid Hatcher is on line two. Should I place them on hold?"

"Yes, please."

"Well," Eugene said with a sigh, "I guess that's my cue to leave." He grabbed the vase from my desk. I hated to see the beautiful roses go. The last time I had received flowers was on prom night. I won't go into how long ago that was.

Before leaving, he turned and said, "When you feel like being treated like a real woman, you know where to find me."

Slamming the door behind him, I mulled over that remark for a second. A real woman. Of course I want to be treated like a real woman. Was it that obvious that I was being ignored?

Pondering the event, I made my way over to a full-length mirror in my office that stood idly by. I had hoped that the mirror would help me clean up my appearance for special business meetings and those last-minute dates that never occurred. Instead, the tall mahogany crested mirror seemed to taunt me. The mirror that was supposed to make me feel visually confident only exploited my love for chocolate. Every ounce gained made all of my outfits appear unflattering. It was obvious that I had put on some weight. Even though I considered myself to be in a relationship, my appetite for chocolate had not subsided. If anything, the fear of losing Cameron had sparked a dependency that only chocolate could pacify. I had the urge to try to lose some weight in hopes that Cameron would find me desirable enough to marry someday. Cameron never told me specifically that he was unhappy about my size, but he didn't have to. Every time we went out in public, his brown, intense eyes would gravitate toward women who were smaller in size or more toned than I. His wandering eye bothered me. After all, I wanted to be the only woman to dominate his attention.

Trying to smooth down my locks a bit, I rushed back over to the desk and picked up the receiver. I took Janeva Blake's call first, a feisty friend I had hung out with. However, as time moved on, our differences caused friction, making Janeva the "wrong" type of friend. Nonetheless, I learned that the wrong kind of friends can be just as instructive as the right kind of friend in light of what not to do in life. At that time, Janeva was a part of my life, and out of respect for our friendship, we chatted for a while. She was trying to coax me to try out some new jazz restaurant that had just opened and to stop by for one of her women gatherings. Not sure how I would feel after work, I told her I'd give her a call back. I enjoyed Janeva's friendship at the time—she was fun and entertaining to hang around—yet she was not the friend built to help sustain the unforeseen issues ahead.

Tribulations in life will either refine true bonds or destroy them, which led me to my friend Astrid, the kind of friend who challenged me to grow and pulled me through the inconvenient stages of life kicking and screaming. Astrid had a tough-love approach, and at times, I did not appreciate her forthright methodology, which often caused conflict between us. Nonetheless, hearing from Astrid could be refreshing, yet only when I was in search of honest answers, which was never, at the time. Reluctantly I took her call on line two. "What's going on, Astrid?"

"I was about to hang up! I've been waiting for a while, and you know full well what's going on, Cocoa!" *Cocoa* was the nickname that Astrid had honored me with, because back then, I could devour any dessert made of the tantalizing, sweet liquid escape.

"Are you coming over to help me with the chocolate festival event?"

Astrid and I had a bond woven through the sweet fate of chocolate thanks to pastry culinary school. However, once I realized that I had developed a love for eating every chocolate delicacy known to mankind more so than mastering the actual art of baking, I dropped out. Astrid, however, turned her love for chocolate into a well-known business opportunity that put her name on the map as one of the most respected chocolatiers in Seattle. When she completed pastry school, without a doubt, Astrid's talents were wholesome for my starving soul yet bad for my expanding waistline. Every once in a while, Astrid would invite me over to her cozy crib to experience her latest sweet creations for the annual chocolate festival held in downtown Seattle. The two of us would meet up to entertain our chocolate addictions while indulging in a glass of Chenin Blanc.

Astrid and I were inseparable at times thanks to our chocolate love affair. However, we had drifted apart due to my unfavorable relationship with Cameron. After I allowed him to move in, Astrid felt as if I had "kicked her to the curb over some random dude," which were her exact words. This was not true. Even though I adored my dear friend, I felt the need to make a bold move toward a lifelong partner for the sake of marriage. I longed to have a baby, and soon. Astrid did not share the same marriage dream, and if our fate had been left in her hands, we would have ended up a couple of little old gray ladies sipping on wine, hoarding chocolate, and hosting a shelter for abandoned cats. I wanted to get married. I wanted a family. The thought of not achieving these goals soon in life frightened me. Yet Astrid was one of those women who could do without a man or dreams of family. As far as she was concerned, men were a waste of time. Astrid often shared that she would rather gain weight eating chocolate than give birth to a child who would turn on her during his or her teenage years.

Even though Astrid was not happy about my pursuit to make Cameron my husband and the father of my children someday, she still honored the fact that I loved helping her with her new chocolate inventions for the upcoming festival. I also sensed that this was her way of trying to save our fragile friendship. "It's that time of year!" she announced. "You think you can break away from Cameron for just one night and help me with the festival? I invited Serenity over, too!"

Even though I wanted to help out, Cameron and I were going through a rough patch. I had to live with the man, and I didn't want to return to house full of tension. It seemed as if we were fighting over the most irrelevant things lately. I really wanted to mend things between the two of us, which meant that I had to turn down Astrid. "Aw, Astrid, that sounds good. I'm in real need of a chocolate fix, but I have plans."

Astrid gave a frustrated sigh. "Look, Cocoa, just because you and Cameron are an item now does not mean you should kick your girlfriends to the curb."

This conversation was mirroring the conversation that I had had before with Janeva. Even though Janeva and I were not close, they both had a similar way of making me feel bad about the men in my life, so much so that at times, I couldn't tell the two apart. Visually, differentiating the two was easy. Astrid was a tall, white, full-figured woman, and Janeva was short and sleek in stature.

Knowing that my rocky relationship was the root problem, I tried to remain untransparent as I explained, "Astrid, it's a combination of things. You are so quick to blame Cameron, but there are other problems."

"Let me guess. If it's not Cameron, then it's your job, right? Are you going to blame your job?" Not allowing me to answer, she continued, "However, I think, that your problem is that freeloading, good-for-nothing waste of time that you're living with. Come on, Cocoa, be honest! That's why you've been avoiding me. You've been too busy taking care of a grown man."

"Please leave Cameron out of this, Astrid. I told you, I've been busy."

"Cocoa, I think you can do better."

"Astrid, I could meet a king with nothing more on his agenda but to please me, and you would still hate him. Face it, Astrid, you can't stand men."

"That's not true. I just feel that you settle, and while you are too busy fussing around with the wrong guy,

Mr. Right is getting away. You really need to learn how to pace yourself, Cocoa. When I was out on the market, men were out for one thing—sex! I don't think anything has changed. How many men are you going to have to go through to realize this, Cocoa?"

Astrid continued talking, not bothering to pick up on whether I was listening or not. At times, Astrid reminded me of the blonde Chatty Cathy doll from back in the day—constantly *jibber-jabbering,* barely taking a pause for air. Ironically, the other daunting truth was that Astrid was a pessimistic woman who had obviously experienced the worst case scenarios in life. In some ways, Astrid was a mystery to me. She could be kind and compassionate, willing to go the extra mile for a friend, and then on the other hand, she could be cold and sarcastic. I had seen her pop pills to calm her inner demons, yet she never bothered to share what made her so sad and untrusting. In my book, Astrid suffered from a strange case of Dr. Jekyll and Ms. Hyde. There was no other way to describe it. When Astrid was sweet, she was golden, but when she became angry...look out!

"Look, I didn't call to fight, Cocoa. I just wanted to find out if you wanted to help out with the annual chocolate festival. And there is something else—I wanted to know if you would attend the grand opening of the new jazz restaurant tonight. I know it's last minute, but I underestimated my workload. I could really use the extra help." She sounded excited about the jazz restaurant opportunity and went on to explain, "I was hired to prepare an array of chocolate desserts for a packed house! I thought it would be fun to enjoy some smooth tunes while introducing my latest creations to a room full of jazz socialites. What do you say? Can you make it? I could really use the help."

Janeva had invited me to the opening of the new jazz club as well, but Astrid had me at the word *chocolate.* The only other comfort aside from the proposal of chocolate that I'd found instantly gratifying was the rhythmic nature of jazz. I could envision moving my full-figured hips to the tender melodies of the baritone saxophone while spoiling myself with strawberries drenched in white chocolate with drizzled, streaming fudge on top.

"Sounds tempting." I realized that I had the rare opportunity to meet up with Janeva and Astrid. Maybe a night out with friends was what I needed. After all, lately, it felt as if I were doing more of the initiating when it came to spending alone time with Cameron. I wanted him to be the one to make detailed plans with me. I didn't understand why I had to be the one who begged for alone time with him. When a man loves a woman, shouldn't he make an effort to want to see her just as much as she desires see him? I pondered, but not for long. "I could really use a girl's night out," I sighed.

"Yes! We all could! Stop by my place after work. We could go over some recipes for the festival, and then we can head to the new jazz spot."

Astrid sounded excited. It was obvious that she missed me. If only Cameron were as enthusiastic to see me. Lately he acted as if I were getting on his nerves. No matter how I tried to please him or be helpful toward him, he seemed to resent me. Hearing Astrid treat me as if I mattered warmed my heart. I realized that a good girlfriend in life can be sweeter than chocolate!

"I can't wait to see you, girl." I did something that I had not done in a while...I smiled.

"We are going to have a blast!" Astrid paused. I could hear her busily rattling pans in the background. "Cocoa, you are going to love these chocolate éclairs! I used chocolate filling instead of vanilla, and I added just a hint of..."

As Astrid explained her latest creation, I received an incoming page from my sister Lamina, followed by the code 911.

"Astrid, I really have to go. I have a ton of work to do, and I just got a page from my sister Lamina. I can't wait to give your new desserts a try."

Astrid paused. I could tell that she was lonely and needed to talk to someone. Sounding a little despondent, she replied, "OK. If you can't stop by, then let me know. I'm also throwing a little get-together. You know, we all haven't met up in a long time—you, me, and Serenity—ever since..."She paused, waiting for my response.

Just then, I understood the root of the sadness in her voice. We had not gotten together much, not since Alison had passed. I too became quiet, only for different reasons that were masked from deep within.

Picking up on my discomfort, Astrid changed the subject. "Um...I think I may have discovered the perfect wine to serve with fudge-dipped strawberries with white chocolate, and this time, I'm adding walnuts with a hint of—"

I had to cut Astrid off. "Sounds good, Astrid, but I really gotta go. I'm running late for a meeting, and I really have to call my sister back."

"OK, girl. Tell Lamina I said hi! You can invite her too if you want! See ya later, girl. Peace!" Astrid just had to end the call with her skeptical words. "Cocoa, I don't mean to be bothersome, but when it comes to Cameron, I smell trouble. I honestly don't know why you let that dude move in with you, Cocoa. Allowing some guy to move in before really having the opportunity to know what he is truly about is relationship suicide. You really need to—"

"Yeah, yeah, I get it, Astrid. Enough already! Please...stop judging me, all right?"

"I'm not judging you. I just...look, we'll talk later." Astrid ended the call with an awkward titter.

I contemplated for a moment, deep in thought about Alison. I really couldn't remember the last time we'd all met up together over a joyous chocolate occasion. Our good friend Alison had been the social butterfly of the bunch. She was always the one to persuade us women to step back from our daily routine and bond with one another. As much as I did not want to start dwelling on how much I missed Alison, just the mention of her name sparked all kinds of cherished memories, and I knew that if Alison were alive, she would not have approved of my relationship with Cameron.

Deep down inside, I knew that I was becoming too obsessed about Cameron's lack of affection for me lately. Maybe it was nothing to fret over; perhaps I was being paranoid. I had been cooped up lately in either one of two places, the office or back at my cold apartment, worrying over my relationship. Calling Cameron on his cell, I left a message informing him that I would be meeting up with the girls straight after work. Just maybe he would get the hint that I was tired of coming home to a grown man who behaved like a careless kid. Maybe he would figure out from the tone of my message that for once I wanted to come home to a responsible, loving man.

From there, I called my sister Lamina. I loved my little sister. She was only three years younger than me, but she acted older and more confident. Lamina was another independent woman who stood up for herself, even against our controlling older sister, Daria. I always commended her for that. Lamina had the strong willpower to fight for a life of her own, and against Daria's better judgment, she moved out way before I did and ended up doing well for herself. Lamina put herself through beautician school and ended up landing an amazing job for an elite production company as a hair and wardrobe- coordinator. Lamina traveled all around the world, working behind the scenes on several motion pictures. Yet the one thing that Lamina could not find success in was the relationship department. It seemed as if difficult relationships ran in the Reed family line like a generational curse. Lamina had been engaged too many times to count! Our older sister, Daria, had given up on men a long time ago. Daria's favorite relationship had to do with the welfare of my own life.

Lamina finally picked up. "Hey, girl, what you doing?" she asked, in haste as always.

"Hey, Lamina! I'm getting ready to head to a meeting. What's going on? You said it was urgent."

"Yeah, it is. Can you meet up for lunch?"

"You are in luck." I looked through my calendar. "I had a client cancel today. Where do you want to meet?"

"Meet me at AJ's Fish 'n' Chips."

"Aw, no, Lamina. Not that grease hole!"

"Oh, well, then, where would you like to go? Let me guess—some high-end, overpriced joint that charges for a glass of lemon water."

"Whatever, Lamina. I'll meet you at AJ's. And what is this about?"

"I kicked Roger's behind out last night. That man can't do nothing right. He's going to meet up with me outside of AJ's."

"Why?"

"To return my house key."

"Are you sure you guys can't work things out? I like Roger. Sure, he's a little rough around the edges. Other than that, he's a nice guy, Lamina. Don't be so quick to let him go."

"OK, Chantel, then why don't you date him? 'Cause I'm done. I'm not like you. I don't let men walk all over me."

"Excuse me? I don't—" I stopped myself, knowing that I would not be able to get my stubborn sister to see my point of view. I just let it go. "Whatever, Lamina. I'll see you soon."

My morning meeting let out early, so I was able to meet up with my sister on time...which really did not matter because Lamina always ran fashionably late. I found a booth facing the window near the parking lot to watch for my sister's arrival. As I waited, an unenthused waitress approached and set a menu down. Without saying hi or making eye contact, she said, "I'll be back to take your order."

Rolling my eyes, I wished that Lamina and I could have met at a different place. I despised bad service, but I decided to suck it up. Peering out the misty window, I spotted Lamina and her soon-to-be-ex, Roger, pull up in separate cars. Without shame, I scooted closer to the streaked window and spied on the two once they surfaced out of their cars within view. Lamina always drove in style. Her flashy candy-apple-red Corvette glistened in the faint sunlight, which peeked in and out of the shadowy clouds. As for Roger, his truck resembled something one would find in a scrap yard, a bit beat up and rusted yet still drivable for the time being.

My sister Lamina was beautiful. She had gotten all the skinny genes in the family, yet for such a tiny girl, she got all of the boldness in the family as well. She wore her hair short and tapered, which she enjoyed dying frequently into different colors of the rainbow. I'm surprised she had any left. Lamina was now sporting a burgundy color hairstyle with violet highlights. She was dressed in a sleek, tailor-made jean suit. Lamina always carried herself with confidence, but a lack thereof characterized Roger. He was cute, with wavy hair and gentle brown eyes. Roger always wore a tank top to show off his colorfully tatted biceps. He was tall, yet his communication skills were not the best, which was most likely the root cause of their breakup.

I watched as Lamina did most of the talking. She was very upset. As she used all kinds of hand gestures toward Roger, Lamina babbled away. Roger looked so pitiful. His attempts to console my sister did not work. Her body language was cold and guarded toward him. The truth of the matter was, Roger was too weak for a strong, spirited woman like my sister. In spite of his tough-guy exterior, deep down inside he lacked the kind of confidence that my sister desired. Once Lamina was done letting Roger have it, she held out her hand. Roger dug into his pocket, and reluctantly, he handed her the key. I watched as he desperately tried to pull Lamina in for a hug, but once again, she rejected his advance. And just like that, Lamina and Roger were over. Roger was visibly heartbroken. Hunched over, he then headed back to his truck. The old lorry took a minute to start up, but once it did, it mustered up enough momentum to peel out of the parking lot.

Lamina entered the restaurant. Of course I played it off, opening up my menu as if I were interested in the greasy food they had to offer. Then I looked up as if I were seeing my sister for the first time. I stood, trying to pretend as if I hadn't observed the scene in the parking lot. I played it cool, embracing my sister. I tried to study Lamina's eyes for a hint of sadness after her breakup, yet there was nothing there. Instead, the cold-hearted woman plopped down. Sighing in relief, she said, "Whew, I'm starving. Did you order yet?" Grabbing my menu, she opened it up and began thumbing through.

"No. I...thought I'd wait for you and Roger."

Lamina got straight to the point. "I'm done with Roger's lazy behind. I kicked him out of my house. He's useless. Do you know that he lost his job—again?! The man can't hold on to nothing, you hear me? No job, no money, no common sense, no dignity, no pride, no nothing. He just can't do it!"

"Lamina!" I gave her a stern glance. "You don't have to—"

Lifting up her hand, she stated sternly, "No! Chantel, I already know what you are going to say, that I was not patient enough with the man. Oh, I was patient enough, trust me. The guy was a raggedy deadbeat horse that could barely break out of the gates, let alone cross the finish line."

"Lamina, how could you be so rude?" I asked.

"I don't got time for that. I'm done, Chantel. If a man can't hang with me, then he has to go. I'm not running a charity center for incompetent, shady men. I'm not getting any younger. If it don't work out, then you got to go! Bye, so long, *auf wiedersehen*, and *arrivederci*!"

"Lamina, you are slamming that poor guy! Every word out of your mouth is hurtful and cruel. Roger could've been the one."

"Yeah, he's the one all right—the one trying to drive me broke and crazy. Look, Chantel, you and I are different people. We had the same mama, but we are not the same people. How many times do I have to tell you that? I don't let people walk all over me like you do."

"Wait a minute. I..."

Just as I was about to address my sister's insolent comment, the waitress appeared. "You two ready to order?" she asked in a bland tone.

"I'm not hungry," I pouted.

"OK. And what about you?" the lifeless waitress asked my sister.

"Yes! I'll take your fish 'n' chips platter lunch special with extra tartar sauce, a side of hush puppies, onion rings, a side of your potato salad, and a large pop, easy on the ice, please." Lamina looked over at me and asked, "You sure you don't want nothing? I'll pay."

I don't know how my sister could eat so much and not seem to gain a pound. That alone made me upset. "No, thank you," I replied sharply.

"Is there anything else?" the waitress asked.

"Oh, yes, hot sauce, please—don't forget my hot sauce."

The waitress jotted down the order, grabbed the menu, and then mind-numbingly shuffled away.

"Why did you pick this place? The service is horrible here," I complained.

"The service may be bad, but the food is amazing, girl. But you like all that fancy stuff, don't you? You like eating at restaurants that serve baby-size portions and charge an arm and a leg."

"I like class, Lamina."

"Whateva!" she huffed. "Like I said, Chantel," she continued, "you are too kind."

"I try to be as nice as possible without crushing a person's spirit. I don't enjoy hurting people. But...I can get mean if I have to."

"Yeah, right. You let Daria walk all over you, and you let your bossy white girlfriend Aspirin walk all over you, too."

"Her name is Astrid, and we've been friends for years. She means well, Lamina. And as for our oldest sister, Daria, I respect her. She has done a lot for us. I don't allow anyone to walk over me. You are wrong."

"Oh, really? How did you get here today, Chantel?" she asked. "Where's your car at?"

"I...well, I..."

"See? Now you sound just like that jackass I just dumped a second ago. You let that trifling, no-good man of yours drive your car? You love that car, Chantel! You've been wanting that ride all your life! Now that you got it, you turn the keys over to that good-for-nothing, freeloading hood? He's no good. I see Cameron around town with different women all the time. The last time I saw Cameron, he was with some blonde woman. She had—"

"That's enough, Lamina! I'm sure you got the wrong guy. Cameron would not ride around in my car with some other girl. And you know what? I'm so tired of you man-bashing! You can go off on your man like that if you want to, but my man is off-limits, and so is my relationship. Look..." I sighed. "Let's just change the subject. Have you spoken to Daria lately?"

"Nope!"

"And why not?" And just as soon as I asked the question, I wished I could have taken it back, for I had now moved on to a subject far worse than then the last, and I was about to get an earful.

"'Cause I can't stand the heifer, that's why! She act like she running the show. She's not my mama, Chantel. Yet you go around calling her Mom! She may be our older sister, but that does not give her the right to try and rule over us! I'm telling you, Chantel, Daria did what she had to do when Mama died, but that gives her no right to try to control our lives. I'm telling you the truth. You let people monopolize your life, friends and family! The only friend who was good to you was that Alison chick, and she's not around anymore. Face it, Chantel, you are weak. You need to be more like me and Robert."

Robert, now that's a name I had not heard in a while. Robert and Lamina were twins, and just like

Lamina, he went off on his own as well. Robert was distant. He did not spend a lot of time around the family. Maybe one of the main reasons was our older sister, Daria, whom I did refer to as my mother out of respect. Lamina and Robert deemed Daria as way too controlling, but I figured that she just wanted the best for us.

"Great! So I'm just one giant pushover!"

"Yes, you are! And your hair, Chantel, is not helping your situation!"

"My hair? What's wrong with my hair?"

"Girl, it's a mess! It's screaming to come out of that puffy ponytail! You've been wearing that ponytail since fifth grade. It's time to let it go. That's just wrong! Nobody is going to take you seriously sporting that ridiculous hairstyle."

"Who are you to give me advice? You are my little sister. Don't you forget that."

"But I have more experience because I don't let anyone get in my way. I live life! I don't stay underneath Daria's rules. Yes, I will admit that there was a time that me and Robert called Daria Mom just like you—still continue to do—but once reality kicked in, we had to break free! I bet you be giving her money, too." Lamina stared at me with her big, intense auburn eyes. "Um!" She shook her head in disbelief. "Girl, you need your head checked. I'm changing the subject. Look, the real reason why I called you here is to let you know that I landed a gig in New York. The job runs for three months or so, and from there, I'm heading off to another location in Ireland. I thought I'd stay there for a while, then head to Germany."

"Germany? What's out there?"

"Oktoberfest, fool." She laughed. "Anyway, I need you to check by my house every once in a while if you don't mind." She slid over the key that her temporary boyfriend had once managed.

Love her or hate her, Lamina was a free spirit. There was a part of me that longed to be more like her and Robert. If they did not like their circumstances, they just up and left. Robert was a mystery, though. He never told anyone where he was. He would call during the holidays, and sometimes he would just pop up out of nowhere for a brief amount of time. My younger brother, Robert, always looked well-groomed and successful. He was just mysterious. Lamina, on the other hand, was more open about her life. She chose the chance to start a new life in a different part of the country within the blink of an eye, and without doubt, she seized the moment.

I watched in amazement as my sister devoured her food. Once she was finished, we talked and laughed about old childhood memories, as we always did when Lamina took long trips abroad. At the end of sister bonding, one of the last things that my baby sister lovingly begged me to do was to stop allowing people to walk all over me...and to run a comb through my frizzy, matted hair.

Lamina's words stuck with me. However, sometimes in life, words are not enough to make a person change for good. I was the kind of person for whom it took unpleasant circumstances to force me to better myself, the kind of unfavorable condition in life that would replay its demeaning version over and over again throughout the corners of mind.

Back at work, my meeting seemed to last forever. I knew we had been over these topics before. It seemed as if some members were talking about the same subject over and over just to hear themselves speak.

I didn't get out of the plant until after six. By then, I was in no mood to go to any jazz club. I was, however, in the mood to submerge my aching body in a rich cloud of sweet, warm, velvety, vanilla bubble bath. I called Cameron again from my cell. There was no answer. Not bothering to leave a message about my change of plans, I ended the call and headed straight home. What would happen from there is an infuriating episode marked in stage one of my life that should have made me ease away from men for good.

The Metro was late. It took me forever to get home. This was ridiculous! I had worked hard all my life to get the perfect car—my jet-black BMW with gold rims—only to end up still taking the Metro, all because I was too weak to say no to my boyfriend who didn't have a car. *I'm a woman! If anything, he should be taking the Metro. Daria would kill me if she knew that I was catering to a man like Cameron.*

When I entered the condo, the aroma of lemon herb chicken filled the air. Sade was playing softly in the background. *Mmmmm.*

Chills ran up and down the nape of my neck. Cameron must have come to his senses; he was finally going to treat me with respect! I floated into the dining room where Cameron was lighting gardenia-scented tapered candles. He had the table set for two. Everything sparkled.

"What's the occasion?" I asked, giving him an overjoyed grin.

Cameron looked up in surprise.

"Chantel! What...what are *you* doing here? I thought you were going out," he said.

"I had a change of plans. Why?" I asked. "What's going on?"

"Um...nothing."

"Then what's all this?" I pointed to the table. Cameron had on the Dolce & Gabbana black double breasted silk suit I had purchased for him on his birthday. I had never seen him wear the outfit; Cameron told me he was saving it for a special occasion. He'd oiled down his arms, and his face was clean shaven. He looked fine, except for the bandage above his left eye.

"What happened to your face?"

"Oh, this." He grinned. "It's a long story, babe. Tell you later."

Perspiration glistened on his forehead. He moved past me, headed for the living room, then turned. "Be right back. I forgot the Zinfandel. I'm gonna run to the store real fast."

"Wait!" I grabbed his arm. Before I could continue, the doorbell rang.

Pulling away from me, Cameron bolted toward the door. I followed closely behind him, curiosity overwhelming me.

"Allow me." Using my God-given curvaceous hips, I forcefully shoved him aside, opened the door, and swiftly stepped out, slamming the entry behind me.

There stood a dazzling woman holding a bottle of Zinfandel. She smiled cheerfully with such luminous blue eyes and perfect white teeth.

"Hi! Is Cameron here?" she asked as if she hadn't a care in the world.

"Yes, he is." I took a deep breath, trying to maintain my composure. "And your name is...?"

"Krissy." She extended her hand. "But my friends call me Kris. You must be Cameron's sister. I've heard so much about you. Your name is Saniqua, right?"

"That's Chantel. Look here, Krissy—"

"Oh, you black girls have such unique names." She giggled. "I had a black nanny growing up. She was so sweet. Her name was Jonisha, but I could never pronounce her name right, so I just called her Mama Jo. Long story short, she ended up quitting because my daddy wasn't paying her on time. After all, Mama Jo had babies of her own to take care of, and she couldn't rely on some deadbeat like my daddy to pay her on time. Now, don't get me wrong; I love my daddy, but he had a gambling problem," she whispered. "From there, everything went downhill. We had to move out of our beautiful home that was like a castle to me into this dinky little shack located in the middle of nowhere. And I had to share a room with my messy stepsister." She sighed and then continued to share her story as if she were on some kind of morning talk show. "Anyway, my fondest memories were of my nanny, sweet Mama Jo. You look a lot like her! Except her wasn't as puffy, though."

My face flushed. "Um, yeah, look, I don't want to converse with you at all, sweetheart. Why don't you wait here? Cameron will join you shortly."

I stepped inside, slamming the door in her startled face. I glared at Cameron, who looked like a mischievous child who had just gotten caught stealing from the cookie jar.

"I can explain," he said.

I snorted. "Save it, Cameron. I don't care to know. Just give me this month's rent. Then get out!"

"I don't have this month's rent. You see—"

I cut him off. "Forget it. Save the lie, OK? Just give me my car keys and get out." Holding out my hand sternly, I waited patiently for Cameron to place my keys in the palm of my hand.

Wiping the perspiration from his forehead, he replied, "I don't have your keys."

"What do you *mean* you don't have my keys?" I shook with rage.

Cameron's eyes shifted back and forth. He held up his hands. "Check this out," he began. "It was a freak accident, babe. I was blazing up a joint—I know you don't like me smoking in your car, but my glaucoma was acting up—and all of a sudden, it slipped out of my hand and fell on the floor. I bent down to get it, and when I got back up, bam!" He clapped his hands together. "I smacked right into the back of a bus! Before I knew it, there was a screeching sound. I was rear-ended. It was a pretty bad pileup! Your car is totaled!"

"You did what?" I screamed.

"Hey, it's OK. No one got hurt. Everyone on the bus was fine, and I just hit my head on the steering wheel. That's how I got this." He pointed to his bandage. "Don't sweat it, Chantel. You got insurance. At least I got out alive." He gave me a foolish grin.

That was it. I had taken all I could take. Cameron had done nothing to fulfill my longing for a mate. It was as if I were taking care of some clueless high-school kid. He never took me out. We never attended church together in hopes of his trying to gain some shred of spiritual values, nor did he show any interest in trying to meet up for counseling involving our relationship. Cameron's inconsiderate behavior played over and over again like a horror film in my mind. At that point, his careless measures spurred me into a dynasty of rage.

"You may have gotten out of that accident alive, but I'm going to kill you! Right now!" With every bit of unsettled emotion rooted in agony, I punched him in his good eye.

Cameron bent over in pain, then squinted up at me, whimpering, "You hurt my eye. I could go blind." Abruptly, his mood changed. Cameron was a man who invested a lot of time in his looks. The prideful thought of resembling a one-eyed monster that would suitably match his personality fueled his anger. Enraged,

Cameron rose to his full six feet five inches and extended his hand to retaliate.

Deliberating quickly, I grabbed an old wooden-handled umbrella off the coatrack and aimed the point at him. *"Go for it!"* I dared.

Cameron's anger quickly subsided as he conspicuously studied my disgusted and outraged appearance. "You're crazy!" he screamed. "Crazy, deranged madwoman!"

Pushing by me, he squirmed his way out the front door. His naïve eye-candy girlfriend followed closely behind. Cameron shouted, "I'll be back for my things tomorrow!"

Locking the door, I began screaming out of sheer frustration. I did not deserve this. I'd taken care of Cameron. I treated him well—better than I treated myself!

My emotions bubbled over into a world of insanity, which ignited irrational thoughts. Blood boiling, I marched into the kitchen, grabbed a couple of worn potholders near the stove, removed the half-baked chicken from the oven, and tossed it out the window. Bawling like a baby, I watched as the rotisserie chicken plunged toward the pavement. I took one last look at Cameron's terrified face as he and his clueless girlfriend fled away from the apartment. Out of humiliation and lost hope, I screamed, "You'll pay for this, Cameron!"

Honestly, I was more afraid than angry. Not only did I not have my car, but I was alone. I hated being alone, a taunting feeling formed by rejection. The only comfort I had was the composed voice of Sade singing "Smooth Operator" meticulously in the background of my callous apartment and throughout my overly anxious mind.

CHAPTER 2

Chantel

I barely slept that night, and my mind would forever replay all of yesterday's ugliness like an embarrassing film that I regretted starring in. Yes, that memory from stage one of my life was officially booked in my memory bank, entitled "The Hall Of Shame." Looking back, I was not shocked that Cameron was cheating on me.

He was a good-looking man. Women were instantly attracted to him. In all honesty, I was down on myself. I wanted to be the only woman in Cameron's life, and I wondered, why was I not good enough for him? Was I not thin enough for him? Or even worse, did Cameron crave a certain kind of quality in a woman that my physical appearance could not meet? Was I not white enough for Cameron? Or was it my skills in the bedroom? Did I lack the kind of excitement that young-blooded men like Cameron desired? Last week he had made a comment on some old underwear that I was wearing. Yes, the underwear was all stretched out and faded, and my bra was dingy. I'm sure that did not turn him on. However, I was comfortable. Nonetheless, I doubt if a whole new underwear set would've kept him interested.

In the end, it's all about performance, and just as I began to dwell on my insecurities in the bedroom department, something worse dawned on me. Here I was, wondering whether I was good enough for Cameron, when a bigger dilemma was at stake, my health. Men like Cameron had the capability to sleep with any woman they desired. I could have had some awful disease. I had no idea who Cameron was sharing his goods with, and with the sexually transmitted disease AIDS being a major scare in the early nineties, I became frightened, so much so that I began to look at my life through a precious image. I instantly desired change, the kind of transformation that made me want to respect myself and give myself the chance to start life anew. And back then, that's exactly what I did. I scheduled a doctor's appointment to make sure that my plumbing had not been compromised. It took a while for me to receive results back in the day. Nowadays, you can pick up all sorts of tests at a local convenience store to determine any kind of illness. Nonetheless, at that emotional stage in my life, I decided to induce change, which would birth a life-changing relationship.

On the day I decided to change my life for good, I called the office and told Yvonne I'd be in later. Throwing on a fitted jacket with matching skirt, I prepared myself for inner change. I boarded the Metro, heading to one of the finest chocolate stores in Seattle, Chocolopolis. Now I realize that my change should have included my addiction to chocolate. However, I had just gotten out a bad breakup, and I needed the comfort of chocolate to see me through.

I could not wait to arrive at the only store that greeted me instantly with sweet rewards in honor of being depressed and vulnerable. Artisanal chocolate was one of my favorite treats. Its makers described it as equal to a good bottle of wine, except *made with some of the finest cacao in the world by artisans who are passionate about creating flavorful chocolate.*

The Metro couldn't reach my sweet destination soon enough. On a mission to fulfill my chocolate craving, I desperately made my way inside. Yes! It was if the sweet aroma of assorted chocolate bars from different regions had been personally chosen for the enjoyment of my very own taste buds. My eyes lit up as I scanned through the array of dark, milk, and white chocolate bars and truffles. Ultimately, my eyes locked in on the ultimate gift that could possibly suppress my inner pain temporarily. My soul swooned at the wide collection of rich milk chocolate bars in a basket huge enough to console my lonely heart. I eagerly purchased the basket of chocolate affection. A huge smile stretched across my face as I envisioned a private meeting between me and my sweet escape.

As I waited outside for the Metro, it started to rain. Even though I held on firmly to my basket full of chocolate bliss, other signs of discontentment sprouted from within. For instance, I was starting to loathe Seattle's rain. I could scarcely keep a decent hairdo in weather like this, and my weight—I was not happy with my body image. *The last thing I should be doing is indulging in chocolate*, I thought. The Metro arrived, and I scurried inside quickly, fearing that my hair would frizz up and that my leather slides would not hold up, either. My arm radiated with pain from where blood was drawn due to a last-minute doctor's appointment. In addition, bumping into the side rail leading into the Metro did not help matters. Locating the nearest seat, I gazed out the window as giant drops of rain streamed down the glass, reminding me of the tears I had cried last night.

A deep, full voice interrupted my thoughts. "Is anyone sitting here?"

I glanced up at a tall, attractive man wearing a black leather coat. He looked as if he had just stepped off the cover of *GQ* magazine.

"No." I smiled weakly, then continued looking out the window, trying to remember where I'd left off in my exercise of self-pity.

"It's a beautiful day, isn't it? There's nothing more exciting than a rainy day in Seattle, don't you agree?" he asked.

"I don't care much for the rain," I replied. "It's hard on the hair, not to mention what this rain is doing to my five-hundred-dollar shoes." I was rather disgusted at this point.

"I love it." He grinned. "I could just strip down to my bare essentials and let the rain take its course all over my body."

Great, I thought. *This guy is nuttier than a Snickers bar.*

"You must think I'm crazy!" His light-emerald eyes twinkled. "That's OK. Your expression gave you away. My name is Brandon." Removing his soft leather glove, he extended his hand.

"Chantel," I responded, feeling just a bit uncomfortable. Yet in the midst of my discomfort, I noticed that this mysterious distraction had a smooth hand and well-manicured nails. *Hmmm...nice,* I thought.

"Chantel. That's a pretty name."

"Yes, we have such unique names, don't we?" I murmured as I rapidly recalled the conversation with Cameron's mystery woman.

"Well, personally, Chantel," he said, removing his other glove, then placing it in his lap, "I think your name is rather beautiful, comparable to its owner."

His response caught me off-guard. All of a sudden apprehensive about my hair, I began combing my fingers through the thick, damp mane. "Oh...well, thank you." Why did I suddenly feel bashful—and especially feminine? I studied the intriguing interruption a bit closer. Thick, black, glossy hair, every strand in place. Strong features, great skin. Captivating heavily lashed, greenish-blue eyes.

"If you don't mind my asking," he continued, flashing a Colgate smile that revealed deep, rather attractive dimples, "where are you headed on this fortunate rainy day with such a huge basket of chocolate?"

Looking at the chocolate, I did not want the stranger to know that I had planned on eating all of it by myself. That would have been so greedy of me. "The chocolate is for our team builder. I'm heading to work. Litton Technologies."

"Really? I have a friend who works there, Eugene Howard. Do you know him?"

Picturing Eugene's unappealing mug caused me to stutter, "Ah, uh, unfortunately. I mean, yes, I do."

"What do you do at Litton?" he asked.

"I'm in human resources. What about you? What do you do?" I asked.

"A Touch of Jazz. It's also a restaurant."

"I know that club! My girlfriends went the other night. Astrid, she's a chocolate chef. She was excited about serving her latest desserts at your opening," I shared, becoming a bit more interested in this smooth diversion.

"You know, I did not get a chance to try any of the desserts; however, I heard that she did an amazing job. By the way, did your friends enjoy the club?"

"I don't know, but I'm pretty sure they did. I haven't gotten the chance to catch up with any of my friends lately. But I'm sure they had a good time."

"The *Times* gave us a great review. You really ought to stop by...when time permits, of course."

The attractive man appeared to gaze into the core of my soul, and something strange from within desired to be with this man in the ungodly way. Hoping that he didn't sense desperation mixed in with my vulnerability after a breakup and my gluttonous love for chocolate, I shook out of this trance in time to notice the bus was almost at my destination. I stood up with my basket of chocolates, yet for some reason, my legs felt weak, causing me to stagger aimlessly onto my feet.

"Well, this is my stop. It was nice talking to you," I said. I felt ashamed for allowing my desperate craving for male companionship devour my thoughts. I didn't need another man in my life. I needed therapy. I needed to go to church on a regular basis. I needed holy oil to be doused all over my damp, fluffy hair until the desire for a man had been purged from my sinful body.

Heart pounding, I struggled to make my way past this now-unwelcome distraction as if nothing had happened. Nonetheless, the tempting gentleman blocked my path. "Would you have any objections to exchanging phone numbers?"

I couldn't believe this! I was done with men. I had my heart set on a new love affair with chocolate. I was going to dedicate my time toward reading the Good Book, maybe even joining an inspiring women's group. I had no time for a relationship. And even though interracial relationships were somewhat the norm where I resided and supplementary accepted in today's society, I myself had never dated a man outside of my own race. So at the time, kicking my game to a white dude was unthinkable! I've got one rule: I won't unlock it unless my ice cream is chocolate! After all, from my angle, there were way too many obstacles to overcome. I'm not at all prejudiced or narrow minded; at that time I was being practical.

"Sorry, Brandon, I...I can't. Thanks, anyway."

Pushing past him quickly, not bothering to look back, I exited the Metro with the speed of lighting.

For the rest of the day, all I could think about was Brandon. I figured I'd never see him again, which in my case was good. I didn't need to be involved in another relationship so quickly after Cameron. Even without diving into an interracial relationship, the hard part would be allowing myself to become vulnerable to trusting any man to heal my broken heart. Desperately trying to erase Brandon from my mind, I searched for a safe digression that would lead me into a new stress-free world without men.

I decided to immerse myself in female friendships. Rather than go straight home on Friday night, I visited Janeva, who shared that she was very impressed with the new jazz club and even more smitten with Brandon, the hot owner with the movie-star good looks, as she put it. However, the moment of truth revealed itself Saturday evening. I had gone into work to try to catch up on a couple of projects, and of course, time got away from me. Even though I was a bit exhausted, I knew that I did not want to wind down back at my empty apartment, so that evening, having decided that a chocolate dessert party with my best friend was exactly what I needed, I made my way to Astrid's quaint condo after a grueling day of overtime.

The front door to Astrid's place was cracked open. I entered the plush living space, cleverly designed to complement her love for chocolate. Espresso-colored lounge chairs with oversized deep-brown throw pillows accented the abode. Soft-russet-colored walls gave her home a feeling of warmth and solitude. Yet the best part was the presence of soothing jazz, which played throughout the space. Lingering in the air remained the rich aroma of unadulterated chocolate.

Following the light laughter leading to a remote deck, I found two familiar women candidly enjoying each other's company. Astrid and Serenity reclined in oversized plush patio chairs while thoughtfully sipping from crystal glasses.

The women gave a cheerful greeting as I anxiously joined in, helping myself to the spread of delicious cold cuts and veggies positioned near the main attraction, a fondue maker elegantly situated in the midst of strawberries and assorted nuts. Marshmallows sprinkled in cinnamon joined an array of sliced bananas, pineapple, and brownies in the center of a round mahogany picnic table. It was nice to kick back in the comfort of those who knew me best. Unlike being in an uncomfortable relationship, I did not have to try to please anyone, and unlike the workplace, I did not have to stress over the need to impress my coworkers to prove that I was worthy of my title. All I had to do was be me, and being me was good enough for Astrid and Serenity. However, that did not stop them from prying into my personal life, and it wasn't long until my pathetic love life became the center of our conversation.

"So, how are things with you and Cameron?" Astrid asked, almost as if she knew the expiration date on my failed relationship.

"Cameron who?" I rolled my eyes while pouring another glass of wine in hopes that it would numb my senses from the interrogation about to take place.

"Trouble in paradise so soon?" she pried.

"Let's just say that things did not go as planned. I really don't want to talk about this, OK? Now, could we please change the subject?"

"Well, I tried to tell you, Chantel, guys like Cameron can't be trusted! Sorry, honey. Moving right along..." she huffed.

Yet given the heavy presence of strong-willed opinions, I knew full well that this conversation was here to stay thanks to Serenity.

My good friend Serenity was an unceasing optimist who hosted one of the most frequently watched morning shows in Seattle. *Good Morning with Serenity* was a local television show that aired Monday through Friday mornings. Serenity collected true stories about any- and everything, from relationships to how to keep a houseplant alive and peppy. However, her main topic of choice was relationships. Serenity was passionate about defining the core of a solid relationship and even more interested in the obstacles that tore them apart.

Serenity was a straightforward African-American woman who also focused on the value of peace. If anyone were to ask Serenity about her mission in life, she would describe herself as being a serenity-driven woman who had dedicated her life to studying the relationships of others in hopes of defining a stress-free life centered around the supremacy of serenity. Serenity's socialite abilities kept her invested in expos and women's gatherings that challenged each attendee to become vulnerable to their deepest insecurities in hopes of conquering their inner fears in search of redemption. My thought-provoking friend spent a great deal of her time diligently trying to encourage those who had lost confidence in a condemnatory world. Based on her research and balanced by her own sacred marriage of ten years, Serenity gave only a few of her critics room to doubt her studied principles, and at times those few who doubted were Astrid and I. Even though we valued Serenity's knowledge and wisdom, we all knew that deep down inside, Serenity had her own demons to conquer.

"Astrid!" Serenity shook her head in a reprimand. "You really should not badger Chantel over her relationships. For one reason or another, it was meant for Cameron to play a significant role in her life. Even though the relationship did not work out, important lessons were still absorbed." Serenity sighed. "I really wish you ladies would come join me for my next women's gathering, or at least stop by the set and sit in the audience to soak up some important feedback. The women there are well versed in perception and discernment. And they are not afraid to conquer vital questions that encourage others to search for the truth in life."

"So tell me the truth, Serenity: how long does it take a person to realize that broke men do not make suitable boyfriends?" Astrid asked with her signature sarcastic grin.

"It's not about the money, Astrid," Serenity adamantly replied. "It's about finding your true soul mate in the midst of trials and tribulations. The questions that you are not willing to honestly ask of yourself are the needed solutions that we avoid in life. What is standing in our way of a loving relationship? Is it money? Status? Addictions? Or pride?"

Astrid gave a sigh of doubt, perhaps because she knew as well as I did that sometimes Serenity's questions gave us all something to deliberate.

CHAPTER 3

Astrid

I honestly believe that most women talk a good game, but when push comes to shove, they are helpless against that deadly Kryptonite known as men.

I considered myself to be different from the rest. I played the fool once in a relationship, and once was enough! After my marriage of five years fell apart, I dove into my own business. Investing in myself was the best investment that I had ever made. I worked hard to become one of the best chocolatiers in the country, and I enjoyed having my girlfriends over to experience my latest chocolate creations.

What I did not enjoy was their constant woes about their tired men problems. This evening was supposed to be filled with eating and joyful banter about good times to come! Talking about men only led me around a winding road off the beaten path straight into the roadblock of depression.

As Serenity attempted to go into another discouraging discussion about love, I had to cut in to save us all. "Enough talk about love and relationships, OK, Serenity? Let's talk about something exciting like the new jazz club I catered the other night. I had the opportunity to serve my newest chocolate confections there."

"You mean Touch of Jazz?" Cocoa glanced over, showing great interest. "Janeva told me about this club as well."

"You missed out, Cocoa. I really wish you would have shown up to help out. It was exquisite!"

I could not help but notice that Cocoa seemed unusually excited about the new jazz club.

"Did you get to meet the owner?" Cocoa asked.

"No, I was too busy, but I heard that he was a real charming guy, which is code for player."

"Astrid, it does not matter what others think. The owner could be a nice guy."

"You of all people should know that every guy has his sneaky dark side. Did your recent breakup teach you anything, Cocoa? So like me, are you willing to take a break from men?"

"Uh-huh!" She thought for a quick moment. "Wait...what?" Cocoa nearly dropped her chocolate-covered strawberry after deliberating the concept. "Do you mean like a diet that eliminates men? No men? At all?!" Chantel asked. "I don't know if I want to do that, Astrid."

"Why not?" I asked.

"Of course not." Serenity jumped in. "Astrid, that's a horrible suggestion! I believe that there is a soul mate for us all! It will take time and diligence to find him."

As I sat there watching Serenity's lips ramble on, I thought, *Why does she always have to voice her logic as if it is the only right concept in this world? Who died and made her Ms. Know-It-All?* I had had about all I could take from Serenity on the subject of soul mates, love, and relationships. After all, this was my gathering!

"Look, Serenity, just because you found the man of your dreams does not make it easy for the rest of us. After all, you seem to put all your trust in your man. But at the end of the day, he's just a man. Your man is capable of being unfaithful, just like the rest of them."

Serenity responded in a rather perturbed tone, which excited me. I don't know why, but I liked getting under Serenity's skin. "Astrid, all marriages have their problems, but at the end of the day, it's a marriage.

The willingness to accept the flaws in a relationship makes it whole."

I allowed the mess-starter inside of me to take over. "Never forget, Serenity, I knew you before you were married, and you were a wild one." I smirked. "And Chantel, you really need to consider laying off men for a while, because we all know that your bedroom has a revolving door through which all losers can walk right in, take care of business, and then bail. Let's face it; I am the only one in this clique who is not hooked on trifling men. You all are pathetic. You can't get it together for one simple ladies' night out without obsessing over men." I paused, took a sip of wine, then continued my condemning attack. "Chantel, I thought you would have learned your lesson after that last guy before Cameron!"

"That's enough, Astrid," Chantel warned. Her face began to perspire. "I shared that with you in confidence!"

"Astrid, you should go lie down. You look a little tired." As always, Serenity tried to defuse the situation.

"No, I'm just fine, Serenity. Now let's see, Chantel...what was his name again? You know, the guy who took your money and spent it on a trip to Vegas with his so-called ex-wife? Remember how I spent the whole night consoling you while you mourned over that loser?" I laughed carelessly. I knew that my behavior was mean spirited. However, I was hurt by Chantel. The fact that she chose some dude whom she barely knew to move in with her instead of choosing me, her best friend—that situation still made my blood boil. Seeing that Chantel had had enough of my torment for one night, I decided to ease up. But perhaps I was too late. I had never seen Chantel so furious. I knew then that I had gone too far.

My dear friend Chantel, whom I had nicknamed Cocoa, had yet to go off on anyone. For the most part, Chantel Reed was a pushover. Cocoa let everyone take advantage of her: tacky men, even her own Daria and Lamina. But I believed that every woman had her breaking point.

Lately I wondered if my anger had to do with Alison. Sometimes I got upset just thinking about her death. I knew that we all missed Alison, and we all dealt with her absence differently, and this was the first real gathering we had had since she'd passed away. Even though we all tried to carry on just as Alison would have done through gift women gatherings and hospitality, the truth was, we fell short without her presence. The simple task of love created to bond women seemed impossible without Alison's presence. After all, Alison had been the only one who could calm my irritable spirit. I could tell that Serenity was trying to be the peacemaker that Alison once was, but in reality, Alison's shoes were too big to fill. And the way I felt was that if Serenity truly had the key to genuine love and lasting relationships, Alison would still be with us.

CHAPTER 4

Serenity

I thought for sure that Chantel was going to go off on Astrid, and I was prepared to intervene. Instead, Chantel took control of the situation by suppressing her anger as she always did, calmly pouring herself a glass of wine and gulping it down swiftly. Then she turned to me and asked in a somber tone to give her a ride home.

On the ride back to her place, Chantel expressed that she should have stayed home, and then the conversation took a strange turn. She began to speak of some guy named Brandon she had met on the Metro. I listened as she reminisced about the handsome stranger's smile, his flawless facial structure, and his deep, rich voice.

Still deep in thought, she shared, "If I could turn back the hands of time, I would have given him my number. I also would have tried to knock some sense into my own head and left Cameron. Maybe I would still be driving my BMW instead of catching the Metro to work and bumming rides off my friends."

"Don't beat yourself up, Chantel. It did not work out and probably for good reasons."

Chantel sighed. "Astrid is so bitter when it comes to men. I never want to be like her, but as time goes by, I'm starting realize why she has become so hostile. I invested so much time into Cameron, so much so that I could actually envision us having children together. Yet as soon as I got comfortable, he started acting up. I was so positive that he was the right guy. Wow! I wish that Ali..." She stopped herself.

"I miss Alison, too, Chantel. After all, she was the one who got us all together. If it wasn't for Alison, we all would be sitting at home trying to think of something to do. I missed her tonight. I think Astrid did as well. Alison was the glue who held us all together, and now look at us. I'm trying to pull Alison's foundation together. I am taking in speakers and really trying to grasp how she would run things. Now, Chantel, I know you said that you wanted nothing to do with Alison's cause, but perhaps you should reconsider. We all have something different to give to this experience."

"No thank you, Serenity. I'm not perfect enough to reach out to women the way that Alison did. I don't want to ruin her cause. I'm just not there yet."

"Chantel, you don't have to be perfect to reach out to other women. All of us are broken, and sometimes our flaws can serve as a testimony in life that can help heal others."

"Serenity, my sister Daria raised me differently. You don't go around telling others your business. That's a sign of weakness. Besides, I'm not sure I can put up with women right now. Just look how Astrid behaved this evening. I know that she is still mad at me for choosing Cameron over her, and I know she still misses Alison as well, but regardless, I really wanted to grab her up by her neck tonight. She annoyed the mess out me."

"Chantel, you and Astrid have been friends for years. That's just Astrid. We all get upset, and Astrid can be a handful at times, and so can I. However, we must remain positive. We all need to grasp something positive from Alison's death, and I think we should promote events together that reach out to women who may be suffering just as she did. Like Alison, these women have nowhere to turn. Don't you think we owe that much to Alison?"

"That sounds good and all, Serenity, but...I'm just not ready yet. I still like to party. I enjoy drinking every now and then, and I don't want to be judged by a bunch of women. I won't fit in. I have to work on getting my life together first, and I should start by taking my mind off men. Who knows? I may even join Astrid and help her create amazing chocolate masterpieces."

"Chocolate? You'd rather go on a mission for chocolate than to reach out to women? You know, I think both you and Astrid are addicted to chocolate."

"What?" briefly studying the look of disapproval on Chantel's face as I entered through the iron gates leading to her apartment. I could tell that my comment rubbed her the wrong way.

"Addicted to chocolate?" she repeated.

"Well...yes! Every time I hang out with you and Astrid, you both fawn over chocolate! Chocolate cakes, cookies, brownies, pies, and cupcakes—you have replaced love and man with chocolate."

"Serenity, that's absurd!"

"I bet you and Astrid could not go one whole week without obsessing over chocolate."

"Hmmm...I can't speak for Astrid, but I can speak for myself. I can do without chocolate."

"Is that so?" I smirked. "Let me know when both of you are up for a little chocolate challenge."

Deep down inside, I knew that addictions ran rampant over the lives of many women, and most likely one of the most alluring addictions had to do with chocolate. After all, I struggled with chocolate addiction myself. I spent many nights getting down with a bagful of milk chocolate Hershey's Kisses. I knew their pain, and as expected, Chantel was reluctant to accept the chocolate challenge, explaining that she would have to fill Astrid in on the details first.

My motive was not to condemn the ladies over their addiction. I was in no position to do so. I too continue to deal with deep-seated issues from my past, haunting memories that are often too painful to remember. And at the time, I tried to suppress these uncomfortable glimpses of the past through the contentment of sweetened foods and alcohol.

What I desired most was to get both Chantel and Astrid plugged into Alison's cause. However, I knew that deep within, it would take more than a chocolate challenge to encourage my stubborn girlfriends to involve themselves with a cause that had the capability to unite authentic woman all over the world on behalf of Alison's genuine love for women.

My Serenity stood as the only safeguard that fought against those painful addictions. My hope was that Chantel and Astrid would break free from any addictions that held them captive, and I knew that the failure to do so would eventually consume them, just as it had consumed Alison.

CHAPTER 5

Chantel

My mind was fixated on Brandon. I dreamed of me and this new love interest on a romantic dinner cruise, staring deep into each other's eyes while a jazz band played the night away. Yet behind every tender reverie was a slither of darkness that would lead into an abyss of taunting judgment overshadowed by my controlling sister Daria. In some occurrences, Astrid would play a cynical role. However, these elusive interruptions diminished in comparison as my mind reflected on the inseparable bond that Brandon and I seemed to share.

Now it was time to face reality. Dressed and perked up by two cups of coffee, I was almost out the door when the house phone rang. I could tell by the nagging ring that it was Daria, the woman whom I referred to as my mother.

Great, I muttered to myself. *Now I'll be late to work.*

Even though I wanted to call her from my cell, she always complained of a bad connection. It had been a while since I had spoken to my sister. Daria had been born and raised in the South. Dealing with the stigma of racism back in the day had caused Daria's heart to become bitter. I had compassion for the pain that my sister endured due to the inconvenience of being born black and a woman back then in Montgomery, Alabama. Eventually I went off to college, for which Daria supported me. Once I entered into a career that stressed the value of equal opportunity, I had to liberate myself from the curse of hatred. Even though my sister preached the need for me to marry within my own race, I would soon find out for myself that love was color-blind.

Landing a job in human resources, I soon realized that everyone, regardless of their race, may have experienced their share of hatred due to matters that were beyond their control. Whether it be race, sex, religion, weight, class, culture, or appearance, we live in a world that thrives on visual standards, status, and greed, depending on the politics or popular beliefs that dominate our society during certain eras. Yet my sister Daria, whom I called Mom, was now imprisoned by her past, a most degrading and grief-stricken history, which made her narrow minded, so much so that she buried herself inside her own pro-black world.

Our mother passed away due to complications after giving birth to the twins. Daria was convinced that due to reasons of prejudice, our mother was denied the surgery that could have saved her life. Daria was furious that the doctors would not perform the vital surgery that our mother needed as soon as possible. Instead, they stated that our mother's surgery would have to take place at a county hospital due to her lack of insurance coverage. However, by the time our mother was transferred to the county hospital, it was too late; she had passed away due to heart failure. I can't remember much from that time. I was just a toddler when my Aunt Wanda and Daria came home with Lamina and Robert, two little crying babies.

My sister Daria, who was conceived out of wedlock in my mother's teenage years, was a teenager herself at the time she dropped out of school to help take care of us kids. We lived off relatives for a while. Once Daria took up a trade specializing in secretarial and business skills, she found a well-paying job in Birmingham, Alabama. Daria became our mother. She was a hard worker, and it wasn't long before she stabilized her own living arrangements, a quaint home where she raised us kids to have moral values. Daria stayed on top of our education. She was also unafraid to try her hand at different trades as she moved on to graduate from cosmetology school and opened up her own hair salon, and that's how my younger sister, Lamina, ended up getting involved in the beautician industry. Eventually, Daria had to close her shop. She had developed carpal tunnel, which made it painful for her to continue styling hair. Even though I admired my sister's strength and admiration, lately she was starting to exasperate me.

Daria had been trying to hook me up with this so-called well-to-do black man for a while now, but I was not interested in her choices. At one time I tried to give Daria a chance at matchmaking, but the guy she tried to hook me up with was old. He looked like a black Orville Redenbacher—red bow tie, red suspenders, and all. It was just wrong. I knew that my sister meant well, and there was a part of me that did not want to let her down. After all, Daria was the only mother I knew, and I already felt as if the twins, Lamina and Robert, had abandoned her. I couldn't do the same. Yet my younger sister, Lamina, believed that I had allowed Daria to brainwash me. I, on the other hand, disagreed. Daria was my earthly mom, and even though I had contact with my natural father, who would fly me out to California every now and then to get to know his wife and my half-sister, our relationship was different. My dad was a nice guy and all, yet he felt like a stranger to me. Daria's nurturing and caring ways reflected a natural sense that I had admired for years.

The rest of my siblings thought differently about Daria because she ended up getting under their skin. Lamina and Robert chose to break free. Nonetheless, every once in a while, Robert would fly in town and stay with Daria for a short while because that's all he could stand. Daria had a way of bugging the peace out of a person, and lately I'd been feeling like the individual she took sheer pleasure in irritating.

Reluctantly, I ran back inside and picked up the receiver.

"Hi, Chantel," chimed in a familiar, sharp voice. "What are you up to?"

"Hi, Mom. How are you?" Why did I have to ask? I *always* regretted asking that question, but old habits die hard.

"I've been doing OK, honey," she replied, "except for these headaches—and I need to get my car fixed. And would you believe it? They cut back my hours at the shoe store! I can barely breathe at night. I hope it's allergies, not an infection. And Robert is supposed to be coming into town. He is going to stay with me for a while, just until he completes some graphic and design schooling. I hope he has enough money to sustain 'cause I'm not running a charity house. I hope he don't think that he going to move in here and eat me out of house and home. I've got bills to pay. Oh well, other than that, I'm doing fine, honey. How are *you*?"

"Yeah, um...I'm doing fine, Mom. You seem a little concerned about Robert, but I'm sure he can hold his own. Mom, you have nothing worry about, and if you should need any help, just let me know. I would love to chat more, but I was just on my way to work. I'm running late." *Maybe now she'll hang up*, I thought. Right.

"So...how's that boy doing?" she asked.

"What boy?"

"You know, the one you have been supporting...Carlos."

"Cameron, Mom. His name is *Cameron*. I mean, *was* Cameron. Anyway, I broke up with him."

"You did? Good. I never liked him, anyway, especially if he did not have the means to keep up with you. I didn't support you through college to end up with some lowlife bum. You should want better for yourself, Sissy."

"Yes, I *know* this, Mom."

"Chantel, I know this nice guy. He aspires to own his own company someday. He came into the shoe store a while back. I got his number for you, and—"

"Oh, OK. Listen, I have to go."

"Wait, Chantel. When will you be coming over for dinner? I'll cook dinner for you both. I haven't seen you in a while."

"Mom, I'll be happy to see just you, but I'm done with men for the time being. I really have to go now. I'll help you out with some money for your car. Just text me the amount."

I couldn't believe I was going to send my sister money to get her car fixed, and I had yet to settle my car situation.

"All right. I love you, Chantel!"

"Love you, too." I hung up, then rushed out the door.

It was raining again, and I'd forgotten my umbrella. Arriving in the sanctuary of my office, I shook the rain off my gear, hung everything up, and turned to spot a vase of pink and yellow roses on my credenza.

That Eugene! I couldn't believe him. He must have heard through the grapevine that it was over between me and Cameron.

I snatched the card from between the soft, green leaves. It read, *Please have dinner with me tonight!* At the bottom, there was a phone number. I crumpled up the card and tossed it in the wastebasket, then punched the intercom button and asked Yvonne to locate Eugene Howard immediately.

While waiting for the little troll to appear, I walked over to the bay window and watched the rain caress nearby clusters of tulips and daffodils. Brandon was right. The rain could be quite beautiful. I wondered if I would ever see him again. *Why hadn't I given him my number?* If anything, we could have been friends. As I sat there contemplating the thought of what could have developed, the maddening sound of the intercom abruptly drew me away from my daydream. Yvonne announced Eugene's arrival.

"You wanted to see me?" he asked, closing the door behind him.

"Yes." I walked from behind my desk, hands on my hips. "Eugene, didn't our conversation the other day mean anything to you? I thought I made it clear. *No more roses.* Just because Cameron and I are no longer seeing each other, do you think you can simply disregard my wishes?"

"Hold it, hold it," he cried. "I didn't send you flowers, and as far as I knew, you and Cameron were still together. So..." He looked at me, deviously happy. "When did you two break up?"

"You didn't send the roses?"

"No."

I wondered who had. Well, it wouldn't be a mystery for long.

"I'm sorry for taking you away from your work only to accuse you of something you didn't do."

"Apology accepted." He smiled. "So, you and Cameron broke up, huh?"

I walked over to the door and opened it. "You're free to go now, Eugene. Thank you for your time, and once again, I do apologize."

He stood there, staring at me with the possibility of hope gleaming in his eyes. "So, do you have any idea as to who might have sent you those roses?"

"No. Goodbye, Eugene." I gestured toward the door.

He began to leave, then turned and looked me up and down. "Well, whoever it is, he sure has good taste in women." He winked, then waddled on his way.

I shuddered and closed the door quickly. Rushing to the wastebasket, I tripped over the leg of my desk and fell onto the coarse carpet. I scraped my knee as I proceeded to crawl over to the wastebasket. I began digging through it as if I were searching for gold. Jumping up once I found the card, I grabbed the phone and took a deep breath before dialing the number.

"Hello?" a man said.

That voice, I thought at first. *I know that deep, rich voice.*

"Hello? Is anyone there?"

"Um...hello." I quivered. "My name is Chantel Reed. I just received flowers from someone, and—"

"Chantel! You got them! That's great. Does this call mean you'll have dinner with me tonight?"

"Who *is this*?" I asked, now dumbfounded. Due to the staticky connection, the stranger's voice sounded muffled, making it difficult to place it for certain.

"You mean you don't know who I am? I must have forgotten to sign the card." He laughed. "It's Brandon. Remember? We met on the Metro."

My heart jumped. *Brandon?* This was actually the first man who had pursued me. Well, there was Eugene, but...I was not attracted to him, so that pursuit did not count. Eugene's pursuit was more like a stalking, which did not make me feel happy...not at all.

"Thanks for the roses," I replied weakly. "They're beautiful."

"You're welcome, doll. So, will you be joining me for dinner tonight? How about ten-thirty?"

"Ten-thirty is kind of late, Brandon. I..."

"Come on, Chantel. I promise you won't regret it. I wish you could see me right now. You've got me begging on bended knee."

I laughed. "Well...OK, OK. Ten-thirty."

"Great. I'll see you then. Bye."

What did I just do? I can't go on this date, can I?

Perplexed in thought, I decided to call the only normal person I knew...well, almost normal. Serenity answered the phone on the first ring, which was odd.

"Hello?" she answered in her usual flustered tone.

"Hi, Serenity. It's me, Chantel. Can you talk?"

"Of course! Are you calling to confirm our chocolate challenge?"

"Chocolate challenge? Ugh...no. Actually, I have date."

"A date?"

"Yes. Remember Brandon? You know, that guy I told you about? The one I met on the Metro?"

"Yes, I remember."

"Well, he asked me out on a date tonight! But I'm not sure if I should go."

"Well, why not?"

Instantly picturing Brandon's gentle smile and his engaging green eyes, I began to smile in a daze. "He is so cute and nice and cultivated." I sighed. "But..."

"But what?"

"Please don't think bad of me. It's just that, even though interracial dating should never raise a concern, Daria is against me dating outside of my race. I'm not sure what I should do! I just got out of a relationship with Cameron, a union that I thought had a chance of leading to something stable. I'm still dealing with my insurance company involving that mindless car accident thanks to Cameron. I really should be getting my life together and focusing on buying a new car. And Astrid is still mad at me. If she found out that I was going on a date, she would be convinced that I could not go a day without a man in my life. Yet I really like Brandon. I just don't want get hurt or manipulated and played all over again."

"Look, Chantel, your sister's prejudice toward white men and Astrid's prejudice toward men in general is not your torch to bear. You have to live your own life, and taking chances through a leap in Serenity is all about making wise decisions that fit what is best for your life."

"You're right.... You're absolutely right, Serenity!" I thought.

"However, if you decide not to go, I am having a dinner party for a group of Serenityful sisters. I will be sharing their stories on a special edition show in memory of Alison. Better yet, you should attend both the dinner party and the amazing show on Alison's behalf. You are more than welcome to join us later on this evening."

"Oh, Serenity, that sounds great. Really, it does, but I'll pass this time around. I will try to make the show, though. I think that it is best that I take a chance and go out with Brandon tonight. Thanks for the advice."

"Of course! Have fun, and fill me in on all the details later."

"One more thing." The question that I was about to ask Serenity felt natural since she had just featured a show on the topic. A clear and precise answer was vague since every woman had her own take on the subject. "If things go well between Brandon and me, how long do you think I should wait before we...well...you know...have sex?"

Serenity paused briefly on the other end. "Chantel, you are asking me of all people, and you know how strict I am involving this subject. I'm old-fashioned. I think you should wait for marriage. If you end up sleeping with this guy and he dumps you and moves on to the next flavor of the week, you will feel bad about yourself. If you wait, it gives him the chance to know you and, most important, respect you. I know this advice seems to be old-fashioned today; however, this wise instruction could end up saving you from a lot of heartache."

I figured that I somewhat respected her words of wisdom, but I was not a virgin, and I enjoyed sex. I was hoping that she would say something like wait two to four weeks max; however, if I wanted that kind of advice, I should have contacted one of my wild friends. Yet I have found that there is certain advice that should not be taken from those who lack moral values. Looking back, I realized that I should not have been so quick to have sex with any guy. Back then, I was so eager to be loved, even if it meant sleeping around. Every guy I slept with ended up making a complete fool out of me. I was definitely going to try taking it slow and saving myself for marriage.

Thanking Serenity for her sound advice before hanging up, I promised that I would fill her in on my new prospect. As I prepared myself for something new, a sense of betrayal overshadowed my thoughts. For the very first time in my life, I was about to go against my sister's wishes, and I knew I was not going to wait for marriage to have sex. That was ridiculous. Asking me to become celibate was like asking me to refrain from chocolate...not happening.

CHAPTER 6

Chantel

The excitement of seeing Brandon for the very first time since meeting on the Metro took on a new feeling of excitement. I left the office about five-thirty and headed for the beauty salon for a hair and nail renovation. Back at my apartment, I chose a fluid red jersey dress with just the right amount of cling and bling to accentuate my curves. The sleek updo complemented the elegant look. Slipping on my strappy red heels, I topped everything off with classic Tiffany flower earrings in platinum, eighteen-karat gold, and diamonds. Daria would flip out if she knew that I was wearing the extravagant earrings she had given me for completing high school with honors. They were such an expensive gift for a high-school graduate, and looking back, I'd have much rather enjoyed the money instead. But my sister always purchased gifts for me that she could borrow in return. I shuddered at the thought that Daria would never approve of my wearing her treasured earrings on an occasion such as this. *Well, what she doesn't know won't hurt her.*

Too caught up in anticipation, I did not give my sister another thought as I studied myself in the full-length mirror. I had to admit that I cleaned up rather well. I tore myself from the mirror, grabbed my purse, then stopped to glance in the mirror once more. *Well, princess, off to the ball we go.*

Just as I attempted to leave, my cell sounded in a familiar ringtone, the theme song to *Mission: Impossible*. That meant that Astrid was on the other line. The only other person I dreaded talking to at times other than my nosy, controlling sister was my skeptical, overly critical friend. Giving a sigh of regret, I answered, "Hi, Astrid!"

"Hi, Chantel! What are you doing?"

"Oh, nothing. I was just..." I felt awful. Even though I did not communicate the fact that I was going to fast from men, I did not tell Astrid no. Part of me felt as if I had misled her into thinking that I shared her feelings by saying nothing at all. To be honest, I was mentally prepared to join Astrid in her mission to refrain from men...that is, until I met Brandon. Searching for a guilt-free cover-up, I continued, "I was just watching TV."

"Anything good?"

"Not really."

"Well, I'm bored! Why don't I come over, and we can make double-chocolate fudge brownies? We can bake and watch a movie. I thought *Charlie and the Chocolate Factory* would be a cute flick to watch."

I felt sorry for Astrid. She was lonely. Even though the movie that we both loved to watch was just a classic kids' flick to most, this was one of our favorite movies. Astrid and I would indulge in our favorite red wine and laugh endlessly together, especially during the Oompa Loompa scenes. The hard part was that even though I knew my friend was lonely, selfishness took over my entire being. I was captivated by the whimsical feeling of being with Brandon. "Wow, Astrid, that sounds great, but I have to meet up with Serenity. I promised that I would help her...tidy up her house...for one of her women's groups."

"Tidy up her house? It's kind of late!"

"Yeah, she's running behind and needed me to help with some last-minute touches. I should really get going. I'll call you tomorrow, girl."

"Well, helping out Serenity shouldn't take too long. What are you doing afterward? You can stop by, and we could find some new delicious chocolate recipes to bake! We don't have to watch that movie. We can watch something else."

"Um...that sounds great, Astrid, but I...I told my sister that I would stop by and help her clean, too. Yep...Daria is having a dinner party tomorrow night."

"Wait...so you like to clean houses now?"

"Well...cleaning...well...cleaning..." My head began spinning as I tried to worm my way through the awful lies. "Cleaning helps out with my anxiety."

"Oh, I see."

"Well, I really have to go. Maybe we can meet up tomorrow for tea?"

"Yeah, sure. But—"

"OK, Astrid, I really have to go." I hung up rather abruptly.

Knowing that the cab driver had been waiting for a while, I stashed my cell in my purse and dashed out the door. I couldn't believe I'd managed to betray my sister's expectations and deceive one of my best friends in one night. Hopefully, Astrid was not able to see through
my horrible lie.

CHAPTER 7

Astrid

I can't believe she lied to me! Cocoa hated cleaning. She has a maid come in once a week to tidy up that little apartment that she has. The only way I could find out if she was lying for sure was through Serenity, and that was exactly what I did, but not before placing my double-chocolate fudge brownies in the oven.

It took a while for Serenity to answer. "Hello!" she said, short of breath.

"Did I catch you at a busy time, Serenity?"

"Not really. I was trying to dust off the top of my ceiling fan. I had to use a stepladder. I'm almost done cleaning. I have a group of amazing women coming over tonight. What are you up to, Astrid?"

"Nothing much. What time is Cocoa coming over to help you clean?" I asked as I leaned on the counter. I began stirring my finger through the large bowl of chocolate Kisses.

"Cocoa? You mean Chantel?"

"Yes."

"I invited the both of you, actually, but Chantel could not make it. She had a date."

"A what?"

"A date. You didn't know?"

"No! I can't believe her!" Nudging the bowl aside,

I gave an infuriated sigh.

"Well...Astrid, if you are lonely, you can always come over and join us. These women are insightful. Their Serenityful stories are inspiring and uplifting. They—"

"Please, Serenity, the last thing I want to do is sit there and listen to a bunch of stories. I have two retirement parties and three weddings to cater this week."

"Well, take a break. Their stories are uplifting, Astrid, and besides, it beats sitting home alone stuffing your face with chocolate. Like I told Chantel, I think both of you are addicted to chocolate."

"What?"

"Every time I hang out with you two, you're obsessing over chocolate."

"Chocolate is my life, Serenity. That's how I make a living, but I am not addicted to it."

"If that is the case, why don't you and Chantel accept my chocolate challenge?"

"Your chocolate what?"

"I call it the chocolate challenge! I challenge you and Chantel to refrain from eating chocolate for one week."

"I can't do that."

"I'm sure you have a vacation coming up soon, Astrid."

"Yes, I do, but I'm not going to spend it running away from chocolate. I use that time to create new recipes."

"Excuses, excuses." Serenity sighed. "Some women escape bad relationships by entering into new ones, and some women resort to eating. Chocolate happens to be a popular comfort choice. You really need to consider surrounding yourself with Serenityful sisters who can support you through supplication and inspiration."

"Look, Serenity, I don't know if I believe in all of that."

"Well, you're serving something."

"What is that supposed to mean?"

"Everyone serves something. I believe your addiction is chocolate."

"That's absurd, Serenity! Look, just because I don't feel like hanging around while you submit to the painful pasts of other women does not make me weak toward anything, not even chocolate."

"Astrid, many women find it freeing to share their pain and how they overcame their trials through the victory of their own Serenity. They don't feel vulnerable at all. These women know that their story could help others.... Astrid?" She paused. "What are you so afraid of?"

"I'm not afraid of anything. I just..." Serenity was the only one who could make me feel so uncomfortable. My guard instantly went up anytime we touched on this particular subject. I had to think of something to say that would immediately end this conversation. "I have to go—my brownies are burning!"

CHAPTER 8

Serenity

There was a part of me that wanted to yell at Astrid. She never gave my women's group a chance. Astrid had changed when Alison passed. I guess we all did. We missed her gentle nature. Alison had a way of reaching out to authentic women. Even though I tried to take over for Alison, the mood seemed so stale. Things became too stifled and structured, which was the opposite of how Alison conducted her surroundings. However, I felt that as if I were becoming better at reaching out to women who were in need of healing.

The event that I was hosting that night was in honor of Alison, and Chantel and Astrid were no-shows. Both of them were seemingly too caught up in their own addictions, not allowing themselves to experience the joy that Alison had left behind. Alison always had women's events going on every week in different locations, but come to think of it, I can't ever remember actually attending an event at Alison's house. I had met Alison's husband once, and he was not nearly as friendly or as outgoing as his mate, but at the time, I figured opposites attract. Regardless, Alison always would find a way to bring women together whether it was at her high-rise posh office or at a unique venue with excellent service. One way or another, Alison always found a way, and I tried to study her hospitable ways and apply her gifts of wisdom to my morning talk show. Tonight I was opening up my home to a group of women whom I valued. I leaned on an inner Serenity that the information obtained from the five lively women would be a key asset that I could apply to the show that I had planned in Alison's honor. And as excited as I was to mend this show together, deep down inside, I felt as if Chantel and Astrid were desperately in favor of tearing my mission for Alison apart.

CHAPTER 9

Chantel

Once the cab reached my destination, I hoped that its musty scent hadn't become embedded in my clothing. There is nothing worse than smelling of expensive perfume with the lingering odor of a cheap cigar.

Funny, I was so anxious to get here, but once I actually arrived, I was reluctant to enter the restaurant. Once I reached the entrance, I noticed a sign in the window that displayed the hours: 12:00 p.m.–12 a.m. during the week, and 12:00 p.m. till 2:00 a.m. on Saturdays. Open for Sunday brunch 10:00 a.m.–2:00 p.m. It was 10:25 p.m. I stood there, wondering if I had made a mistake. Maybe I should have taken a break away from the dating scene and concentrated on my career. Besides, I had just gotten out of a dysfunctional relationship. Just as I was about to dig in my purse in search of my cell, I heard the door unlock.

Brandon, looking taller and more muscular than ever, grinned and whispered, "You're not having second thoughts, are you?" He gave me a piercing gaze. Without waiting for a response, he continued, "I had to close this place down early just to spend time with you." He studied me carefully. "And it was worth it. You are absolutely stunning, Chantel, a work of art."

"Thank you." I smiled. Whatever reservations I had seemed to melt away. Just looking at Brandon gave me a sense of security.

"Come on in, Chantel." He led me into the exquisite foyer of the restaurant. Spacious burgundy chairs lined the castle-inspired space. "I'll be right back. You can have a seat or take a look around. I won't be long." He disappeared around the corner.

My friends were right. This place was extravagant. Beautiful paintings of well-known artists adorned the walls: Dizzy Gillespie, Lena Horne, Sonny Rollins.... On the center wall, I spotted a painting of Billie Holiday. Wearing a long, baby-blue evening gown and a white gardenia in her hair, she was leaning against a piano. I was in awe. I studied the astonishing artwork.

"May I help you with something?"

I turned to find a dark-skinned woman with long, jet-black hair draped from the back of her head. Her dress revealed a nicely toned body. She probably worked out religiously, but her face seemed hard and rather masculine in form. She looked at me as if I had some kind of mental disorder.

"I'm Chantel Reed. I'm here with..."

"She's here with me, Sylvia." Brandon came up from behind. "Chantel, this is Sylvia. Sylvia, Chantel."

"We met," she hissed coldly, keeping her eyes on him. "I thought you had a business meeting." Ooh. If looks could kill!

"Well, you know me, doll," he smoothly replied, ignoring her message. "I love mixing business with pleasure."

"Yeah. I of all people should know that," she snapped.

"Sylvia, could you please excuse us? We have private dinner plans. Feel free to show yourself out."

She gave Brandon a look of death, then rolled her eyes at me before storming out of the restaurant.

"Please excuse Sylvia," he explained. "She is one of the hostesses. Good help is hard to find."

"Look, Brandon, I hope I didn't come between you two, because if—"

"Don't worry, Chantel. You don't wear it well. Your smile is what I want to see." He flashed his infectious grin. "Come with me."

He took me by the hand and led me down a broad corridor. The floor was blanketed with plush burgundy carpet. Paintings of Miles Davis, Louis Armstrong, Charlie Parker, and B. B. King; singers from back in the day such as the Godfather of Soul, James Brown; and Motown artists Diana Ross and the Supremes, Smokey Robinson and the Miracles, and the Jackson Five decorated the walls.

"Watch your step," he warned, pointing to the stairs. He led me down into an enchanting ballroom with a single table set for two sitting in the center of the room.

Hand in hand, we walked toward the table, and he carefully seated me. A vase of exotic orchids set off the table, covered with a creamy lace tablecloth and set with gold-rimmed china and sterling flatware. Above us hung a gleaming crystal chandelier.

A live band nearby played Nat King Cole's "Unforgettable." This seemed like a dream, and I didn't want to wake up. This reality outdid any fantasy I could ever have imagined. A waiter appeared and poured champagne. We toasted each other.

"May I bring in the appetizers?" the waiter asked.

"No, not yet," said Brandon. "First, I would like to dance with the lady. May I?"

Brandon extended his hand toward me. As I stood, my gaze was fixed on him as if I were in a trance of some kind. We began slow dancing. Brandon caressed my back, then began kissing the side of my neck softly. I'd never been treated so royally and so sensitively.

Everything seemed wonderful, but I knew this was wrong. I wasn't going down the same old path again. Halfheartedly, I pulled away.

"What's wrong?" he asked.

"Brandon, this is certainly more than I expected, but...if you're looking for a one-night stand, you're with the wrong woman. I'm saving myself for marriage. If you want me to leave, then I'll do so. I'm sorry, but that's just the way things are."

"I can respect that, Chantel. There is no need for you to go." He smiled tenderly. Then he caressed my face, holding me close once again. *Heavenly*. I began to question myself. *Can I do this? Can I keep my promise?* This was not going to be easy. Not at all!

CHAPTER 10

Chantel

The next day, I slept in late—well, I wouldn't really call it sleeping. It was mostly daydreaming about the incredible evening that I'd spent with Brandon. Words could not express how much fun I'd had. Brandon was everything that a woman desired: attentive, exciting, refined, thoughtful, intelligent, established, and surprisingly single, which did make me wonder. Why was a guy like Brandon not married by now? Then again, the same thing could have been asked of me. I had a great-paying job, I love to cook, I can take care of myself, and I hadn't gotten married yet, either. I considered our meeting to be marked by fate. The only obstacle that could have sabotaged my doubts was my very own firing squad of cynical friends and family members. As I sat up in bed, fearing what they would think, my cell rang. The first one to fire her bullet of doubt was my sister Daria.

I answered in an ill-fated tone. "Yeah, Mom, what's up?"

"What's up? Now, is that any way to talk to me, girl? Never forget, I have looked after you since birth."

"Sorry, Mom, I just got up."

"It's almost noon, Chantel. Why aren't you out of bed yet? Are you sick?"

"No, Mom, I'm fine."

"Then why aren't you at work?"

"I decided to work from home today, Mom."

"Oh, well, when are you coming to see me? You know that driven young man I told you about?"

"Yeah," I responded dryly, hoping that she would sense the lack of interest in my tone. "What about him?"

"Well, he is dying to meet you, Chantel. I told him that you would be over this Saturday!"

"Mom, it is very inconsiderate to make plans without consulting me first."

"I am consulting you. Right now."

"You did not ask me first."

"Well..." She sounded hurt. "This never bothered you before."

"Yeah, I know, but it bothers me now."

And as always, my sister's hurt instantly turned into anger and an all-expense paid guilt trip. "What is wrong with you, Chantel? I have always tried to look out for your best interests. Ever since Mom passed away, I have tried to fill her shoes. You are so ungrateful!"

"I don't mean to be, Mom. It's just that—"

"Look, Chantel, I have put a lot into you meeting this eligible young bachelor. It's not like you can go on one of those televised dating shows because you're black. A black woman does not have a chance; it does not matter how successful you are. Now, you need to be here on Saturday! This is a great catch."

"If this guy is such a great catch, then why don't you date him?"

"It's not about me! Why are you being so difficult?"

There was no getting around my reality. I had to tell my sister the truth whether she approved or not. "Mom, I'm seeing someone," I blurted out.

She seemed surprised. "You are? Well, Chantel, why didn't you say so? I'm a little skeptical. You lack discernment when it comes to quality black men. Does this one have a job?"

Even though it was not written in stone that Brandon and I were a couple, the chemistry between the two of us was undeniable. Brandon and I were meant to be. "He's a really nice guy, Mom. He has his own business, he's well established, and—"

"Get to the bad part," she interrupted. "How many kids does he have?"

"None."

"Has he ever been to jail?"

"No!"

"Has he been married before?"

"Not that I know of."

"Then what's wrong with him, Chantel?"

"Nothing is wrong with him. He's perfect for me."

"Well, in that case, why don't you bring him over for dinner on Saturday? I'll make your favorite homemade mac-and-cheese, yams, fresh-baked rolls, and—"

"Mom, I have something to tell you, and you might not like it—no, I'm sure you won't like it."

"What is it?"

"The guy I'm seeing is white." Sinking under the covers, I prepared myself for the ongoing shrill that was about to take place.

"You mean to tell me that you are seeing a white boy? Chantel, are you crazy? After all that our family has been through dealing with hatred and prejudice, you mean to tell me that you are seeing a white boy? Girl, have you lost your mind?"

"It's not like that! Brandon is—" I tried to explain, but she cut me off.

"No! No! Absolutely unacceptable! Chantel, you need counseling."

"What?"

"Counseling! I know this great therapist. She can cure you of your problem."

"You want me to see a therapist because I'm dating a white man?"

"I think you have given up on our black men, and I can understand why. Weariness can happen every so often. Her name is Imari. She is a wonderful sister who can provide you with the closure that you need to move past this white man. I'll text you her information when I hang up. You need help, Chantel."

I was fuming. My sister was such a control freak! I couldn't take it anymore, so I let her have it. "And do you know what you need, Daria?"

"No, Chantel. What do I need?"

Throwing all motherly respect right out the window due to my deep-seated anger, I said, "You need to get a life!"

CHAPTER 11

Astrid

Chantel finally returned my calls after three text messages. "I can't believe you lied to me, Cocoa!"

"I'm sorry, Astrid, it just..." She paused for a moment and then continued in a flustered tone. "It all happened so fast. I wanted to tell you, but I couldn't think straight at the time. But now that I've gotten a chance to know him better, I think this may be the one! Can't you be happy for me? I really like this guy."

"That's not the point, Cocoa! You were committed to taking a break from men. We were supposed to get involved in a chocolate escape! Who knows? This could have been an opportunity for us to go into business together. I've been looking for a business partner, but I can't get involved with someone who I can't trust."

"Astrid, please! Daria just laid into me and now you. I can't take this anymore."

"Well, you brought this on yourself."

"So I want a man to call my own. I want to get married and have kids! This could be the guy who I end up spending the rest of my life with."

"Yeah, right!" I huffed. "I wish I had a dollar for every time I've heard that line. You are wasting your time, Cocoa. He's going to end up hurting you just like Cameron and the guy before him. Aren't you tired of playing games?"

"I'll tell you what—I'm tired of being judged by you!"

Chantel hung up. And then I realized that it was impossible for me to end a phone call cordially. This problem used to pertain to men only, and now it had evolved to women.

I was furious with Cocoa. The fact that she could not pull herself away from a man in order to heal from her last relationship was unwise in my book.

Later on that evening, I stopped by Serenity's office, in a beautiful high-rise building that overlooked the city of Seattle. The most stunning sight was being able to view the Space Needle from the bay window. Our last encounter hadn't ended well, with my making up a lame excuse about burning my brownies and hurrying off the phone. Even though I understood Serenity's logic in life, she was the only one who invited me over to hang out with either her or her so-called "authentic friends," or join her at her unique office for a light dinner and drinks.

Serenity was as hospitable as they come. Her office was inspiring and cozy; you could tell that she spent a lot of time there. Serenity ran an innovative business that encircled artists of every kind, mainly women, ranging from poets to writers, illustrators, performers, and inventive businesswomen. Serenity's walls were decorated with historic magazine covers, such as *Time* magazine's 1953 cover of actress Audrey Hepburn, *Life*'s 1969 cover featuring model Naomi Sims and the line "Black Models Take Center Stage," and a 1968 cover with Coretta Scott King;

There also were framed quotes from Proverbs with the wisdom of King Solomon as well as inspirational quotes from famous leaders and poets such as Maya Angelou, Nelson Mandela, and the Dalai Lama. Serenity's office also featured artwork, including an illustration by our mutual friend Camila of a woman's profile boldly outlined. The hair was streaked and was formed perfectly around her oval face. The contour did not have eyes or a nose. The curved, full, red lips emphasized the thought-provoking piece. Scrolled on the bottom of the picture, insight from the artist read as follows: *The layers of a woman are complex. Her ability to practice patience and discernment is an art within herself.*

Serenity looked professional wearing a sleek black dress with striking heels. Her thick, black, shoulder-length hair was smooth, with not one strand out of place.

As we sat near the bay window sipping on white wine, I had to ask, "What is that picture about?" I pointed to Camila's creation, which captured my attention the most.

Serenity smiled. "Camila drew that picture for me, actually, during a time that I was trying to define my self-worth in life. She has the ability to capture my thoughts through a simple drawing."

"What does it symbolize?" I asked

Serenity placed her glass down on the nearby desk and walked over to the illustration. "Well, notice that this woman does not have eyes, which means she is blind toward visual judgment. She does not have a nose, which means she cannot be tempted or misled by scent."

I thought, *She would not be able to smell a delicious chocolate dessert, either.*

Serenity continued. "The one true thing that she has are her full lips, which are curved, symbolizing that life is not perfect, yet her lips remain sealed, which is exceptional given the fact that most women are highly opinionated. Her closed mouth represents peace. Even though she may not be happy about her circumstances in life, she values peace above all. This woman does not rely on what she can see, nor is she led by the aroma of a fine scent, for that matter. She relies solely on her instincts through the conviction of expectancy or hope."

The interpretation of the mysterious artwork inspired me to think about my own circumstances and quest for peace. Even though I didn't like the obstacles that hindered my path or the manner in which most of my girlfriends handled their personal relationships, this did not mean that I had to sacrifice my inner peace, whatever that might be.

From there, Serenity and I got on the subject of the chocolate challenge.

"Look, Astrid, I want to apologize if I offended you by bringing up the chocolate challenge. I know chocolate is your life! You are a very talented woman. I just thought that perhaps you could use a little break from the business, that's all."

Serenity was right. Even though I enjoyed the freedom and comfort of owning my own business and creating new recipes, at times I suffered from chocolate burnout. I knew that I had to take a break eventually in order to regroup. I never wanted to grow tired of the business. I wanted to turn my business into a franchise that could stand the test of time. Nonetheless, I needed balance.

"What is the chocolate challenge about?"

"It's escaping from the demands of life. If we are not careful, certain circumstances, people, or jobs can turn into gods. In other words, you can become trapped and unfulfilled in life. The chocolate challenge is refraining from chocolate or anything else that may take up a lot of time, replacing those gods with exercise and positive thinking, or in my case, intimate prayer. I asked Chantel if she was up for the challenge as well, but for obvious reasons, she's not."

"I'm not happy with Chantel right now," I shared.

"Why not?" Serenity asked in surprise.

"She abandoned me for that guy who is going to use her up, just like all the rest of them."

"Astrid, that's not right! Have you ever been in love?'

"Yes. Or so I thought. But it ended horribly. I'm trying to protect Chantel, but she keeps repeating the same stupid mistakes over and over again."

"Astrid, you can't protect people from themselves. Give Chantel room to make her own mistakes. Only then will she be able to make smart decisions. Your job is to be a good friend. She needs you."

I had to ask about Serenity's church life. I've never been a person sold on church, only because the churches that I attended in the past seemed fake to me—women sitting up there with plastic smiles in public but behind closed doors not any better than the rest of us.

"Do you go to church a lot, Serenity?"

"There was a time when I went religiously, but then there came a time when I felt that I had been fed with the Word to the point of completeness. I did not want to turn into a mundane churchgoer. It was time for me to go out and share my spiritual knowledge with others. I have met some amazing women, Astrid, women who express themselves through the art of cooking." Serenity pointed to a colorful picture of a variety of food, ranging from tequila-lime shrimp to tabbouleh to my favorite pastime, sweets.

"I know of an amazing woman who resides in Canada, one of the best cooks I have ever known, besides you, of course, Astrid." She smiled. "She loves her family and expresses her love through cooking. However, there is a deeper desire that every woman craves. Our ability to search for that inner completeness either pushes us out of our comfort zone or leaves us impotent through our fears of disappointment. My girlfriend in Canada strives to break free, which is why we are still friends to this day. I realize that I don't bond well with stagnant people, and in return, they do not respond well to me, for that matter. I'm trying to push them forward, and they fight to stay exactly where they are. I wonder where our friendship will lead us, Astrid."

Absorbing Serenity's concepts, I fixed my attention back on the illustration of the solemn yet anxious-looking woman. I wondered if I could be a woman who kept quiet during troubling circumstances. Time will tell...I guess.

CHAPTER 12

Serenity

I had not seen Isidora in months. Isidora was a free spirt who loved to travel and do her own thing. She was searching for the perfect relationship, having to be the one to initiate the desire for true companionship. We met up at the park for a midday walk among the oaks, conifers, camellias, Japanese maples, and hollies. On the shores of Lake Washington, the Washington Park Arboretum was the perfect place to take in nature while escaping life's dark impressions.

"I'm so tired of inconsistent men!" Isidora blurted out in sheer frustration. Isidora was a natural beauty. With blonde hair and blue eyes, she resembled the classic all-American girl. Her desire for purpose greater than the confinement of this world set her on a path that was different from the rest.

"Either they're crazy or boring. Where is the perfect man with a balance who is centered around a greater purpose?"

"Well, Isidora, that takes time."

"How long? There are so many things that I want to do. I want to travel around the world. I'm ready for the perfect guy.... Where is he?"

"Patience, Isidora."

"I'm tired of waiting. In the meantime, I keep making the same mistake over and over again with a guy who does not know what he wants. One minute he is ready to commit, and the next minute, he's not. I can't live like that."

"Do you care for this guy?" I asked.

"Yes! And that's what sucks! Because I care, James can manipulate my heart. I never know when he's up or down. It's exhausting."

Isidora had been dating James, whom she had met through a mutual friend. She and James had the same interests, such as hiking, sightseeing, and traveling, and they both were seeking out Serenity. Isidora was a take-charge kind of woman when it came to seeking out her Serenity. And James was more laid back, she explained. They attended church almost on a regular basis in the beginning of their relationship. In spite of their similarities, certain insecurities threatened to drive these two apart.

Isidora was a woman who diligently searched for true love but had a hunger to fully understand her purpose in life. I can remember many times running into Isidora at Serenity-based functions where she would arrive by herself or be the last to leave.

Isidora was driven when it came to attending Serenity-based conventions. On one occasion, she and I attended an African-American Serenity-based conference where there were not many white women in the audience that night, yet Isidora's spirit was dialed into the minister's. The subject of fear resonated with the spirit-filled congregation of women who wore lavish hats. Many nodded, and some shouted out, "Amen!" and "Praise the Lord!"

The lively young female minister said that the power of Serenity could overcome fear through perseverance in the storms of life. She acknowledged that we are God's children, and just like our own children, we fear many things and seek comfort from grown-ups in times of worry. However, the lesson cannot manifest its full purpose within us without the existence of trials and tribulations.

The understanding that Isidora embraced from that sermon seemed to make her feel more secure than the comfort of insecure men. Isidora was one who desired to be filled with serenity and peace. There was nothing else in this world that had the power to uplift Isidora's spirit.

Knowing that Isidora desired a higher understanding of love from a maker that surpassed all worldly knowledge made her quest all the more complicated at times. Just like the rest of us, Isidora was only human. Yet Isidora's dedication and personal understanding of a Serenity purpose seemed to separate her from other women who seemingly knew God only through the Serenity of others. Some of these women did not have a personal relationship, which showed in a robotic hypercritical light.

That day, Isidora and I prayed amid the serene surroundings while birds chirped freely and the soft breeze rustled through the trees. I found it interesting how nature itself, created by the same being, could be so calm while deep within the heart of humans stalked a restlessness, a longing for a sense of direction and resolution.

CHAPTER 13

Chantel

The following weeks seemed perfect. Brandon and I were inseparable. We were a perfect match, yet something inside me did not feel at peace. My relationship with Astrid was shaky, but on the other hand, my relationship with Serenity was fine. Brandon and I took our relationship a step further by joining Serenity and her husband on several dinner engagements and movie dates. Even though my relationship with Brandon seemed flawless, something just wasn't right. After work and on weekends, as we walked along the beach or I joined him on a serene cruiser escapade, our relationship resembled one of those shameless black-and-white perfume commercials—no pun intended. Our inviting dinner cruises on Elliott Bay outshined my expectations!

The experience was exceptional. A turn-of-the-century elegance embraced us both. We enjoyed memorable dinners and pleasant strolls on the deck, savoring the Seattle waterfront and skyline. We shared piña coladas and danced the night away. We did it all.

Brandon and I were the perfect interracial couple. *Interracial*. Why did that bother me? For some reason, I was uncomfortable! I don't know if it was because my sister disapproved of our relationship or because Astrid was upset with me. I wanted to be able to fully include Brandon in my life, but I also wanted acceptance. I needed some advice.

Serenity would only encourage me in her typical way, which was all good until it was time to put

Serenity into action. Without my consent, my sister had texted me the number of a therapist, but I didn't want to go that route. Astrid was too bitter about men right now. Then I thought of my friend Nataliyah! A vivacious blonde who spoke her mind and lived passionately within her own convictions, Nataliyah was married to a man named Abhay—I'd never bothered to ask what ethnicity Abhay was, nor had I bothered to look up the origin of his name. Abhay was a handsome gentleman with a glistening bronze complexion and was soft-spoken. This made sense since Nataliyah often did most of the talking. They complemented each other well.

I phoned her, and we met up for tea at a Teavana. Nataliyah arrived before her aerobics class.

"Hey, girl, are you OK?" she asked.

"Yes." I sighed. "I just need some advice."

We put in our order: mint green tea with honey for me and passion tea for Nataliyah. After we were served, we walked outside and sat on a nearby bench.

"What's going on, Chantel?" she asked, her face full of concern.

"I don't know where to start. I...I don't know how to say this. I'm not even sure that I should tell you. I feel at this point I need to share this information with someone." I felt uneasy about what Nataliyah might say. I did not want Nataliyah to think that I was against interracial dating. I also did not want to offend her by talking about my insecurities, whatever my hidden dilemma might be. "I don't know if I am afraid of what people might think. Promise me this will remain confidential. You see, I'm—"

"Stop!" Nataliyah grabbed my hand, then moved closer. "You don't have to tell me anything more. I already know what you're gonna say, Chantel."

"You do?"

"Yes, I do. You're pregnant? And that deadbeat guy you were dating dumped you?" Nataliyah shook her head in a concerned gentle motion.

"What?" I asked, not knowing whether to laugh at the thought or the expression on her face. She was trying be understanding in spite of her conservative background.

"Chantel, you have been my friend for a while now, and with all of the craziness that is going on in this world—men turning into women, women turning into men, dogs turning into cats—"

"Dogs turning into cats? Nataliyah, I don't—"

"It's a figure of speech."

"Nataliyah, I'm not pregnant!"

Nataliyah paused, then took a quick sip of her tea. Her face took on a calm demeanor. "Thank goodness! I was running out of things to say to you."

I regrouped my thoughts for a second, then continued. "So here is my situation. I'm seeing a guy who I really like. He's smart, handsome—the whole entire package!"

"Oh! Well, that's great!" Nataliyah gave an energetic clap of approval.

"Yes, thank you. But he's white, and my sister is against me dating outside of my race."

"What does your sister have to do with this? Your relationship is between you and your new man, not your sister. Three is a crowd." She smiled.

"I know, but my sister..."

"Chantel, you have to do what is best for you, not your sister."

Out of curiosity, I asked, "Have you and your husband had any issues being a biracial couple?"

"Yes, at times. My husband's background has traditions that I have never experienced, and sometimes that can be a bit challenging on my end, being that I'm a white girl out of the suburbs of Detroit. But I've always had an interest in different cultures and music, so I feel comfortable. Besides, it wasn't my husband's skin color that attracted me to him; it was his honest love for me that brought us together. I was searching for a false sense of love through broken men...until I met a man who showed me a godly form of love. From there, my relationship through my Serenity led me to a mate who loved me unconditionally. Through that bond, we were able to start a family together."

Nataliyah spoke of her husband through a genuine core of gratitude. Yet her life brought about another concern—children. Nataliyah and Abhay had a beautiful daughter named Sofie, who was the perfect combination of both of them. Sofie had her dad's skin tone and striking features similar to Nataliyah's bone structure. Her curly brown locks, intermingled with streaks of natural blonde highlights, accentuated her hazel eyes.

Even though children are a rewarding blessing, I wondered what obstacles my children would face having a black mom and a white dad. Of course, Seattle was diverse, full of children from various backgrounds. Yet the thought of my kids being judged due to their background scared me.

I had to ask. "Has Sofie run into any problems due to her diverse background?"

Nataliyah thought for a second and then sighed. "The most recent event that I can think of had to do with a routine errand to the grocery store. Sofie had wanted me to buy her some candy, and I don't allow her to have sugary treats, so I put my foot down and told her no. I had to practically drag my child out kicking and screaming. As I tried to get Sofie into the car, I was approached by a rather intimidating black woman. She was wearing some kind of store badge which indicated that she managed the store. She was accompanied by a couple of security guards. With a strong tone the woman asked me if Sofie was my daughter, and of course, I told her that she was. Yet it wasn't until after they heard Sofie refer to me as 'Mommy' that they backed off. I was upset! Kids throw tantrums all of the time! I could not believe that these people thought that I was trying to kidnap a child! I was upset!" Nataliyah gave a look of frustration.

I thanked her for meeting up, and even though she gave me an honest glimpse into her life and how she viewed the core of her own unique relationship, there was a nagging uncertainty that longed for a deeper understanding of how to move forward. Being in a biracial relationship should not have bothered me to this extent. I knew that there must be something festering deep within my being that tormented my soul.

The following morning, I made an appointment to see that therapist.

CHAPTER 14

Chantel

The morning of my therapy appointment, I woke up a complete wreck. It had been raining for the last couple of days, and my hair was untamed. Without time to put some effort into the mess on top of my head, I tried to slick it back into a ponytail, but it was still a bit puffy, and I had run out of gel. I took off for work already frustrated.

I was a bit reluctant to share my thoughts with a total stranger, so I asked Astrid and Serenity to come with me. Fully aware of the confidentiality agreement between therapist and patient, I still had my reservations. It was true that I had tried everything in the past: relationship gurus, even psychics. I can remember one psychic who told me that I was coming back in my next life as a wild horse. She told me that I would live my life wild and free—yeah, right! With my luck, I would probably come back as horse crap covered in flies.

While immersed in paperwork, I realized that I had slacked off the last few weeks so much that I had Yvonne hold my calls and reschedule my appointments, which would allow me the time to catch up. Still, my mind kept going back to Brandon. I could not keep from smiling every time I thought about him. We had not had sex yet, and that too was a concern because I could feel temptation kicking in. Just as I was about to indulge in a very inappropriate daydream, I heard people arguing outside my office. Seconds later, the door flew open. Eugene burst in, followed by Yvonne.

"I'm sorry, Chantel. I tried to tell him you were busy, but he insisted on barging in."

I asked her to excuse us while I got to the bottom of this unexpected appointment. "And to what do I owe this surprise visit?"

Eugene, dressed in a white smock, took off his protective goggles. He was obviously infuriated. "Well, for starters, Chantel, you can tell me what's going on with you and Brandon."

"What? Who told you about Brandon?"

"We met up at the Blue Robin for a game of pool last night. Brandon told me about this breathtaking woman he had met on the Metro named Chantel from Litton Tech! He went on bragging about your amazing relationship and how he wined and dined you. What's wrong with you? Are you out of your mind?"

"No, but you are!" I snapped. *Who does he think he is, my sister?*

"Let me get this straight. You would rather date a white boy before even giving a brother a chance?" He pointed at me. "When he dumps your sorry behind, what's next? Women?"

"You are out of line, Eugene."

"No. I'm out of patience. I care for you, Chantel. All I ever wanted from you was a chance to show you what I had to offer."

"You don't even *know* me," I disputed, my frustration rising.

"So give me that chance." His face dripped with perspiration. He reached in his smock for a handkerchief. "After all," he continued, "you keep giving everyone else the opportunity...first drug head Cameron and now John Boy!"

"That's enough, Eugene." I rose from my chair, grabbing hold of a pen to try and control myself. "I'm going to have to ask you to leave right now. I don't appreciate you barging your way into my office unannounced, and I really don't appreciate you sticking your nose into my personal affairs."

Eugene's face became distorted with anger. He yelled, "Guess what women like you get? *Absolutely nothing!* I could have given you *everything*, Chantel. All Brandon's gonna do is use you and then dump you like common trash. But, hey, you're obviously immune to that kind of treatment. Y'all always screaming you can't find a good black man! All you want is a good black man. All these men are losers or in prison or ugh—you women!" Eugene began pacing. "All along, you women refuse to give highly educated, hardworking, respectable, devoted, righteous men like myself a chance. Nooooo, you women chase after hoodlums, no-job crackheads that you end up taking care of, or better yet, men who are in and out of prison! Ten babies later, you're collecting government income, living off of thick government bologna and cheese. The thug has up and left you. Only then do you come looking for a guy like me to take care of you and your little thug-like offspring."

Eugene drew in a deep breath, then pointed at me. "Well, no more! I've had enough! Ya hear? No more! I speak for every sophisticated black man who is sick and tired of being used by women like you! I'm done with you, Chantel Reed. That white dude is already dragging you down. Just look at you—your hair is tore up!"

Oh no, he didn't! It had been raining off and on all week, and yes, my hair was a little unruly—but tore up?

Speechless, I stared at him. Clearing my throat, I placed the now-dismantled pen onto the desk. Taking the time to pull down on the hem of my blazer, I gently but anxiously combed my fingers through my disheveled hair and then responded coldly, "Eugene, you are way out of line in the workplace. How dare you! I've tried to spare your feelings, but clearly you don't give a care about mine. The bottom line is I don't *like* you!"

My heart pounded. I felt as if it would pulsate right out of my chest. "You're short, boring, and older than the average men I date. I suggest you get yourself a young, naive little girl who needs a sugar daddy and pay her to date you! Better yet, if you are really tired of being used by women like me, why don't you do all the men like you a favor by funding a sugar daddy foundation for short, dumpy men such as yourself who can't find a woman? Now, please leave my office."

"I feel sorry for you, you!"

"And I feel sorry for you. However, if you don't leave my office right now, I'll have you thrown out by security, and then I will file a complaint for ongoing harassment. It will take only one push of the button!" My quivering finger hovered over the security key.

Shuddering with anger, he threw open the door and stormed out. Yvonne stumbled in from eavesdropping. She quickly ran back to her desk, removing her prying self from Eugene's heated path. The awkward man slammed the door behind him.

A few moments later, Yvonne's voice trembled over the intercom. "Chantel, are you OK?"

"I'm just fine, thanks." I sighed. "Please excuse me. I have a ton of work to do."

CHAPTER 15

Chantel

Hesitant but determined, I fought my way through traffic to meet up with my best friends, Astrid and Serenity. I knew Astrid was angry with me, but we could never stay mad at each other for too long. Astrid could not see the logic behind spending money on some stranger to analyze my problems, but she wanted to be there for me. Astrid had been through only one breakup in her life, "and that was enough to last me a lifetime," she reminded me. I was one who believed in soul mates. Astrid shared that she respected my journey and wanted to support our friendship. I think that every woman should have friends who support them in every area of life. After all, this world has enough critics. Even though Astrid said that she had a good hunch about how sad my story would end, even though she was in pain, she still supported me due to our loyal friendship, which consisted of me, her, and the sweetness of chocolate. Who knows? Maybe Astrid was hoping that this therapist would talk some sense into my head, and then we could go back to our previous plan—no more men and a lot of chocolate!

And then there was Serenity. Serenity was upset that I could not find a "godly" counselor to confide in. It was good to have Serenity by my side since she had met Brandon several times. Serenity seemed to like Brandon. And both Brandon and Serenity's husband seemed to get along. They had even met up a couple early mornings to go golfing. I thought Serenity could shed a positive light on Brandon, to show that I was not being biased. I did fear that Serenity's holy-rolling ways might get in the way of the therapist consultation, and for that concern, I warned Serenity not be too preachy. Serenity needed to understand that not everybody had the same driven purpose in life.

Once I reached the high-rise office complex, I entered through the towering glass doors, which led into a cozy reception area with a nice aura. Standing next to Astrid and Serenity, I had to give them both a warm hug. Astrid's eyes seemed stressed, but I was touched that she was there for me even though she had yet to find her perfect companion in life. As usual, Serenity, though beautifully and professionally dressed with every strand of hair in place, seemed anxious and confused.

"Thank you for coming, girls. This means the world to me. Astrid, I know I lied to you, and I apologize. I just—"

Cutting me off, she responded, "Don't worry about it. I'm here for you. Part of me hopes that the therapist will tell you to abandon men for good, and the other side of me feels curious."

Thirty minutes later, the secretary ushered the three of us in.

While the office was subdued, I thought she had too many plants. It reminded me of a jungle. At least she wasn't dressed like Tarzan, or should I say, like Jane.

Her tall and sophisticated secretary dressed all in black introduced us. "Imari, this is Chantel Reed and her close friends, Astrid and Serenity." She gave a quick nod and then left, closing the solid oak door behind her.

"Why don't you ladies have a seat?" Imari pointed toward three oversized cream-leather chairs.

Tiny but compact, Imari wore a three-piece black African dashiki outfit. She resembled Eartha Kitt; in fact, I expected her to purr at us. "Now, just to let you both know," she confided, "I usually do not allow friends to attend the session due to confidentiality issues, but since you were adamant about having your friends Astrid and Serenity present during our first session, I bent the rules. The influences of friendship can also shed some light on the choices you make in life."

"Thank you, Imari." I smiled uncomfortably.

Imari glanced down at the notes that her secretary had handed her before leaving. "So, Chantel, what seems to be the problem? From the forms that you filled out, I can see that you are well-established in life; however, relationships with the opposite sex have been an issue."

"Yes. I'm in love with a white man, and I...well...I don't want anyone to know just yet. The only people who do know are my best friends, Astrid and Serenity. My feeling may have a lot to do with my sister Daria. She is not in favor of me dating outside my race."

Imari began taking notes. "Have you ever dated outside your race before?"

"No."

"What is it about this new relationship that makes you feel so uncomfortable?"

"I guess I'm afraid of how my sister will respond and how his family may respond."

"Why are you in this relationship, Chantel?"

I looked aimlessly around the room for a second and then focused back onto Imari. "Curiosity, I guess. And I'm...well...getting tired of letting black men take advantage of me—the majority of them, that is."

Even though Astrid was supposed to be there for quiet support, she just had to start talking. "I know I am supposed to be here for support, but I can't hold back," she said. "Chantel, that's ridiculous! The guy you're dating could end up taking advantage of you, too. Being a jackass is a state of mind; it has nothing to do with race."

Serenity chimed in. "I agree. Our job is to love one another regardless of skin color."

Imari studied the three of us for an awkward moment. "I see that you all have your own views, most likely developed from your own personal struggles." Focusing her attention back on me, she continued writing and then asked, "Do you have any friends who are in an interracial relationship?"

"Yes, and it's beautiful. All of the couples I know are the perfect match. I'm just not sure that an interracial relationship is the perfect match for me."

"Does it make you uncomfortable to be with this gentleman?"

"No," I answered quickly.

Imari studied her notes. "What made you start this relationship?"

I pondered for a moment. "I wanted to try something different. Curiosity, I guess."

Imari glanced over at me for a second. Her piercing brown eyes seemed to stare through my soul. I felt uncomfortable, as if I were being judged, and feared that this meeting might be a mistake.

Imari peered over at me as if she were trying to examine the core of my being. She then glanced back down at her notes. "Hmmm. Your situation is understandable and quite common, Chantel. Many women are going through exactly what you're experiencing. Nothing to be ashamed of, I assure you."

Not quite understanding what she was saying, I felt my forehead wrinkle and my lips purse together.

"Chantel, I must inform you that you suffer from CB," Imari said.

"CB?" *Is she calling me a crazy...b...?* I thought. *This may be true, but that does not seem appropriate.*

Imari could sense the tension in the room. "Calm down, my dears. In other words, Chantel, you have a scenario otherwise known as *chocolate burnout.*"

I was baffled.

"It's simple, Miss Reed. You're tired of dating inside your own race. You desire to experiment outside the box. And there's nothing wrong with that, my dear."

"That's ludicrous!" Serenity voiced in an upset tone. "There is no such thing as chocolate burnout. It all had to do with the character of the man, not the color. I dated my husband for years before we married. Not once did I judge him based on the color of his skin. I think you are stereotyping black men."

Imari responded, "Some black men seem to believe that black women have a certain preconception of them, similar to how Chantel may be feeling toward her black male counterparts. I am not speaking against black men by diagnosing Chantel with CB. Serenity, in your reality, this issue does not exist. You shared that you are happily married to a black man. But in the lives of some black women, the struggle is real." Imari took a deep breath as she searched for the right words of understanding. "Serenity, all I'm saying is that in order for Chantel to get past this mental hurdle, it may be helpful to give her challenge a code name."

"But the code name 'chocolate burnout' seems ludicrous. I can see if it had to do with maybe an actual addiction to chocolate of some sort, but to associate race with that particular word seems offensive."

"I don't think it's offensive, Serenity," I intervened. "After all, I've been led by my sister Daria, a woman who took over the role of mother, to confide in black men ever since I started dating, and from where I'm standing, black men don't seem to have a problem dating outside their race. And over the years, some black men have gone so far as to portray black women in a negative light. I think I may have CB. I'm tired of being mistreated by black men. Serenity, just because you found a dedicated black man does not mean that every black woman is destined for the same outcome as you."

"Chantel, I think this whole session is useless," Serenity protested. "This woman is filling your head with a bunch of nonsense."

"Serenity, at this point, I think you should be quiet," Astrid chimed in. "We are here to support Chantel. You are running up her bill by running your mouth."

"Astrid, I'm not running my mouth. I'm being honest. Imari has not mentioned any Serenity-based resources to get Chantel on the right track."

"It has nothing to do with Serenity, Serenity!"

"Ladies, please." Imari hushed the room. "I will not overcharge Chantel for this session, Astrid. Serenity, I have read every Serenity-based book from the Bible to the Koran, and I have discovered that having Serenity is something that must be practiced on a daily basis." Observing the cross around Serenity's neck, Imari asked, "The cross that you are wearing...are you a Christian?"

"I believe in God and His Son, Jesus Christ, and the Holy Spirt. However, I don't approve of the way Christianity is being portrayed in today's time, but I do consider myself to be a follower of Christ."

"Serenity, your Serenity is a constant journey that you may be hiding behind due to personal addictions or past hurt."

"I resent that. I'm not hiding behind my Serenity. I am committed to my belief!" Serenity yelled.

"Why? What are you hiding from? What are you afraid of?" Imari asked.

Astrid seemed a bit amused by Imari's questioning. She smirked, "Yeah, Serenity, what are you afraid of?"

Serenity glared over at Astrid. "This is a waste of my time. This is not about me; this is about Chantel. I'm going to go wait outside." Serenity leaped up and stormed out of the room.

"Wow!" Astrid piped. "I don't think I've ever seen Serenity that mad before. I kind of like it! I get so tired of her positive Mary Poppins side. This is a nice change." She smiled deviously.

"My intent was not to upset Serenity," said Imari. "I just wanted her to realize that we all have issues that we either try to mask or confront. Astrid, if you don't mind joining Serenity out in the waiting room, I'd like to finish up this session with Chantel in all confidentiality."

"Sure." Astrid gave me a wink and headed out the door.

Looking back at me, Imari stated firmly, "Chantel, your friends obviously care about you. I can see this, and Serenity, well...Serenity has a different way that she would like you to handle your situation. Masking the problem through her own religious beliefs may be heartfelt in her eyes, but it may not be the answer for you." She sighed. "Chantel, your journey is personal. It's between you and your own passions in life, which can be explored to the fullest only through your own intimate understanding." And then Imari asked a question that threw me off guard. "Chantel, tell me more about your good friend Alison. She played a significant role in your life. Is this true?"

Feeling uncomfortable, I answered, "Yes. Alison was like a sister to me, Serenity, and Astrid. She had time for everyone. Alison was so kind and understanding."

Imari asked, "Chantel, in the questionnaire that you filled out, it says that you respected Alison's opinion. How so?"

I thought for a moment. As I began to visualize Alison's lively features, her vision brought a peaceful smile to my face. I could see her fair skin, her vibrant smile, and her thick, curly deep-red hair complemented by her warm brown eyes. "Alison was always there for me. She made everything seem so achievable. Her understanding seemed to surpass all human knowledge. She made everyone around her feel OK about being imperfect. Alison also started up an outreach program that encouraged and celebrated women. Now that she's gone, Serenity has tried to take over. Astrid and I wanted to help out with her organization as well, but it was way too time consuming, so Serenity took charge instead. Serenity means well, but the organization is now nothing like when Alison ran it. Nothing is the same since Alison left."

And then, Imari asked the dreaded question. "What happened to Alison?"

"I...I don't want to get into this. I just can't."

"OK, Chantel, when you're ready." She gave an understanding smile, moving on with the session. "Chantel, it is clear that you leaned on Alison for emotional support, but eventually you will have to face life on your own, unafraid to make mistakes." Smiling rather intensely, she said, "Chantel, if you are going to date outside your race, do it right. Experience every avenue just as you would with a man of your own culture. Meet his family, and have him meet yours. But whatever you do, don't stray from your own culture.

After all, this man is also in search of change." She smiled. "Chantel, only then will you know if this relationship has a chance of succeeding."

Imari placed her hands on top of a spotless desk and looked directly into my eyes. "In other words, it's time for you to get your feet wet, if this experiment doesn't work, you won't bother trying again. However, if it does work, then your mission is accomplished. You will have found your mate.

"Go ahead, Miss Reed. Step out of your glass cage," she urged. "Too much chocolate is not good for certain black women. Look around you. Black men have explored different options for years looking for their significant other outside of their race. So why can't more black women do the same? One would never know, but my parents were biracial."

Imari's head was covered, so I could not examine the texture of her hair. Observing her attire, I thought she was an eccentric black woman.

She went on to explain her background. "My father was Jewish, and my mother was black. My parents are both gone now, but they taught me the most important values in life are to embrace ourselves and to treat everyone with respect. Where would I be if my parents chose to stick with their own race?"

Imari gave an unwavering grin and then responded with deep principle. "We live in a visual world, my dear. This world of ours is filled with tainted perceptions that reflect negatively on the flawed concepts of beauty and wealth. The balance of true love is lost within the bowels of hype and fantasy, leaving many people to question the accurate meaning of the words *love* and *respect*." Imari grinned encouragingly. "Chantel, don't worry about other people. They are forever judging. Serenity views relationships through her belief. She does not believe in chocolate burnout because she has not walked in your shoes. This problem is real for you, at least for now. In order to delete this issue from your life, you must challenge this situation head on. If it is meant to be, the issue will dissolve, and you will look at Brandon beyond the color of his skin. True love is color-blind. But to many, they can't help but to see love through the barrier of cultural confinement."

Imari had given me a lot to think about. I wanted to tackle my issue head on, but I did not want to do it alone.

Later on that day, the three of us ended up stopping by Liam's, a festive family-owned Chinese joint that we all used to enjoy every so often for a girl's night out of dinner and drinks. It was there that I lost what little cool I had left by pleading with Serenity and Astrid to stop by my sister's house for dinner with Brandon. And if that went well, I would also try to persuade them to join me in meeting Brandon's parents. I did not want to do that alone. Astrid and Serenity were my security blanket. I knew that if my friends were with me, my sister Daria would be on her best behavior.

Serenity was the first to turn me down. "I can't this weekend, Chantel. Ray has a social event at work. Maybe the four of us can make plans for dinner?" she asked while scanning over the colorful wine list in search of her favorite apple mixed drink.

Astrid responded as if she could not wait to take out all of her frustrations, so I prepared myself for the endless rant about to take place. "OK, Chantel, first of all, you know I don't really want to meet this guy. I think you are diving in way too deep, girl. You need to take time off and enjoy being single for a second. And second of all"—Astrid looked around—"why are we here? This used to be Alison's spot. Everything about this place reminds me of Alison."

"Is that such a bad thing, Astrid?" I asked. "I talked to Imari about Alison, and—"

"You discussed Alison with that strange woman?" Serenity pulled her eyes away from the menu. "Why? You just met her!" She was visibly upset.

"Alison was a big part of my life, Serenity. Let's face it; Alison was special to all of us!"

My heart began to race. Alison was an emotional subject. The wounds within in us ran too deep to hide. Knowing the personal pain that each of us carried inside, I tried my best to break the tension. Switching the subject, I went down memory lane in search of happier times. "Remember the first time we met Alison? It was hilarious." I chuckled softly. "She was covered in chocolate, remember?"

Serenity's anger seemed to melt as she recalled that day. "Yeah, I remember as if it were only yesterday. The chocolate fountain that Alison was working on exploded. Chocolate was spewing everywhere. It was such a mess!" She laughed out loud. "But we all managed to help her shut that thing down... . Well, at least I did! I don't know what you two were doing." I laughed.

"I had just gotten my new apron, and I was trying to stay as clean as possible" Astrid laughed.

Thinking back, I shared, "And I didn't know whether to open my mouth and try to catch the chocolate in my mouth for the bizarre reason that it is actually a reoccurring all-time favorite dream of mine. I often dream that chocolate rain drizzles from the sky. To think of it...if rain truly tasted like chocolate, I couldn't care less about my hair. I'd be standing outside all day long with my mouth wide open," I admitted as I sat there visualizing the blissful thought.

"You guys remember when Alison wanted to open a Chinese restaurant that only sold dessert?" Astrid laughed. "And her menu was plain awful!"

"Yeah, it was!" I recollected. "Alison had some crazy ideas all right."

"Yes, she did!" Astrid busted out with laughter in a crazy manner that only the thought of Alison could initiate as she looked back on the moment in time. "She wanted to serve chocolate-covered egg rolls, licorice lo mein topped with some kind of milk chocolate sauce...and some other crap that no one in their right mind would dare eat."

Reminiscing about Alison was the highlight of the evening. And yet deep down inside, I wondered why Alison chose to leave the way that she did.

"Looking back," Serenity sighed, "that was the most vulnerable moment that I have ever seen within Alison...you know, the day that she came looking for help with that out-of-control chocolate machine. I wish she would have continued to stay as open with her problems. Then maybe we could've—"

"See, there we go again." Astrid cut Serenity off. "Every time we hang out, we end up talking about Alison. Can we please change the subject?"

Astrid was right. We always ended up talking about Alison. The memories were always fun in the beginning, but then reality set in. Alison was gone, and she wasn't coming back.

Changing the subject, I sank back into my own selfish concerns by revisiting the point at hand. Even though what I was about to do was so unlike me, I did it anyway. I shamelessly begged Astrid to join me and Brandon. "Astrid, please come with me and Brandon. I can ask if he has a friend for you. He's a handsome guy. He may have a normal friend that you can date!"

"No! Chantel, I'm done with men! I don't understand why you want me to tag along, Chantel. Why?" she asked. "So that you can prove to Brandon's family that you are down with white people? Why do you need me there?"

"Come on, Astrid. That's not it, and you know it. I don't want to do this alone."

Astrid sat for a moment staring intensely at me almost as if she were trying to figure out if I was truly sane or not. Astrid began fidgeting with a pair of wooden chopsticks. "OK! I'll go, girl." She shook her head doubtfully. "You are such a plain!"

"Thank you, Astrid!" I gave a smile of relief.

As ludicrous as my own logic may have appeared to Astrid, I was relieved to have her there for me. However, looking back, it all turned out to be one big, costly mistake!

CHAPTER 16

Chantel

Imari had told me to get my feet wet, not to drown myself, but I generally do what I want, and this time I brought my friend Astrid along for the ride.

Business was slow for my friend. However, she was lucky enough to book a couple of major dinner events for a wealthy socialite and a talented businessman, which gave her a little breathing room to relax and think of new chocolate recipes to add to her extensive list. I was getting a little concerned about my waistline. I really loved chocolate just as much as Astrid, but it was starting to show. Between helping her test different recipes and my own job, I did not have time to exercise.

Astrid often talked about flying out of country. She wanted to fly off somewhere exotic or take up a new hobby too, but instead, parked her behind on the couch and ate chocolate—all kinds of chocolate M&Ms and Hershey's Kisses. I'm not going to lie. I too had a love for chocolate on every level when my relationships ran dry. I knew my friend had to find a life outside of her chocolate addiction, and oddly enough, the desire for a man never seemed to enter her thoughts. Astrid was married once upon a time, which she considered to be one of the biggest mistakes of her life. The second one was agreeing to tag along with me.

In the end, Imari's advice led us into one hot mess. Astrid agreed to tag along and meet Brandon's parents. She also agreed to have dinner with me, Brandon, my sister Daria, and our half-brother, Frank.

The following Saturday, we all met up at my sister's house.

Brandon tried to impress my sister Daria with a dozen white roses along with a bottle of her favorite wine. It was hard to tell if Daria was impressed or not. Daria was a tough nut to crack. She rarely smiled, and even when she did, she still looked upset.

Daria had put together a fantastic meal: baby back ribs, fried green tomatoes, mashed potatoes, homemade bread, and sweet potato pie for dessert. I noticed that my half-brother Frank was not interested in conversation. As he sat there stuffing his face, he didn't bother to look up from his plate.

Only a few minutes into the meal, Daria patted her lips with her napkin, then asked, "So, Brandon, how long have you been white?"

"Mom!" I yelled.

Daria was a bit flustered. "I mean, uh, living in Seattle?" She shrugged.

Brandon flashed that charismatic grin that I had been introduced to when we first met. "I've lived here for almost twelve years. However"—he took a quick sip of merlot—"I've been white all my life!" He chuckled, yet the tension raised by Daria's disapproval hung over the room like a taunting dark cloud.

"Look, Brandon, I'm not much for small talk, so I'm going to get right to the point. What are your intentions with my sister?" Daria asked, squinting her beady little eyes at him.

"What do you mean?" he asked.

"Oh, I think you know what I mean. There are plenty of women out there for you to mess with. Why not Astrid? She's a blonde. They have the most fun, right? Why not stick to your own kind?"

Astrid's face turned beet red. "Wow!" She let out an annoying, high-pitched laugh. "It's impossible to stay silent at this very moment, and let's face it—Chantel, you are afraid of your sister," she huffed.

Astrid was right. Even though I longed to tell my sister off, when push came to shove, I was not capable of doing anything else other than sitting there with my mouth wide open in complete and utter shock.

Astrid went straight into battle. "Daria, I am totally capable of finding my own man, thank you very much. I don't need a matchmaker. I choose not to date at this time because I am too busy running a successful business. I would also like to state that your sister and Brandon are two grown adults. If they want to date, they should be allowed to do so without your expectations hovering over their decision. It's rude and intrusive."

Daria replied without pause, "Astrid, I want the best for Chantel, and I don't think Brandon is suitable."

"Why? Because he's white?" she asked.

"No," Daria responded. "Because he's not Mr. Right."

"Who are you to decide who is right for your sister? She should be able to—"

Daria cut Astrid off, as she often did when she felt threatened. I also noticed that my sister's eyes appeared to have a glazed-over look, which meant that she had been drinking her favorite white rum imported from Jamaica. "I don't know why Chantel asked you to come here, Astrid. This is between me and my sister." My sister turned toward me and asked, "Honestly, Chantel, do you even have any black friends?"

"Daria, what kind of question is that?" I asked.

"Well, do you? Because I don't believe I've ever seen you hang around anyone of color."

"I do have black friends, Daria. Serenity is a good friend of mine. I tried to invite her to join us, but she declined, which I'm beginning to believe was a smart choice on her part."

"Serenity? I met that woman before. The Jesus freak? That's not a real black woman. Serenity has been brainwashed by society. I feel that if you had more true black sisters encouraging you to date within your race, this would have never happened. Serenity is not one of us."

Astrid's face was now beet red. "Serenity is convinced of her belief, just like you are convinced of yours, Daria," she said firmly. "Serenity has nothing to do with the subject at hand. Again, Daria, it is Chantel's choice to date whoever she chooses to date."

"Well, I'm with Astrid." Frank spoke up and then carried on by singing "It's Your Thing" by the Isley Brothers. "Do what you wanna do. I can't tell ya who to sock it to... . Come on, Chantel, sing it with me!"

"Shut up, village idiot!" I yelled. Turning to Daria, I said, "How dare you insult Brandon this way? The world is changing, Mom. Times are different from the days of Dr. Martin Luther King, Jr."

"If you two were to have children, they would be considered black. How do you feel about that, Brandon?" Daria asked in a disgusted tone.

"I'm more concerned with raising respectful and happy children. I couldn't care less about what this world thinks," Brandon answered smoothly, showing no signs of uneasiness.

"I think you're foolish for getting involved in this type of relationship, Chantel. I have invested so much into you. I would like you to marry within your race and raise children who have a solid foundation in their heritage."

"That does it, Daria!" I rarely got mad at my oldest sister, but when I did, I refused to refer to her as Mom, and to show my disapproving rage, I would refer to her by her first name. Slamming my hand upon the table, causing the silverware and glasses to rattle. "I am so tired of trying to live up to your expectations. You never put this much pressure on Frank!"

Daria glared at Frank for a split second and then said, "Frank is a lost cause, and you know this, Chantel." She huffed as she reached for her glass of wine.

Frank just sat there, eating and humming to himself as if he were content being mocked in front of people.

"I'm done. I can't take it anymore. If you can't accept Brandon, then I can't accept you," I said.

"Chantel!" Daria batted her eyes as if she could not comprehend what she was hearing.

"No, Daria, I'm serious. I can't live like this anymore!"

Rising from the table, I made my way out the door, and Brandon and Astrid followed. Of course, Brandon, always the gentleman, thanked Daria for the invitation, which was more than I could even consider doing.

Oh yes, that entire evening was a hot mess, but not nearly as messy as the evening over at Brandon's parents' house. That gathering was a complete and utter nightmare.

CHAPTER 17

Chantel

Brandon's folks lived on Mercer Island on a beautiful little estate overlooking Lake Washington. The evening started off awkwardly as Brandon's mother instantly mistook Astrid for his girlfriend.

"Oh my!" She looked her over and examined her thighs. "She's nice, Brandon. She has some good childbearing hips." She smiled.

Brandon immediately cleared the air. "Oh no, Mom. This is Astrid, a good friend of Chantel's."

Then, taking me by the hand, he presented me front and center. "This is Chantel Reed."

The look on Mrs. Wilmington's face was inexplicable. She stared at me as if she were observing an odd statue in some gloomy wax museum. "Oh, well, I...oh," was all that she could utter.

The awkward evening continued as we sat around an elegantly appointed dining table and began a sumptuous meal prepared by their personal chef and served by their housekeeper, Edie.

Brandon's family consisted of his mother; his stepfather, Brady; and his younger sister, Megan, who was twenty-one.

Reaching for her fifth glass of wine, Brandon's mother inquired, "So, dear, tell us a little about yourself."

Fidgeting with my napkin a bit, I looked over at Astrid, who gave me a warm, familiar smile, as friends do. It may sound silly, but I was glad that my friend was there. I looked over at Brandon. He too gave me a look of comfort. Still fussing with my napkin, I finally placed it over my lap. "Oh. What would you like to know?"

"What does your family do, dear?" she garbled softly, a smile pasted on her insipid face.

"I work in HR for a well-known company in Seattle."

"Oh...well, you're quite beautiful. Isn't she, Megan?" She stared condescendingly at Brandon's sister.

Megan, a rosy-cheeked girl with every strand of her hair flawlessly in place, responded in a high-pitched little voice, "She is really pretty for a black girl. You don't look all ghetto like the girls on one of those rap videos. Do you like rap music?"

Astrid responded, "Are you kidding me?"

"No, Astrid," I responded, "I got this." Gritting my teeth, I could feel the tension brewing in the room.

"Megan," Brandon's mother cautioned, taking another swallow of wine, "do not stereotype. I'm sure Chantel likes all kinds of music."

Answering sharply, I said, "I prefer Negro spirituals. I enjoy humming them while I pick cotton in the backyard."

"Wait...excuse me?" Brandon's mother asked.

My stomach felt as if it were tied in knots. I glanced at Brandon, whose hands covered his face.

His mother ran her words together yet continued in her cultured tone. "Did I say something to offend you? You should be happy that I invited you to sit at my table. I never—"

Brandon cut in. "Mother, please, don't say another word." His tone was dry and direct.

"What? I just—"

"Mother, don't say another word," he demanded.

I started to feel warm. I had to leave the room. Placing my napkin on the table, I stood. "Excuse me. Where is your restroom?" I asked.

"The *powder* room is upstairs, dear. Two doors to your right." She mustered up a drunken smile that accentuated her weathered face. Too much golf? She was definitely the snobby, country-club sort.

"Thank you." I mimicked her plastic smile, then excused myself. As I left the room, I peered around the corner to watch from a distance.

"What's wrong, Brandon?" asked his mother.

"You and Megan are offending Chantel. There are plenty of attractive black women in the world."

She reached for yet another drink. "Well, I'm *sorry*, Brandon. I don't go roaming the streets looking for them. She happens to be sitting right here. I just thought—"

Astrid intervened. "I'm not bothered one bit by your ignorance, Mrs. Wilmington. I am concerned for your young daughter. You should teach her to be more respectful toward other people who are not rich and white like you."

Megan piped in, "I was just asking a question. I did not mean any harm."

"Some people might not take it that way," Astrid snapped.

"Don't you get upset with my daughter, white trash!" Mrs. Wilmington's voice grew louder. "You must be one of those white girls who wants to be black. It's
a shame. She has an attitude, Brandon—most of these sold-out white women do!" she huffed. I'd never seen Astrid so livid. I became dizzy as Brandon's mother continued to vent. "What happened to Emily? She was a nice, purebred white girl. Her father was high up on the food chain. She was born with a silver spoon in

her mouth. What happened? You made the perfect match together."

Brandon sighed. "Emily was a drunk, completely out of control."

Mrs. Wilmington shook her head somberly. "You two were the perfect match."

"The only thing that matched was the color of our skin. Forget it, Mom. Just drop it, all right?"

I ran up the stairs, entered the bathroom, and leaned against the door for a while. Finally, my breathing slowed to a normal pace. I walked over to the mirror. *What am I doing here?* Taking a deep breath, I took my hand and smoothed my updo. Then I ran my hands down the sides of my dress, checking out my attire. This evening was another disaster. I couldn't believe I had wasted my valuable time on these people and had invited my best friend to watch me fail. I could have been at home, just Astrid and I indulging in a chocolate-fudge brownie with extra nuts.

Opening the door, I took a deep breath and prepared for anything this Addams family might say or do. As I approached the head of the staircase, I spotted Brandon's stepfather, Brady, stationed near the banister.

"Are you OK?" he asked, his face beet red, one side of his long-sleeved shirt pulled out, the other side tucked in his pants. He walked toward me, reeking of booze.

"I'm fine, thanks. Excuse me."

He blocked my path. "You'll have to excuse Barbara. She can be such a nag. That old bag, I'd get rid of her if I could, but she's my meal ticket, if you know what I mean!"

I flashed Brady a tight grin. "I hear ya. It's OK. Really. I'm fine. Please excuse me." I aimed to maneuver around him. His sturdy body blocked me like a solid oak tree. He wouldn't let me pass. Just then, I spotted Astrid from behind.

"Chantel, are you OK?"

The drunken man removed himself from my path, allowing Astrid to make her way toward me.

"Is everything OK?" she asked. "I came up to check on you. I'm ready to go, girl."

"Me too," I agreed.

We both proceeded to make our way downstairs. Abruptly, Brady grabbed my backside, giving my rear a solid squeeze, then a pinch.

"You know," he said, laughing boisterously, "Brandon sure has good taste in women, especially you chocolate ones. I sure would like a taste."

My reflexes were quick as I slapped his pudgy, unshaven face. The sound echoed throughout the hall.

Rubbing his face, he grinned, not at all intimidated. "Brandon's got himself a feisty cup of hot chocolate, huh?"

My eyes filled with tears. As Astrid and I both darted down the curved staircase hand in hand, I hoped that I wouldn't break my neck trying to race down the windy steps in high-heeled shoes.

We finally reached the dining room. "Brandon, let's go now."

Brandon rushed over. "Chantel, what's wrong?"

"Your stepfather needs to learn how to keep his hands to himself."

Brandon glanced over at Astrid. Out of complete discomfort, she looked away to avoid eye contact.

Brandon's face became distorted and turned red, and his eyes became a sea of raging blue. "I'm gonna kill him!"

"Wait a minute, Brandon." His mother leaped from her chair. Stumbling over to him, she grabbed his arm. "You don't know Brady's side of the story. I watch those rap videos! This jungle bunny could have backed it up on him or whatever they do. You should have never brought this ghetto woman and her white-trash friend into our home!"

"Mother, I don't *need* to know his side of the story. Your husband wakes up in the morning drunk, and he stays drunk!"

"Watch your mouth, young man," she scolded.

Just then, Brady sauntered in. "What's all the commotion?" he asked as if he'd just arrived home from church.

Brandon approached him. "Did you try to force yourself on Chantel?"

"No!" Brady said in denial, but Brandon refused to back down.

"That's not what she says."

"I was just kidding around, son. I couldn't resist. She's got a lot of junk in her trunk, if you know what I mean. I just grabbed a quick feel, that's all."

I watched Brandon's body seethe with rage. He drew back his fist and punched Brady, causing the man to topple backward so forcefully, he shattered the top of the dining room table, falling through the frame and onto the floor like a rag doll.

Brandon's mother screamed as she ran over to her husband and knelt down beside him. "Call 911!" she cried. Megan fumbled around with her cell phone as she tried calling for help. "Look what you've done, Brandon!" his mother shouted, sobbing hysterically.

"Look what *I've* done? He's a drunk! So don't even think about pinning this on me! You will never see me again until that drunk is out of here." Brandon grabbed Chantel by the arm. "Let's go."

Once we were outside, Astrid could not contain her feelings. "This is a nightmare! Chantel, you need to end this relationship right here and now!"

"What?" I asked.

"Astrid, I'm sorry for that mess. Really I am," Brandon said.

"You two are not right for each other!" Astrid told us straight out. "Chantel, I think you need to move on. You don't need a relationship right now."

"I don't want to end my relationship! I love Brandon." I turned to him. "Could you please wait for me in the car? I'll be there in a second."

Brandon looked dejected, different from the self-confident businessman I knew. Without a word, he made his way to his car as we took off toward Astrid's vehicle.

"You don't love him, Chantel."

"I do! Don't you see? We both stood up to our family members. Now all we have is each other. I found a man willing to stand up to his mother for me."

"You are making a big mistake. Chantel, he's going to use you and dump you, just like Cameron!"

"Stop it, Astrid!"

"No, I won't! I won't be there for you when he dumps you! I'm tired of trying to heal your wounds. You have to make a choice."

"Are you asking me to choose?"

"Yes! I think you need a break! Why don't you spend time with me? You can help me with my business."

"I don't want to be alone, Astrid! I don't want to be some dried-up woman sitting at home eating chocolate all day. I have chocolate burnout—on every level!"

"You think I'm dried up?"

"I think you're scared to take a chance. Relationships scare you."

"Look what just happened in there. It should scare you too, Chantel."

"I love Brandon, Astrid."

"You don't love Brandon. You love the thought of being in love. I'm done, Chantel. Take care."

With those words, my best friend got in her car and took off, alone.

CHAPTER 18

Serenity

I had just hung up with Astrid. She sounded so lost, and she was furious with Chantel and me. Of course, she felt abandoned because Chantel had run off with Brandon, leaving her alone. Ironically, she was upset with me for suggesting prayer. Astrid told me that God had betrayed her, and every time I spoke of Him, it was a painful reminder.

It was true that Astrid had a lot of hang-ups in life, as she had confided in me about her painful divorce. Astrid was unable to have children. Even though she had tried to hold her marriage together by trying to conceive, her efforts led her deeper into despair and disappointment. During this dark moment in her life, she noticed that her husband was slowly slipping away. Astrid tried everything to keep her husband from giving up on the marriage, from expensive vacations and counseling through their church, yet nothing worked. Eventually, her husband found comfort in the arms of one of the couple's dearest friends, a woman they both new. A fellow church member whom she had confided in had betrayed her, and to make matters worse, this woman was pregnant, and the father was Astrid's very own husband. The wounding thought that her husband and friend could hurt her in such a way broke her spirit. Trust was now an elusive thought that ceased to exist in her deceptive world.

Astrid called looking for answers. Deep down inside, she did not want to see another friendship slip away. None of us had had any control over how Alison left our lives. Even though a woman's friendship is not an intimate relationship between a man and a woman, it was the death of a sisterhood bond.

Astrid was hurt. In despondency, she shared that she did not want to see Chantel, and I felt as if she was pulling away from me as well. I tried to persuade Astrid to help coordinate one of the greatest events for women—which had meant so much to Alison. I tried to do everything that Alison would have done, which included inspirational speakers and the opportunity to present different mentors whom she knew would be the perfect ones to speak to the lives of such broken women—yet there were times when all of us would become angry with Alison. After Alison left, everyone fell apart. It appeared as if Astrid wanted nothing to do with Alison's cause. After all, what kind of friend would allow her personal pain to rule over their lives without reaching out for help? My fear was that Astrid would abandon the need for female bonding by staying cooped up behind closed doors, trying desperately to escape through her chocolate desires.

Watching my girlfriends wilt away made me desperate for answers. Every woman was in search of closure, which cannot be achieved without the sovereignty of forgiveness. Still, how can one forgive without the vulnerability of being betrayed all over again?

CHAPTER 19

Chantel

The long trip back to my condo was quiet. Once there, I started a fire. We sat close to each other, each holding a huge mug of hot chocolate topped with marshmallows.

I noticed then that Brandon's right hand was swelling. Rushing to the fridge, I gathered ice in a plastic bag and placed it on top of his bruised hand. "Look, Brandon...I'm..."

"I hope you're not even *thinking* about apologizing. None of this was your fault. My family is psycho—that's all there is to it. The only good thing that came out of this whole ordeal is when you told Astrid that you loved me. Did you mean that?"

Feeling uncomfortable for a split second, I thought that perhaps I should have waited awhile before blurting out such a serious statement. "I guess I should have waited before I—"

"Chantel, I love you, too," he confessed.

Brandon glanced at the clock on the wall. "It's already midnight. I'd better get going." He caressed my face gently. "Look, I'm going to have to leave to visit my dad and brother in England in a couple of weeks."

"In England?" I asked.

"Yeah, my dad met my mom while he was on business in New York. My mom used to be normal, believe it or not. My dad met her at a business conference. The two hit it off and eloped. Before you knew it, they had started a family. I have a twin brother. His name is Landon, and he has Down syndrome."

Brandon stared into the fireplace for a moment, then turned his attention toward me, his eyes intense. "My mother took it hard. Even though she tried to make her marriage work by moving to England to be with my dad, too many obstacles threatened the marriage. Her inability to accept a child with disabilities was a burden, and one day she made the decision to file for divorce. My mother took me with her, and we moved back to the United States."

"Brandon, I'm sorry!"

"No, don't be. I fly out as often as I can to see my dad and brother. My dad was too overwhelmed with work to take care for Landon, so my dad found one of the best facilities not too far from him. I visit him when I'm in town, and they take good care of him."

"Brandon, I'm sorry. I—"

"Chantel, please don't feel sorry for me. I wanted you to know because I would like you to come with me. I want you to meet my dad and my brother." He gave a warm smile. "I love you, too, Chantel. I want you to meet them."

"Oh, Brandon, I would love to, but two weeks is so soon. I'd have to have more notice. I'm so honored that you would even invite me!" I smiled contentedly.

Reaching in his vest pocket, he pulled out a key and a Post-it note with the address. "I thought that's what you might say. So when I get back, I want to take you somewhere special." He handed me the key. "Not only is this the key to my condo, Chantel, but you can consider this to be the key to my heart as well."

The air filled with passion as we began to kiss. As much as I wanted to give into lust, Serenity's words of waiting for marriage first rang throughout my mind. I had made an oath to myself. I planned on keeping it.

Pulling away, I whispered, "I will be waiting your return with open arms."

Chocolate Burnout

CHAPTER 20

Chantel

I was proud of myself for being able to hold to my promise. I felt like a rejuvenated virgin. Yes, I am only human, and I had urges as well. However, I wanted to do things right this time around.

Brandon had been gone for only seven days, but it seemed as if he had been missing in action for seven months. I went by his condo as he had asked. It was incredible! Stylish and elegant, the light-filled space reflected scrupulous attention to detail. From the natural stone floor trimmed in rich wood and the opulent carpet underfoot to the stunning floor-to-ceiling windows, this condo spoke of cultivated wealth and sophistication.

I did as Brandon requested and took care of his sprawling colorful plants and his aquarium full of exotic fish. I hated to leave. Brandon's condo felt like a vacation away from home. Long white-chiffon curtains draped from the surrounding bay windows overlooking the bright lights of Seattle. I never got tired of the breathtaking view, and I never got tired of obsessing over Brandon.

While Brandon was gone, I kept myself busy as I poured myself into my work. I also began working out at the gym and trying to cut back on the chocolate. Chocolate reminded me of Astrid, and the girl was not taking any of my calls.

One long Friday evening, I entered my apartment feeling exhausted after a long day of meetings and conference calls. It was one of those dreadful days during which I had found myself dreaming of having a twin to do all the dreadful things that I hated. If I had a twin, I'd make my double attend these boring business meetings, dental appointments, gynecology appointments, and bad blind dates, if need be.

As I settled down in my cozy leather chair, the doorbell rang. I glanced at the clock on the wall—ten p.m. Who on earth could be stopping by at this time of night?

Peering out the peephole, I was unable to make out the image of the person. "Who is it?"

"It's me, Chantel."

The voice was rich and deep, familiar, yet I could not place it. "Who is me?"

"It's me, Chantel. Cameron."

I felt my heart skip a beat. *What does he want?* Leaning against the door, I answered, "If you're looking for your belongings, I left them at the front office. I gave them to Debbie; she put them in storage. The office is closed for the evening. You might want to—"

"No, Chantel, it's not about my clothes. I need to talk to you."

About what? I wondered.

"Come on, Chantel; let's not do this through the door. Can I please come in? Please, Chantel?"

Against my better judgment, I allowed my ex-boyfriend into my home. Closing the door behind me, he flashed his player grin. Back in the day, I felt weak from that conniving beam. But this time, I was not falling for it.

"Are you here for your video games? Because I left them with Debbie."

"No, Chantel, I came to see you. Girl, you look good."

I knew he was lying. I had just gotten off work, and it was raining. My hair was a mess, and I was wearing a plaid dress I'd purchased at a closeout sale two years ago. Combing my fingers through my tangled hair, I demanded, "So, why are you here?"

"I miss you, girl." He reached to pull me close. I pulled back.

"I'm not a fool, Cameron. Tell me the truth or leave. I'm in no mood for games. I had a long day, and I'm tired. I want to take a long, hot shower and go straight to bed."

"That sounds good to me," he said, toying with me and attempting to pull me near once again.

I moved back. "Get to the point, Cameron, or leave."

"OK, OK." Shoving his hands deep into his pockets, he gave me one of those sad, apologetic looks. "I need a place to crash for a few days."

"Oh, really? Why don't you ask Miss Sunshine, the woman you ran off with? Let's see...what was her name?" I pondered for a moment. "Oh yes, Krissy. What happened to Krissy, Cameron?"

"Ah. Chantel, you still stuck on that? That girl is history. I don't have nothing to do with her anymore. She was nothing special." He shrugged.

"Nothing special, huh? For nothing special, you sure did get all dressed up in the designer outfit that I bought you for your birthday."

"You still trippin' over that?"

"No, actually, I'm standing right here in front of you listening to a whole bunch of lies." I placed my hands on my hips. "Nothing special, huh? That's why you fixed up my dining-room table and took out my good china and candles to entertain some other woman? This is my condo, which I pay for, and all the time you lived here, you never went all out for me. Not only that, but the real shock was that you could cook!"

"Ah, Chantel, you still—"

Raising my hand, I intervened. "Yes! I'm still trippin'! I'm still everything that would describe the word *angry!*"

"Come on, baby." Once again, he reached out to console me. "Give me a chance to make it up to you."

"Don't you 'baby' me, Cameron! No. It's too late. I have someone else."

"Oh, it's like that, huh?"

"Yes, it's like that. So why don't you go back over to Krissy's house and stay there?"

"I can't. She kicked me out."

"Oh, really. Why?"

He confessed like a reprimanded schoolboy. "I couldn't come up with my share of the rent money."

"Hmm...she catches on fast. Unlike myself. Kudos for her!"

"Come on, Chantel," Cameron pleaded. "It's late, and I don't have anywhere else to go. Can I please stay here? I'll be gone by tomorrow. I plan on moving to Phoenix. I have this buddy of mine who drives a truck. He's going to give me a lift out there." He smiled reassuringly. "I'm going to make a fresh start. I plan on rooming with my brother Reggie. Come on, Chantel. I would take care of you if you were in this position."

"I seriously doubt that," I huffed. Yet the kindhearted side of me caved in. Brushing my fingers through my hair, I agreed to let him stay. "But only for tonight, Cameron," I warned. "I want you out of here by tomorrow."

Cameron flashed a wide grin. "Thanks, babe. How about a hug?" He opened his arms to me.

"No! You can sleep on the couch. You know where the sheets are. I'm going to take a shower."

I felt as if I were stuck in an odd dream as I entered my bedroom, slightly closing the door behind me. I couldn't believe I was allowing Cameron to stay here. Thinking about the events of the night, I carefully stepped out of my clothes and took off my stockings. Wearing only my lingerie, I returned to the bedroom door and peeked out to check on Cameron. I was caught off-guard as I watched him strip down to his black buttock-hugging Calvin Klein briefs. I could feel my face perspiring. My heart began racing. I had to take control of my thoughts. Feeling ashamed, I gently closed the bedroom door and locked it.

While showering, it dawned on me that perhaps I had finally found a meaningful relationship with someone whom I did not have the heart to disrespect. Could I finally be in love? Was Brandon the one? As I contemplated the question at hand, I shortened my usual extensive and in-depth shower. Once I got out, I dried myself off. In many ways, my bathroom was my sanctuary. The cozy surroundings decorated with scented candles and warm chocolate tones throughout calmed my nerves. Taking a moment to clear my head, I decided that I did not want Cameron to stay here for the night. Even if I had to pay for him to sleep in a hotel somewhere else, I was willing to do so.

Fearing that Cameron might be going through my things, looking for something to pawn, I hastily dressed in the most unattractive night attire that I could possibly find, a flannel pajama set from three years ago that reminded me of something the mother might have worn on *Little House on the Prairie.*

Entering the living room, I noticed that Cameron was not on the couch. I heard noise coming from the kitchen. Following the clatter, I found a barely dressed man fixing a sandwich. Heading over to the counter, I pulled up a bar stool and sat down.

"Cameron, I don't think you should stay here for the night. I really think I may have something real here, and... I just don't want to mess it up."

"Something real? You mean with the white dude? Now, Chantel, I did not know you had acquired a taste for vanilla ice cream." He smirked as he continued to spread Miracle Whip on a piece of wheat bread.

"Vanilla ice cream? What are you talking about?" Just then, it dawned on me. "Wait a minute. How do you know about Brandon? Did Eugene tell you about us?"

"Naw, I haven't spoken to Eugene in a while."

"Well, then?

"Dude came by here while you were in the shower."

My heart trembled. I combed my fingers through my crimped locks. "Brandon was here?"

"Yep." Cameron sensed my distress and was enjoying every minute of it. "Yeah, he came by here. He must be in love."

"Cameron, what did you tell him?"

Cameron continued to spread sandwich spread on another piece of bread. "I told him the truth. That you were in the shower." He gave me a taunting wink.

I noticed that Cameron was still wearing nothing but his briefs. My eyes widened. "Cameron! Did you answer the door in your underwear?"

Cameron laughed. "Why, of course I did. I'm proud of what my mama gave me." He stood back, spun around, then proceeded to twitch his pecs. "This is one tight package. I had to show the old boy what he was up against, ya know what I mean?"

I couldn't stand to hear anymore. "Get out!" I screamed. I grabbed a pot off the hanging rack and threw it at him. Cameron ducked, still smiling.

"Ah, come on, Chantel, why ya gotta—"

"Get out!" I screamed, throwing another pot aimed at his head. *Ugh—I missed again!*

"Hey, can I at least finish making my sandwich?"

"No! You get out, or I'll call the police! I mean it. I want you out!" I reached for a frying pan this time. Cameron got the message.

"OK, OK. Just let me put my clothes on."

Running into the other room, I grabbed Cameron's clothes and shoes and threw them outside.

"Ah, now, come on, girl, why you got to throw a brother's clothes out like that? I'm indecent."

"Go on, Cameron. Go out there and show Seattle what yo' mama gave you." I grabbed my umbrella, but this time I poked him in his high, bouncy rear end until he was completely out. Locking the door behind him, I heard him scream.

"You're crazy, Chantel Reed! It won't ever work between you and that white guy, anyway, because you're a psycho black woman!"

I quickly grabbed for my cell phone. I had not checked my messages at all for the day. I had three messages: one long-winded text message from Daria, one text message from Serenity about some kind of event that she was throwing for women, and a text from Brandon. It read, *Hey, babe. I know it's late, but I took an early flight home. All I could think about was you, Chantel. I need to see you. I hope you don't mind, but I'm going to stop by for a while. You make coming home a real treat. I'll see ya soon. I love you! Bye.* Heart. Heart. Smiley face.

It was then that I could feel my own heart sinking into the pit of my stomach. I cringed, thinking about Cameron and how he must have boasted in front of Brandon. I had to go see him. I tried to call him on his cell, but I knew he was deliberately not answering. Calling a cab, I headed straight to his condo.

I rang the doorbell. I could hear jazz music from inside. I continued to ring the doorbell.

"Brandon! I know you're in there. I can hear music."

"Go away, Chantel!"

"Brandon, I have a key. If I have to, I'll use it. Please, let me in."

Brandon swung open the door. His eyes were red.

"Oh, my...have you been crying?"

"Don't flatter yourself, Chantel. I'm on London time. I haven't been getting much sleep." He shook his head in disappointment. "So what's the deal? Am I not black enough for you?"

"Brandon, don't be ridiculous. Please, just here me out. Can I please come in?"

"Five minutes." He allowed me inside. "So who is he, Chantel?"

"Brandon that was my ex-boyfriend. He didn't have a place to stay, so I was trying to help him out. But...I knew I should have said no. I wish I would have." I began combing my fingers through my hair. "Brandon, nothing happened, I promise you! He was sleeping on the couch. And I was taking a shower. I had a long day at work. I had an awful meeting to attend; it lasted for hours. I was in and out of conference calls. I was not thinking straight. But after my shower, I asked him to leave. I was so tired, I was not thinking straight."

I was tired of explaining, but I felt that if I stopped talking, he would stop believing, so I kept talking compulsively. "You have to believe me, Brandon. I would never do anything to jeopardize us! Cameron is a complete idiot. I would never go back to a man who has no respect for me. Look at me!" I pointed to my attire. "I must love you. I took a cab at midnight looking like a crackhead. I'm wearing *Little House on the Prairie* flannel pajamas, and I don't have a stitch of makeup on, yet I'm here with you, trying to convince you that I love you!"

I began to sob. Hiding my face in my hands, I had finally run out of words.

I felt his soft, strong hands touch mine and pull my hands away from my face. He kissed me on the cheek ever so tenderly.

"I believe you, Chantel." We kissed ardently, and yes, my flesh wanted more. "I'd better get you home, Chantel. It's late," he whispered.

"I don't want to go home. I want to stay here."

"Chantel, you don't have to—"

"Shhh," I whispered, kissing him unreservedly.

That night, I gave up my newfound celibacy. It was official. I'd fallen head over heels in love with this man.

CHAPTER 21

Chantel

I avoided Serenity's phone calls and text messages like the plague. I had broken my promise to stay celibate, and the worst part of it all was that I did not care. I am a modern woman. Asking me to be celibate is like asking me to go a week without chocolate!

The chemistry between Brandon and me was electrifying. I have never experienced such an attraction. We seized every opportunity to make love, and I enjoyed every moment. Afterward, he would never make up some sorry excuse and take off. He would lie in bed with me and hold me. He conversed with me, rubbing my back gently while taking the time to make sure that I was happy and satisfied. Brandon's love for me made me look at my life differently. I found value within myself through our exclusive romance, and I was not about to allow one of Serenity's guilty lectures deprive me of this feeling. I had not heard from Astrid, either. I was sure she was boarded up in her apartment, sulking in a world of chocolate.

I was certain that I had the real deal, and I was not going to allow the opinions of others invade my thoughts. These days, I was good at ignoring Daria as well. Daria would hit me up for money every now and then. She had gotten laid off from work, and she needed help until she could find another job. I don't know why I called it a loan; it was more like a handout. My sister never paid me back, but since I had it to give and she'd done so much for me growing up, I did not mind helping her out. Her will to rule over my life still drove me insane.

Lately, Daria had kept her distance, and for one hopeful moment in time, I thought she had finally decided to let go and allow me to make my own decisions in life. Of course, that was not the case. Old habits were hard to break. When it came to Daria, I would have to find the courage to fight for control of my own life.

Brandon and I had been going strong for a while now. We were inseparable, and sadly, Astrid and Serenity were girlfriends of the past. I had not spoken to them in months. Daria was looking for yet another handout. This time around, my sister asked to "borrow" two thousand dollars. Looking back, I should've asked her, "What for?" I realized that I should have asked a lot of questions instead of walking blindly through life as if I were living in some kind of fairy tale. Yet at the time, I figured that God was finally smiling down on me and I deserved happiness, never thinking that my sister was nesting away money for an unforeseen prearranged wedding.

My sister took advantage of the fact that I was jaded by this new romance. I was lost in the concept of inseparability. Brandon and I did everything together! We laughed and had fun like most happy couples. Most important of all, we dreamed together about a lasting relationship. I no longer stressed about having chocolate burnout. Brandon was the man for me. I was content.

Eventually, reality set in. Brandon had scheduled another trip to London to see his dad and twin brother, who lived in a facility for adults with special needs. Even though I'd promised to go with him this time around, I had to decline for health reasons. For the past couple of weeks, I had been suffering from dizzy spells and sometimes blackouts. Luckily, I was at the office or with Brandon when these unsettling disturbances would occur. Finally, Brandon talked me into seeing a doctor after I had one of my dizzy spells over dinner one evening. The earliest appointment was during Brandon's time away in London. I begged him to let me go with him and said I'd schedule an appointment when we got back, but Brandon was concerned and insisted that I see someone as soon as possible. So I stayed behind.

Yet through the midst of it all, Brandon seemed worried about something. He was usually so transparent and happy-go-lucky, yet lately, he seemed preoccupied. I had asked him several times if there was anything wrong, but he would only change the subject. Looking back, I should have been more persistent.

CHAPTER 22

Chantel

After dropping Brandon off at Sea-Tac International Airport on Sunday, I headed to the supermarket to pick up a few things.

While pushing my shopping cart through the store, I noticed that I had an admirer. His ebony face grinned at me from the bakery, through laundry supplies, the drugstore, the meat department, and all the way to fresh produce. Following me to the checkout counter, the stranger waited until I was finished and paid for his protein shake. It wasn't long before he approached me as I loaded my groceries in the car.

"Can I help you with your groceries?" He grinned.

Looking deep into the handsome stranger's dark hazel eyes, I thought he looked familiar. In every way, the stranger reminded me of my first love, Martin!

Just then, his voice and signature grin confirmed my memory of the guy I had lost my virginity to. Martin was a ladies' man, and he had a sparkling personality. All of the ladies loved being around him, and   the men loved hanging with him. We had been high-school sweethearts, and we had planned to get married straight out of high school. However, Mom/ my older sister, Daria, made sure that those marriage plans did not go through by moving us out of Alabama and here to Seattle. I hated her for that, but looking back, I'm glad that she had made that decision. We were too young.

The stranger's name was Leo Diamond Hunter, who bore a distinguished and striking appearance. The clean-shaven brother had the body of a track star, which gave him a robust appeal. Toned and very muscular, he was not bad to look at. Not that any of this should have mattered because I was madly in love with Brandon. Yet I couldn't help but study the handsome stranger once more. He almost seemed too good be true! Studying his exterior even closer, I couldn't help but notice that he was well over six feet tall. His skin was dark and smooth. He had teeth as white as pearls, and his smile was flawless.

"I couldn't help but notice you in there. You are *something* else." Diamond began loading my groceries into my newly purchased Town Car. I had finally settled things with the insurance company and had been able to find a decent car to get me around town again. Even though my hair was styled and my skin shined from a spa session, I still felt insecure.

He was now studying my figure, which I did not like. I had just indulged in chocolate chip pancakes with extra chocolate chips and heavy chocolate syrup. My pants were actually cutting off my circulation. *I should not have eaten those chocolate pancakes*, I thought.

"Thanks." I smiled, silently giving him points for being so generous with his compliments. "Bet you say that to all the women you meet in supermarkets."

"No, you're the first one," he responded in all seriousness. "Forgive my forwardness, but I have to ask, are you seeing anyone?"

I felt as if I were on *Jeopardy!*, searching for the right answer.

"No."

Why did I say that? Brandon's plane is probably just taking off.

"May we exchange phone numbers?"

I felt as if I were in a trance. "Sure." *What am I doing?*

"I'll call you tonight." He smiled, turned, and strolled away. I couldn't help but watch him leave. He looked just as good from the back as he did from the front.

Driving out of the huge parking lot, I decided that when he called, I wouldn't answer the phone. However, my selfish desire overpowered my principles. I ended up taking Diamond's phone call. We talked for hours, going over old times and reminiscing over old friends. Diamond had a great sense of humor, and he looked good on paper, aiming to make partner at a prestigious Seattle law firm. Diamond was both intelligent and witty. I could not help but think that my sister Daria would definitely approve of this guy! I could envision my sisters making wedding plans just by my describing this guy via text.

Having convinced myself that I was just chatting with a friend, I accompanied Diamond that evening to a comedy club. We laughed endlessly. We dined at a renowned sushi bar, sharing seafood and endless laughter. I enjoyed Diamond's company; he was refreshing.

The topic took a different turn when I asked him about his parents. Diamond shared that his dad had passed away. I could relate to this part, having lost a parent at an early age. His mother sounded like someone I would not care for. I hated to be judgmental, but she reminded me of Daria. Diamond shared that his mother, Mrs. Franklin, had been married five times. All of her husbands were deceased. At first I thought she was killing them off, which is a horrible thing to think, I know, but apparently they had all died of natural causes.

Yet Diamond still spoke well of his mother. "My mom is still my mom. You know, she can be a bit overbearing, as most moms can be at times, but she only wants the best for me. She keeps hounding me to get married and give her some grandbabies now."

"Well, I bet she is proud of you."

"Yeah, I guess so. So, Chantel, do you want kids?"

"Huh? Well, I'm getting older. It's about time that I start settling down. I need to find the right mate first."

"Yeah, you know, I love kids, Chantel. I would like to have a houseful someday soon."

All of a sudden, I began to feel guilty, sitting there talking to this guy whom I had just met about children. Even though Diamond reminded me of a guy I had had feelings for long ago, deep down inside, my heart belonged to Brandon. Steering off topic, I asked, "So, what do you think about interracial dating?"

"What?" I could tell the question had caught him off-guard as he placed his napkin down in thought.

"Interracial dating. What do you think about that?"

"Well...in today's time, that really shouldn't be an issue. People are attracted to whoever makes them feel complete. Personally, I have never dated outside of my race. All the women I connect with happen to African-American women. I have nothing against the interracial couple who make the decision to bring biracial children into the world. What I do have a problem with is culture."

I rolled my eyes. He was starting to sound like Daria.

"Chantel, we as African-Americans have been stripped of our culture. I feel that we should work on embracing where we come from and truly focus on raising strong black men and women to reflect our beautiful heritage. I think once our image is diluted, it becomes hard for our children to identify who they are as individuals, causing them to become insignificant in the eyes of a proud world that basks in cultural distinctiveness."

He chuckled, exposing his deep dimples. "When I do get married—I say *do*; I live positively!—I would like to be with a woman, preferably a successful black woman, who desires to have children and who values the instruction of a hardworking man. By being educated, this woman is aware of what she wants and is motivated to make a better life for herself and our kids."

Taking a sip of wine, I continued. "So you would never consider marrying outside your race?"

"I don't know, Chantel. I was raised by a black woman whom I adore and respect. I could never abandon the black woman. The black woman is a part of me. She lives right inside here!" He pointed to his heart.

I had to admit, part of me admired the adoration that he displayed for the black woman. I was often consumed with some of the negative publicity that black women endured. Educated black women were not showcased enough, but then again, I have noticed that lately every ethnic group has faced ridicule to some degree. Nonetheless, I was infatuated with Diamond! Which made me ponder, *Is my chocolate craving returning?*

Afterward, we ended up at his place. As I stood on the dimly lit balcony overlooking the beach, I realized I'd gone too far. The moon shining on the water gave it a dazzling brilliance. The waves pounded against the sand. I felt an aching pain in my head beginning to throb. *What am I going to do?*

Diamond dimmed the lights even more, then turned on a soothing jazz tune.

And yes, before I knew it, we were kissing fervently. He quickly stripped down into his sleek boxers. Slowly, he began to undress me, yet my mood was disrupted as random pictures of Brandon fluttered through my troubled mind. *What am I doing? This is wrong. Completely wrong!*

"No! I can't, Diamond." Pushing him away, lured by a false sense of love, I realized that we had made our way into the bedroom. Running out, I turned on the lights and began searching for my top and shoes.

"What's wrong?" he asked.

"I'm sorry, Diamond. I can't do this. I think you are a wonderful, successful, talented, young, sophisticated guy. I always dreamed of hooking up with someone like you! And if only I had met you sooner, this would have been perfect, but unfortunately, you're too late! You see …"— I was desperately trying to find my other high-heeled sandal—"I'm involved with someone else. We're very much in love. I don't know why I let things go this far. Please forgive me."

Buttoning up my jacket, I asked, "Have you seen my other shoe? Diamond, could you please help me find my shoe? And then could you please take me home?" I began to panic. "If not, just let me call a cab."

We found my missing shoe on the balcony. Diamond dropped me off without incident, a perfect gentleman. I apologized once more, and he agreed never to call me.

CHAPTER 23

Chantel

The rest of the week, I kept thinking about how close I'd come to deceiving Brandon. I was so distraught that I actually forgot to show up for my doctor's appointment. I tried to find another doctor to see me. Brandon would be upset with me if he found out that I had missed the appointment.

I felt like such a fool. I valued our relationship too much for such carelessness.

On Friday, I drove through thick fog to pick up Brandon at Sea-Tac. He seemed withdrawn. "What's wrong?" I asked.

Silence. I figured he was suffering from jet lag. When we arrived at his condo, I tried to be affectionate, but he pulled away and stood looking out the window.

"Brandon, what's wrong? Wasn't the trip a success?"

"My trip was fine, Chantel. Everything went nicely. What about you?" He walked over to the bar and mixed himself a drink. "How did things go while I was away? Anything interesting happen?"

"Not really...but I missed you."

"You missed me? Yeah, right." He laughed sarcastically.

"What's that supposed to mean? What's wrong with you?"

"Didn't Diamond keep you busy enough while I was gone?"

At a loss for words, I thought, *How on earth does he know about Diamond?* "How did you...?"

"Your sister Daria paid me a little visit. She dropped by the club before my trip. Your devoted sister, the one you call Mom, wanted to put our relationship to the test."

"What? Brandon, what are you talking about?" I asked.

"She challenged our relationship, Chantel! Daria was so sure that if a successful black man stepped into the picture, you would leave me in a heartbeat. Daria told me that you desired to be with a black man but settled for me in the meantime. Even though I was secure in our relationship, she was positive that you were not. Chantel, I trusted you. I thought that you were just as dedicated to our bond as I was, so I accepted her little challenge. I told Daria about a friend of mine named Diamond, a smooth, established black man whom I was sure your sister would approve of. I pulled up some information about him, Daria looked it over, and she was blown away by his success, and the fact that he was a black man only added to her approval."

"Brandon, that's ridiculous! My sister would never sink that low."

My mind fluttered in and out of thought as Brandon bitterly spoke. "Daria insisted you couldn't be that content, that deep down inside, a successful black woman desires a victorious black man. I accepted her challenge. I lost."

"You did what?"

"I had to do it, Chantel. I had to find out if you were really devoted to me. Obviously, you're not. Your actions were stupid. Leo could have been any black man just looking to satisfy his needs."

"I didn't do anything! I stopped before anything happened."

"Yeah, I know that you were comfortable enough to take your shoes and your shirt off!" he yelled.

Reaching behind the bar, Brandon pulled out a small black jewelry box and opened it. There sat the most beautiful sapphire ring I had ever seen.

"This was to be yours. I planned on asking for your hand in marriage, Chantel. I fought against my mother's wishes for you!" Eyes full of rage, he continued, "To say the least, my plans have changed. Indefinitely." He threw the ring against the wall.

My heart filled with pain, and I began weeping. "Brandon. Please! I love you. I never meant to—"

"You really made quite the impression on Diamond Chantel!" Brandon shook his head in disbelief. "Diamond's been gunning after me for a while now over some girl who meant nothing to me in the past. That punk had the balls to tell me that he could see himself with you! Do you know how sick that made me feel?"

"Diamond can feel whatever he wants to for me, but I don't feel the same way, Brandon."

"It does not matter, Chantel! Your actions showed differently that night! You know what? Just...get out, Chantel. Now," he stated calmly at first.

"Brandon, please, let me—"

"Get out before I throw you out!"

Before leaving, I pleaded, "Brandon, you had no right to accept such a challenge. You should have talked to me! You had no right to do that!"

"It is over, Chantel!" he screamed. "Get out! I don't want to see you! Get out!" His face was full of rage.

It was over and fully my liability. I realized that I was no better than Cameron. I felt ugly, inside and out. How could I have been so foolish, so immature?

The next couple of weeks, my emotional pain was so intense that I became physically ill. I still had not made an attempt to go in and see a doctor over the dizzy spells that I had encountered for months now. And I had yet to confront my sister or Diamond over their devious scheme. I was so afraid of a vicious side that was rising up in hatred against my own flesh and blood. I was in mourning. I was unable to eat much or sleep, and my stomach ached and stretched with pain. At night, I tossed and turned, my spirit full of anxiety and discomfort.

I called Brandon's number just to hear his voice on the answering machine at his club. In my mind, I replayed all the good times we shared, the passion we embraced. We were so right for each other! These memories were all I had as a keepsake. The hate I now had for the woman whom I had once looked up to as a mother figure was unspeakable. I had no respect for her, so much so that I would no longer refer to her as Mom for now on. I would call her Daria, just as my younger siblings, Lamina and Robert, referred to her. From now on, I would treat Daria like the enemy that she always was.

CHAPTER 24

Chantel

Weeks passed. One Monday morning, my secretary reminded me, "I'll be taking my vacation soon, so you'll be getting a temp for two weeks while I'm gone."

That particular day, I was out of it. I still had not followed up with a doctor. I felt so lightheaded, so dizzy.

"That's fine. I hope you enjoy your trip. Is there anything else?" I asked, trying to appear normal.

"As a matter of fact, there is. Are you OK? I've been noticing that..."

Her voice became faint, and the room started spinning. I tried to perk up, but the sensation was extremely powerful. And yes, just like that, I blacked out.

"Ms. Reed! Ms. Reed!"

Where was that voice coming from? Was I dreaming? I opened my eyes. What was I doing in bed? A man in a white jacket stood over me. His nametag read *Hewlett, M.D.*

Panicked, I looked around. There was an IV in my arm. What was I doing in a hospital?

The doctor helped me to a sitting position, then grabbed his clipboard off the table. "You were severely dehydrated, Ms. Reed, so we had to give you an IV to get fluid back into your system. We also took some blood and an ultrasound." He hesitated, looked at the floor, then right into my eyes. "Um, Ms. Reed, you need to know that..."

Oh, no! He's gonna tell me that I have some kind of illness! There was a time when I was careless when it came to having sex. *I should have had Cameron checked out. What if I'm HIV-positive?*

"You're pregnant," he continued. "You are carrying twins! You should have been on bed rest weeks ago. The ultrasound confirmed that you're three to four months along."

My stomach had been a little bloated and had swelled up a bit. I thought I might have had a tumor! Or the least of my worries, eating way too many chocolate desserts! However, I was so depressed, I didn't care if I lived or died. I was more concerned with my broken heart than my bloated stomach.

"When was your last menstrual cycle?"

"I don't know," I answered, head spinning.

"Was your cycle normal?"

"Well, come to think of it, it wasn't." It would come and go, but it was not normal. I thought it was stress! *Four months? Twins?* My body ached. I had chills and awful headaches. And I had to force myself to keep food and fluids down. I began to wonder, *Am I oblivious or what?* I began crying. *That's why my breasts are sore. That's why the smell of meat makes me want to vomit. That's why I have to pee every five minutes!*

I was diagnosed with hyperemesis gravidarum, or severe morning sickness, which made me wonder, why did they call it morning sickness when it occurred morning, noon, and night? I also developed pneumonia, for which I was hospitalized. In the midst of it all, my doctor told me that I had to keep down fluids and that I had to find a good obstetrician. He gave me options such as adoption, yet I could not do that. Even though my life was upside down, I wanted my babies.

The emotions going through my head were unbearable. I knew that I was in bad shape, and yes, I heard the words that no pregnant woman wanted to hear: "We are keeping you here until you are better and to make sure that you and the babies are stable enough to go back home. But even when you do return home, you will need someone to take care of you." I was an independent woman. I was not used to having anyone take care of me. I was the one who took care of other people. I was the reliable one, and now my body had a life of its own; it was fighting against me.

The doctors gave me medication to stop the ripping pain and pressure within my stomach and uterus. The doctors gave me medicine to help me hold down fluids. I was also given medicine to stop the discomfort that pressed down like a steel weight upon my chest. My ears stopped up at times. I tried to read the nurse's lips. Eventually resting became easy. I rarely took medication, and now I was loaded down with prescriptions that I had never heard of. I was happy to have the pain stop. Resting was easy to do as I faded in out of sleep, yet it was a heavy rest, one that I was unable to control. My spirit ultimately felt as if it were stuck within my body. The medication used to ease my pain and prevent me and the twins from stress paralyzed my thoughts. I became numb at times toward my own conscious feelings. I could barely feel my own movement or the growing change that the twins were forming from within my body.

My assistant must have called everyone on her list because I received visits from people whom I had never wished to see again. The very first visit was from Daria. I was too weak to even fight, so she did all of the talking.

"I knew something like this was going to happen, Chantel," she warned. "You know what you need to do!

I know you must be angry with me, and if you were in any condition, you would probably lay into me real good, but you have to know that I am looking out for your best interests." She paused, then looked around. Slowly, she moved toward me. My vision was blurred, but I could make out her conniving image, and I could hear her selfish motive.

"Diamond is willing to marry you even though those twins are not his. You need to marry Diamond. Diamond reached out to me after things blew up between you and Brandon. We met up several times for lunch. I even invited him over to the house. Diamond told me that things got bad between him and Brandon. They are no longer friends. Diamond has feelings for you, girl. It was love at first sight. I think that Brandon was meant to come into your life, Chantel, so that you could meet Diamond. Brandon literally led you to a jewel, honey. At first I was not sure that Diamond would want you because you had babies by another man, and his friend of all things, but he is such a saint. He told me that he did not care. He is willing to raise those babies as if they were his own. I'm going to start planning the wedding, Chantel. We will wait until after you have the babies. We will get you ready for marriage within a month. I love you, Chantel! Everything I do is for you, little sister."

Bending down, she kissed me on my forehead. If I only had had enough strength, I would have tried to grab hold of her neck and choke her head right off her body.

Not knowing the date or time, I was still fading in and out of consciousness. Next to arrive was Brandon. He seemed sad. "I know you are carrying my babies, Chantel. I had a keen hunch; that's why I wanted you to see the doctor. I want you to know that I will do everything in my power to make sure that those babies are taken care of. Your sister told me that you plan to marry Diamond! Wow! I guess I never could trust you, Chantel. How could you even think of taking up with my bitter ex-friend? Don't my feelings mean anything to you?"

He paused, and through blurred vision, I watched as he paced around the room. Even though the drugs were fighting to control my spirit, I could still sense Brandon's deep sorrow. I could feel something distant shielding his being. Even though our lives were in strife, I longed to make peace. I wanted to comfort him, but my soul was trapped inside a seemingly lifeless body.

"I have a lot of thinking to do. I just need time. I'm taking off to clear my mind for a while. I'm back to London to spend time with my dad in the midst of all of this chaos. The old man is sick. I've been seeing someone in London to talk out my problems. I've been seeing this person for a while to help me cope with some things that have been going on in my past. To be honest, Chantel, I'm not sure I would make a good father, but I'm going to try. I just have a lot of things to sort through. And now that you're taking up with Diamond, it makes things a lot easier for me to leave. Sometimes I wish I had never taken your sister up on that offer. But if it hadn't have been Diamond, it would have been someone else."

I wanted to tell him not to leave, but I was stiff and so indolent, all I could do was watch him leave.

Serenity stopped by several times, praying over me. Holding a big black Bible, she touched and prayed over my stomach and anointed my hospital room with holy oil. She told me that she would be back, and if I had had enough strength, I would have told her not to come. She was annoying the heck out of me.

And then there was Diamond. Daria had talked Diamond into coming. I was angry! There was nothing that I could do about my anger, which had bowed to the submission to lethargic drugs.

"I know this is so soon. Chantel, the first time I laid eyes on you, I knew that I wanted to make you mine. I know what you are thinking—how could I betray my friend? To be honest, Brandon and I were never really good friends. I'm willing to choose my soul mate over friendship any day of the week. I'm willing to be the best father. You'll see. Your sister is going to help me find the perfect ring for you. It'll all pan out; you'll see."

Walking over to me, he bent down and kissed me on the forehead. I despised him. He smelled like betrayal. He left the room just as sly as he had entered my life.

I was very sick, and the only people I wanted to see were my younger sister, Lamina, and my younger brother, Robert. The only other person I wanted to see was Astrid, but she was a no-show. The only person I longed to see was Alison, but death stood between us. And at the time, I was more than willing to leave this life's deception for a life filled with peace.

CHAPTER 25

Chantel

I lay huddled in my hospital bed. Still a bit groggy, I could feel my own strength fighting the medication and my own spirit slowly surging back into my body. I was starting to feel somewhat normal despite carrying twins.

An unlikely visitor stopped by. It was Eugene.

"Why is it so dark in here?" he asked as he headed for the windows. He opened the draperies and was shocked at what he saw. As daylight hit my swollen face, he gasped. "What is going on, Chantel? You look awful!"

"What do you want?" I mumbled.

"I heard what happened."

"Yep! I'm pregnant with twins. And you were right, Eugene—he left me."

Eugene's face was full of remorse. "I never meant for this to happen."

"This is hardly your fault."

"Chantel, you look...please let me help you."

I noticed that Eugene was clenching a white paper bag. He placed it near my bedside. "It's your favorite. I snagged the last one." He smiled proudly. "It's a chocolate-fudge-brownie cupcake."

For some reason, that announcement perked me up a bit.

"I love you, Chantel."

I did not want Eugene to love me, especially when I felt so unlovable. "Eugene, how can you love me? You don't even know me...not really." I began crying.

"Believe me, you don't want to know me. I'm not worth the pain."

"Give me a chance, Chantel." He knelt beside me, his soulful eyes full of passion. "Let me love you—you and your babies!"

His request melted my heart. Even though my sister was set to marry me off to Diamond, I was not sold on her plans for my life. I decided to give in to Eugene. I'm glad I did. Eugene felt safe. I knew I could trust him, but one question remained: could I trust myself? Eventually I would have to confront my sister, Diamond, Brandon, and Astrid. What would be the final outcome of my decision, I wondered. Was I taking advantage of a good guy for my own selfish reasons?

CHAPTER 26

Astrid

Serenity begged me to come with her to visit Chantel in the hospital. I knew that Chantel was too proud and wouldn't want anyone to see her in such a vulnerable condition, and I myself was still in no mood to deal with the outside world. I was keeping a low profile. I had taken on a couple of orders through my website, but my heart was not in it. I had reached my ultimate fear—chocolate burnout! I had lost my zest for creating new, delicious chocolate treats. Nothing motivated me anymore. However, Serenity's phone call did inspire me to make a chocolate treat for Chantel in hopes of lifting her spirits. Serenity had been calling Chantel and visiting her in the hospital as well. She was sure that a visit from me would make Chantel's day, and so reluctantly I agreed to meet Serenity at the hospital.

Serenity was an hour late, and by then, Chantel had filled me in on all of the details. I was not happy about her decision to allow Eugene to help her out with her pregnancy. Again, Chantel had run into the arms of a man in search of protection. Even though I felt this way, I was tired of expressing my feelings, which only seemed to fall upon deaf ears. I decided to let Chantel be Chantel and support her whenever I could in her time of need without judgment.

Yet someone who was not willing to go along with Chantel's plans was Serenity. Serenity finally came rushing into Chantel's room wearing a cycling outfit and holding onto a helmet right as Chantel was about to sink her fork into a slice of one of my chocolate lovers' cakes layered in rich frosting with a chocolate-covered cherry on top.

"Don't eat that, Chantel!" Serenity screamed.

"Don't worry, Serenity; I already said grace." Chantel gave Serenity an annoying grin, as if to say, *Please do not interrupt me while I'm trying to get my chocolate groove on.*

"No, it's not that. I've been reading that too much is not good for the babies. It could crowd out the healthy food and add calories, not to mention the caffeine that is found in some chocolate."

I had to interrupt. "Serenity, leave the girl alone. She's pregnant—with twins! Let her enjoy herself. Let her splurge a little."

Serenity refused to listen. "I think you should take up bike riding. I just biked all the way down here!"

"Serenity," I said to dispute her, "you are an hour late, and you smell a little tart."

Serenity sniffed the pit of her arm. Frowning a bit, she replied, "OK, so I smell like a goat. But cycling can be rejuvenating."

"I don't want to bike ride, Serenity!" Chantel was becoming upset. "I just want to enjoy your company while eating cake. I have a lot on my mind. I'm afraid!"

"Of what? You have great friends who will help see you through this!"

"Yeah, right!" Chantel laughed. "Do you know that Brandon has a disabled twin brother? I'm carrying twins, Serenity! What if one of them comes out needing special attention? I'm not equipped for that."

"You have to lean on God, Chantel! He is more than able to equip you with the desires of your heart. I have a friend named Natasha, who gave birth to a child that required a lot of attention. Natasha and her husband did not give up hope on their son. They went on to see their son through countless operations, through sickness and pain. Through the power of love, that young man is breaking down barriers and living life. He is not confined to his wheelchair. He does not hide behind closed doors. He went off to college, and he is living a beautiful life! Just because he was born with a life-threatening disability does not mean that he allowed circumstance to rule over him. Natasha and her husband persevered through love. I can recall Natasha telling me that God gave her a son with special needs because He knew that she had the love he needed to survive."

Serenity walked over and grabbed the fork and the slice of cake out of Chantel's reach. "Chantel, I am trying to help you!"

Chantel screamed, "And I am trying to help you, Serenity! If you don't give me that cake, I am going to get out of this bed and toss your crazy behind out the window." Chantel pointed to the window, which was fourteen stories up. Serenity stared at the window for a second. Without a second thought, she placed the cake back within Chantel's reach.

"I need my fork, too, Serenity," Chantel demanded.

Not only did Serenity give Chantel's fork back, but she delicately handed her a napkin as well.

To be honest, I was bit upset with Serenity. Who was she to come in here preaching as if her life was so great? At times, I felt that Serenity judged us and could be too preachy, and I took the opportunity right then and there to let her know.

"Life is so simple for you, isn't it?" I began to vent, pushing Serenity into an even more awkward position. "Things are not as easy as you make them out to be, Serenity. Chantel is alone with twins. What I would have given to be able to have children! You know I miscarried twice. Words can't describe how devastating that was for me. I had no one to turn to. You have an answer for everything through hope! But hope does not work for everyone."

Serenity responded to my anger with empathy. "Astrid, I can only imagine how alone you must have felt. Through much research and from hearing from women who have suffered miscarriages, I know you need someone one to talk to. It seems as if you still have trouble coping with your loss. Anytime you need someone to listen, I'm here for you."

"I don't know what I need, Serenity, but maybe you should give Chantel and me the freedom to figure things out on our own instead of always trying to fix us. I don't think that's your job, so you should accept our wishes and mind your own business."

"I agree!" Chantel added. "You can't just stroll in here and take cake of a pregnant woman! Are you insane?" She waved the fork filled with chocolate frosting.

Serenity's feelings were hurt so much that she left immediately afterward. Chantel and I watched from the window as she made her way out of the hospital. She mounted her bike and steered it out into the busy street in an out-of-control manner. Cars honked, and angry motorists cursed her wobbly biking skills as they swerved past her efforts to regain control. The only comforting thought I had at that moment was that Serenity was near a hospital, so if she did get hit by a car, she could receive instant medical attention.

"How are you holding up, Astrid?" Chantel asked as we watched Serenity try to make it across the street without killing herself.

"OK. Better than you, I guess."

"Yeah." Chantel chuckled. "Look, Astrid, I wanted to apologize for—"

"Chantel, don't. Look, I'm responsible for my own happiness. You should be able to go out there and find happiness without me standing in your way."

"Well, a lot of good that did me. Look where I am." Chantel sighed.

"It does not matter where you are now. You followed your heart! Sure, I can be a bit bitter toward men, but that's something I have to deal with."

"I know it does not look like it, Astrid, but I'm trying to get it together."

"I know you are—we all are—but getting through the obstacles is a big part of it. I'm going to give you time to figure it out, girl. If you need me, I'm only a phone call away."

Giving Chantel a genuine embrace, I left feeling better than I had in months. That day, I truly decided to give my friend the time to deal with her own problems while giving myself the liberty to move past my own pain.

CHAPTER 27

Serenity

"I can't believe how awful those two treated me at the hospital, Camila!" I vented as we worked on the women's expo to be held in Phoenix. Camila was working contentedly at the drafting table. She looked stress free dressed in white and stationed near the bay window of our high-rise office. I wished I could be as content as Camila, and it appeared as if Camila had been hoping for the same.

Setting her pencil down, she removed her flamboyant red-framed glasses that she wore only while working on art projects. She gently placed them on the table. "Serenity, I know that you are hurt, but not everyone is going to run their lives as you do, and you will have to accept that. You expect everyone to do things according to your design, but we are all structured differently.

"When I'm designing furniture, I'm excited about the texture and the nature of the wood. Each piece has a unique quality. I don't try to design all of my pieces the same because that takes away from the wood's natural form. People are the same way, Serenity. You have to allow them to be who they are and learn from their own mistakes so they can learn how to develop value within themselves."

Camila was right. How many times had I tried to fix my friends or even my husband to fit into my mold? I desperately wanted to see them do well in life—I was honestly trying to help—yet I hated being the kind of woman who constantly tries to control others out of fear.

I'd had a friend named Eva. Everything started off great. She introduced me to a ton of women in the community. I hit it off well with most of them. As time moved on, Eva began feeling insecure due to my friendships with the other women. Eva disclosed her disapproval many times throughout our friendship and tried to manipulate and control me out of fear. Yes, fear—of what other women were saying about me, of dealing with the personal lives and mistakes that these other women were making. The fact that Eva was so condemnatory toward these other women made me question our relationship. I always believed that Eva and I had a rare friendship that could not be compared to any other alliance. I had Serenity in our bond. Yet Eva's insecurities tore us apart. I did not want to be the kind of woman who has to dominate her friends. After all, my passion was to keep Alison's vision alive. Alison had a gift that reached out to women through acceptance and honesty. Alison would say, *"Don't allow anyone to make you feel guilty about finding the good in certain people. Due to their own insecurities and hang-ups in life, your godly gift is their weakness."* It was those words that helped me move away from Eva. Chantel and Astrid seemed to drift off into their own lives, abandoning Alison's cause altogether.

I figured that many women can feel helpless in their relationships with other women at times. True female bonding is vital to help us through this confusing thing called life. Sometimes you don't know what to do, whom to trust, or how to respond to a friendship that is on the brink of being torn apart. In times such as this, you must move on and do what you know how to do in order to survive emotional destruction.

I can remember attending a beautiful conference with my friend Isidora to see the inspirational Christian author and speaker Joyce Meyers. I couldn't help but notice the packed auditorium. The crowd spilled into an overflow area. Joyce glowed in the spirit. Even though she was recovering from hip surgery, she was alive and kicking. Her grandson shared his testimony about how during his trials, he had a praying grandmother who revealed that when you don't know what to do, you keep doing what you know how to do. Don't allow problems to derail you.

The only thing I knew how to do at this point was to pray in secret. I realized that if I wanted to really help my friends, I had to stop preaching at them, something that Alison never encouraged. For example, there were times that Alison and I would start praying for women. Yet looking back, I wondered why Alison never took the time to pray for herself or her situation. I wondered why I never took the time to reach out and pray for her pain. Alison was good at making her life seem so strong and secure, but deep down inside, she had insecurities and problems just like any other woman. Alison was just better at hiding her issues. But in the end, every dark entity comes out into the light.

CHAPTER 28

Chantel

I was starting a new chapter in my life, so I had to make important changes to secure the well-being of my twins. I had thought about staying in my sister Lamina's house, but it was not child friendly. It was a flamboyant abode filled with closets full of shoes, purses, breakable souvenirs from around the world, and bottles of imported wine. My younger sister's home was perfect for a single woman who never ever dreamed of having kids. I had to find a home with childproof locks and equipped with nanny cams. I was able to find a secluded condo so that Daria could not trace my whereabouts. I also denied all visits from her while I was at the office and rejected most of her phone calls; however, I kept just enough contact through texts to make her believe that there were no hard feelings. My reason for doing so was vengeance. I know that it was not my place to seek revenge on anyone, but I was angry at Daria for plotting against me. I was going to get back at her and Diamond for what they put me through. I couldn't blame Brandon for being insecure enough to go along with Daria's plan. My sister has a way of manipulating most people.

Nonetheless, I had to make sure that I focused all of my attention on having a healthy pregnancy, and of all people, Eugene was a big help. The man treated me like a queen. He stopped by and did all the cooking and still found time to hunt down all my favorite cravings. He rubbed my aching back and swollen feet. He even participated in my Lamaze classes. Nothing seemed to thrill him more than feeling the babies kick.

Although I was happy to have his loving support, I still longed for Brandon. Not once throughout my pregnancy did I hear from him.

One Wednesday morning, Eugene and I went grocery shopping. As I stood in front of some shelves trying to decide what kind of bottled water to buy, my water broke. Just then, Eugene came strolling toward me.

"There you are," he said. "What kind of ice cream do you want? Orange sherbet or Rocky Road?"

"Eugene, my water just broke," I said calmly, my heart beginning to do double time.

"Oh, that's OK. I'm sure it was an accident. Go ahead and grab another bottle. They won't make you pay for it. I'll go find the janitor and have him clean this mess up." He began to turn away.

"No, Eugene. My *water* broke! The babies are coming!"

He stopped, then turned toward me, eyes enormous. He dropped the ice cream into the cart, pushed it to one side, and grabbed me by the hand, muttering, "We've gotta get out of here."

As he led me outside, he began telling me to breathe, just as in Lamaze class. He started breathing with me. I wasn't even having contractions, but it made him happy, so I breathed deeply. He helped me into the Blazer, and we shot out of the parking lot.

When we arrived at the hospital, Eugene grabbed a wheelchair and rushed me inside. He told one of the nurses that I was in labor. I had been able to work up to thirty-five weeks before my doctor instructed me to relax more. Now at thirty-seven weeks, I was heading into the delivery room.

Eugene stood by my side during the C-section. He was there for the birth of Isabella and Isaiah, born at 1:30 and 1:41 in the afternoon. My girl was six pounds, and my boy was seven pounds, or "seven up," as they called him. Serenity and Astrid arrived to see my new obligations in life. Serenity brought in a giant Moses basket big enough to rest both twins inside. The basket was filled with diapers, bottles, baby blankets—everything but the kitchen sink. The babies were healthy and came home with me after two days. The twins were well worth the wait, with their father's fair complexion and deep dimples and the cutest wavy brown Afros!

Before we left the hospital, Brandon paid us a surprise visit, his arms full of pink roses, balloons, and stuffed animals. "How are you feeling, honey?" he asked.

Honey? I thought. *The nerve of this guy, not to have anything to do with me while I was carrying these kids and having the audacity to show up now!*

"How do you think I feel?" I asked weakly and a bit uneasy. Looking up at Brandon, I realized how much I'd missed him. Yet he had betrayed me. I was close to tears. "What do you want?"

"I came to see the babies...and you, of course. They're beautiful, Chantel. They are a perfect combination of the both of us. And I love the names." He began tying the balloons onto one of the bed rails.

"Why are you *really* here, Brandon?"

He stopped. He looked different. I saw something I'd never seen before: the sadness in his eyes had changed them from rich green to sorrowful ocean blue. "I want a second chance. I want to be a father to my kids. I've spent the last months doing a lot of soul-searching, and I know this is what I want."

"You did a lot of soul-searching, all right. Several months' worth."

"I understand your anger, Chantel, but please give me another chance. I'll do whatever you ask of me. You can't tell me you don't love me when you've been carrying my babies."

"Why, Brandon? Why have you come back? How do I know it's for good? How can you expect me to trust you?"

"Chantel, last week my biological father died of pancreatic cancer. He wanted me with him during his final days. During that time, he apologized for allowing my mom to take me instead of stepping up to raise me and my brother together. That was one of his biggest regrets." Brandon paused, then looked out the window, watching the rain drip gently on giant evergreen trees.

Turning back to me, he whispered, "I don't want to make the same mistake Dad made, Chantel. I want to be a real father to my children. I promised him I wouldn't repeat his mistakes. But above all, Chantel, I never stopped loving you." He began pacing. "I let fear control me instead of love. Please take me back. Please."

Kneeling down, he reached into his pocket and pulled out the beautiful ring he'd shown me months earlier. He took my left hand and placed it carefully on my ring finger. "Will you let me be a husband to you? Please, Chantel, say yes."

Conflicting emotions raced through my mind. I was in no condition to make such a crucial decision and told him I needed time to collect my thoughts.

CHAPTER 29

Chantel

Weeks had passed by, and I had not allowed Daria see her niece and nephew. I granted her access to the twins only through brief videos or pictures through a private social media site. I hired a nanny to help out with the twins, which my sister was against. She wanted to move in with me to help take care of the babies, but I'd rather have jumped off the Space Needle before I'd have allowed that backstabbing woman into my home. I felt awful for harboring bad feelings toward my sister, but back then, teaching her a lesson was the only emotion that consoled my bitter heart.

Eugene came by almost every day. He adored the twins. He changed their diapers, gave them their bottles, and burped them. I couldn't just let him go, not after all he'd done for us...

Could I?

I needed advice, so I took counsel from Tia, a life coach and a very wise woman who had been married for many years before her husband passed away last spring. She had raised three of her own children and had opened her home up to foster children. I admired Tia. She was not too preachy like Serenity, and she was not too cynical like Astrid. Most important, she was not overly judgmental like Daria. Tia was compassionate and understanding; she weighed the truth on an honest scale.

We sat down in my kitchen, enjoying a fresh pot of coffee one morning. We had not seen each other in a while, so we caught up some. Finally, I asked the question. "Tia, what should I do?"

Tia had always challenged me to solve my own mishaps in life; however, she was aware that I had a huge problem. Grabbing my hand, she said, "Chantel, no one can make those decisions or answer your questions except you. Brandon is the father of your children. It appears that you still carry a torch for this man. Is he allowed to make a mistake? After all, he is human. The only time mistakes become unacceptable is when they become habits."

"I know, Tia, but what about the children's cultural background? They will be diluted. At least Eugene is a strong black leader for my children."

"People are going to always have something to say about interracial relationships. My husband being half-Irish and half-Italian and I being a black woman raised quite a few eyebrows back in the day when interracial dating seemed to be a sin to most people in the South. Many of my black girlfriends believed that I should've stayed within my own circle, but I was looking for love, and I knew that the kind of companionship that I was seeking did not exist within my circle of African-American people. I happened to find the love of my life outside of my heritage. Some women are hung up on the desire to marry a strong black man, and some men and women are bitter toward their own race due to negative circumstances that could happen in any cultural background. Some black women complain that most of the black men they meet desire only white women or Latina women. Well, say that at the end of the day, longevity wins. You can create the perfect man or woman in your head, but can they stand the test of time? That's the real question. Real love is color blind, Chantel. Love is also an action, not a feeling and not found in appearance. If that person is willing to fight your battles and love you in a reciprocal manner, you have found your mate. I lot of men and women get caught up in fantasy love. At the end of the day, reality will set in."

Tia took a sip of her coffee and then reminded me, "Don't forget, Chantel; those are Brandon's children as well. They have two great backgrounds to learn about. It is important to raise good God-fearing children with great moral values. Through Serenityful guidance, you will raise excellent human beings who will soar on eagles' wings regardless of any cultural differences. Never forget: fear thrives on confusion. I look at fear as the devil, the father of lies.

"As for Eugene," she continued, "he appears to be a wonderful man and good friend. Perhaps that's all he ever will be. Even if you don't reconcile with Brandon, you will only end up finding someone else as physically attractive. Even though beauty is only skin deep, I don't think you are in love with Eugene. You can't make yourself love someone. Out of pity, you will find yourself trapped, and the results will become costly in the end. Eugene will heal."

She grabbed my hand, stating sternly, "He will find someone else to love. His whole being represents love. Eugene is worthy of adoration! And God will not allow His most vital request of all to go without gratitude."

Tia handed me a slip of paper. "One of my favorite Bible verses to back it up is Colossians 3:14: 'And over all these virtues put on love, which binds them all together in perfect unity.' Consider going back to Brandon if that is what you want. Nothing in life is guaranteed, and any relationship you care about is worth fighting for."

I spent the night tossing and turning. Finally, I made my decision. It was tainted with mixed emotions of guilt, remorse, and the most damaging of all, anger.

In spite of Tia's heartfelt advice, I handled things my way, which led me on a costly journey

CHAPTER 30

Chantel

The following morning, I asked Eugene to meet me at the park. He showed up promptly. We sat on a bench. My heart pounded. "Eugene, I want to thank you for being such a good—"

"Chantel, stop! I've had something on my mind for a while, and I've finally worked up nerve enough to ask." He got down on bended knee and brought out a petite black-velvet box from his pocket. He opened it to reveal the most delicate antique engagement ring.

"Chantel Reed, will you marry me?"

I caught my breath, then began crying.

"I know this is kind of sudden," he said, "with all that you're going through. This was my great-grandmother's ring. I want you to wear it. We can wait awhile and perhaps for now just set a date."

"Oh, Eugene. You don't understand. I can't marry you. I've decided...to...marry Brandon."

"What?" Eugene staggered to his feet, staring down at me in disbelief.

"Eugene, I'm going back to him. Please don't take this the wrong way, but he is the father of my children."

"The man's a sperm donor, Chantel. That's all he is. He left you for almost nine months! He left you! He thinks he can just walk back into your life?" Eugene began pacing. "And you're gonna let him? Please don't do this, Chantel."

My heart filled with sympathy for this gentleman whom I had used shamelessly.

"You're a wonderful person, Eugene. I will forever be in your debt." I couldn't look him in the eyes; the pain was unbearable. "You're a good friend, but that's all you will ever be. You could never be anything more."

Eugene bowed his head. When he looked up, tears streamed from his eyes. "You have truly hurt me this time, Chantel. Never again."

He tucked the engagement ring back in his pocket and walked away.

I could do nothing but sit and ponder in great sadness. Had I done the right thing? What would I do if Brandon abandoned me again? Even though I told Eugene that I would marry Brandon, deep down inside, I was still hurt by his actions. I couldn't do it.

Later that day, I met up with Brandon at a nearby café. Things got heated. I shared my decision not to go through with our marriage.

"So what are you going to do, Chantel? Are you going to marry Diamond? I told you that guy has had it out for me since day one!"

"Well, you should've thought about that before you sabotaged our relationship by trying to test it."

"I told you that was a stupid thing to do! I'm sorry! We have kids now, Chantel! We need to move forward."

"That's what I'm trying to do!"

"Oh, by stringing Eugene along, too? Word around town is that he wanted to marry you too. What kind of game are you playing, Chantel? Is your life some kind of bachelorette reality television show? You are playing with real emotions! When you run out of men, what next, Chantel? Are you going to start online dating and continue to expose our children to a long list of rejects?"

As I sat there looking at Brandon, I noticed that he was not the same man I had fallen in love with. He had not shaven in weeks. He looked disheveled. Leaning back into his chair, he stared at me as if he were trying to examine my motives. No longer with a look of adoration, the glint in his eyes remained dull. He looked tired, as if he were gazing at a tedious piece of art that was now a waste of time.

"Look, Chantel, I'm giving you the opportunity to make things right." He sighed.

I knew Brandon was going through a lot, but I could not see past my own pain at this point. Looking back, I wish I would've have taken the time to understand Brandon's pain. I will admit there were areas in our relationship in which I lacked compassion. I yearned for the man I had fallen in love with. I still cared for Brandon, but it became obvious that he was now exhausted by our relationship. At least this is what I had discerned to be true at the time.

At the end of the day, Brandon and I both knew that we had acted responsibly. We agreed to settle our differences like practical adults, to arrange suitable visitation rights for the sake of our children. Yet no matter how hard two adults try to maintain a civil relationship, I would soon realize that there is something about a breakup that forces the irrational side to take center stage.

Regarding my final decision, let's just say that I knew what I wanted to do, which made no sense to anyone else but me.

The next day, I met up with Diamond and Daria. Daria insisted that we meet over at her place for brunch. What a nice spread she presented: lox and bagels, mini veggie quiche, egg and hash brown casserole, fruit salad, and fresh-squeezed orange juice. Even though the spread was delightful, the company disgusted me, but I managed to suck it up.

"I am so glad you agreed to finally see us, Chantel." Daria gave me an embrace. I cringed, knowing that the only reason why she was hugging me was that she was controlling my life again...at least that is what I led her to believe. The fact that she had invited Diamond over to discuss my future made me despise her only more. Trying my best to control my emotions, I had to control my temper as I listened to this careless self-seeking human being that I had once looked up to as a mother. Daria continued, "I only wish you would have brought the babies with you. I have yet to see them, and I'm sure they would love to meet their father to be." She gestured toward Diamond, who looked well groomed. His appearance might have been attractive to any other woman, but because I knew what he was all about, his appearance turned my stomach.

"I can't wait to see those kids. My mom went out and purchased her future grandbabies a ton of gifts that I think they would love. I've never seen her so excited to be a grandma."

I could not believe this. I wanted to lash out at these two con artists for plotting against me and for Daria to go so far as to plan my wedding to some guy I hardly knew. It made me livid. To think, as I was laid up in that hospital room trying to fight for my life and the lives of my unborn babies, my so-called sister was behind the scenes trying to map out my life. *How low can a sister go?* I thought. But I knew that if I wanted to make things work according to my plans, I had to play along.

"The kids are with Brandon. They were a little under the weather, but as soon as they get better, I will invite you over, I promise, Daria."

"Oh, you're still calling me Daria?" she asked in a rather sharp tone.

"I'm sorry. I meant Mom," I quickly corrected myself, not wanting Daria to pick up on any bitterness that I harbored toward her.

"That's more like it!" Daria beamed. "I'm going to let you two lovebirds reunite. I'll be in the kitchen if you need me, Oh, and don't worry about Frank. He finally found a job and won't be back till later on this evening." She winked.

As soon as she disappeared around the corner, without pause, Diamond began to plead his case. "Chantel, I know this was a mess how everything went down. I only wish we could have met on natural terms. But honestly, the minute I laid eyes on you, I knew that you were the one I wanted to spend the rest of my life with. You are everything I always wanted in a woman. You are full figured. I love women with meat on their bones. You are smart and intelligent. You now have kids! That's an already-made family."

"Wait, Diamond, your ex-best-friend is the father of my children. We were supposed to get married. Don't you have any concerns about being partly responsible for our breakup?"

"Chantel, Brandon and I were more rivals than friends."

"So, is that what I am to you? Some kind of game?"

"No, of course not."

"Don't you care about your friendship? I know Brandon is partly to blame as well, but he is the father of my children."

Diamond's eyes turned sincere. Even though I've known men to put on a good acting game, there was something about Diamond's plea for my affection that almost made me feel differently toward him.

"Chantel, I'm just looking to complete my life. I have money and a successful business, but I want more! I want more. I'm craving to be a father. Now, you're making Brandon out to be some kind of saint. I know the guy. He has his addiction."

"Don't we all suffer from some kind of addiction?" I asked.

"I can see you suffer from falling in love with the wrong kinds of guys."

"OK, and what's your addiction, Diamond?"

"I fall in love with women who fall for the wrong guys." He paused for a moment. His eyes were soft and brown, and his gaze seemed to hold sincere compassion for my pain. Unlike Brandon, Diamond seemed to care at the moment. He went on. "I did not respect Brandon in the first place for asking me to try and seduce you. I figured he must not have loved you that much if he went to such lengths to try and test your Serenity through some other dude. I would never agree to such an evasive scheme if you were my woman. When I met you, I knew that I wanted to offer you more than games. I want to offer you a true relationship. I want to be a good father to your kids."

"Brandon thinks that you are trying to get back at him for something that happened in the past. Is this true?"

"Chantel, I don't play games. I aim to keep what is in the past in the past. I want to make you and your kids my future. Let's move forward together."

I was ready to move forward...just not with Diamond. But in hopes of a quick resolution, I agreed to the unthinkable.

CHAPTER 31

Astrid

"Say what? You have got to be kidding!" I screamed in disbelief. "You're marrying Diamond? Why?"

Chantel had asked Serenity and me to meet her at her favorite seafood restaurant. It was a beautiful day, and for once the sun shone brilliantly in the sky, piercing through the tall evergreen trees. The only bad part of this day was Chantel's announcement.

"No, I'm not kidding. I've decided to marry Diamond."

"But why?" Serenity asked, just as dumbfounded as I was.

"I have my reasons."

"Is it because he's black?" Serenity asked. "Do you think that just because Diamond is black that he would make a better parent for your kids? Because if you do, that's absurd."

"No, Serenity, that's not it at all. Just trust me on this one. I have my reasons for wanting to marry Diamond. Now, I would kindly appreciate it if you girls would do me the honor of being my bridesmaids."

"No!" Serenity protested. "I don't want you to marry that guy. He tricked you into trying to deceive Brandon. Why would you want to marry a man like that?"

"Serenity, please don't judge me."

"I'm with Serenity on this one, Chantel," I said. "Why would you want to marry someone who deceived you?"

"I can't explain all that right now. Please, I need you guys to be there for me," Chantel begged. "Serenity, please, if you agree to be my bridesmaid, I will attend your expo in Phoenix. I promise. I'll take the twins with me if I have to."

Serenity seemed to instantly reconsider once she heard Chantel's offer.

"And Astrid, if you help me out, I'll turn over the catering job to you. I know business has been slow lately. This will be the perfect opportunity to make some good money and network."

"Chantel, who's paying for this wedding?" I asked.

"Daria."

"What? Where did she get the money from?" I asked.

"Apparently, Daria has been nesting away her money and investments. Daria has quite the savings due to a couple of wise reserves."

"This does not sound right, Chantel. Something is not right about this whole thing. It sounds so...wrong." Serenity shook her head in disbelief. "But if attending your strange wedding will make you feel better, then I'll do it, but I will hold you to attending my event in Phoenix."

"It does not seem right to me, either, Chantel, but I'll do it for you."

"Great!" Chantel lifted her glass of iced tea and smiled rather deviously. "Cheers, ladies!"

CHAPTER 32

Astrid

Even though I did not believe that Chantel truly loved Diamond enough to marry him, I went along with her wedding plans. It actually felt nice to work on a big project. Business had been a little slow lately. The only active engagements happening in my life up until now were my eating habits and bizarre dreams. In one, I was overindulging in a triple-chocolate pound cake. My face was covered in chocolate as I devoured the oversized dessert. I looked a mess—there was chocolate everywhere! There was chocolate in my hair, on my white apron... . I never stopped once to grab a napkin. I just kept eating.

Another reoccurring dream portrayed me on some crazy game show in which the host had me choose between door number one and door number two. No matter what door I chose, a giant bar of animated chocolate awaited. Behind the other door was a group of topless men of every color. I could have had my pick from an assembly of well-toned and good-looking men. Now, any normal woman would search through this group and choose her perfect mate from the pack. Not me: I ran straight for the chocolate and started doing some kind of crazy happy dance.

I would wake up so confused after this repetitive dream. Would the dream ever change? Deep down inside, I longed to choose from the men displayed in front of me, but I just couldn't navigate myself in the right direction. I'm sure Serenity would have told me that my dreams had to do with some kind of hidden chocolate addiction. Now I feared that she could be right.

CHAPTER 33

Chantel

Well, the time had come. Today was the big day. I was set to marry Diamond. My sister had hired one of the best wedding coordinators in Seattle. The venue was gorgeous. The after-party was set outside with tons of white tents laced in lights. You would have thought that a well-known celebrity was about to wed. My dress was extravagant: an Alençon mermaid-style strapless gown with a sweetheart neckline, elongated bodice, gathered-tulle skirt, and a chapel train. There was even a low flower at the left thigh. It was a romantic dress full of beautiful detail and priced at $3,630. Sadly, this was not the dress I would have chosen for myself, but since my sister was paying for the wedding, I allowed her to do as she pleased.

My sister's favorite color was maroon. So all of my bridesmaids wore maroon dresses that fit very nicely. Of course, the only attendants I was only allowed to choose were Astrid and Serenity. My sister handpicked five of her own friends. The men wore tailored suits accented with maroon bow ties. My babies were not present. I left them with Tia, who was not invited because my sister did not approve of her strong-willed ways or her interracial marriage to a white man whom my sister believed to be racist. My sister Daria was delusional. She thought that when Tia and her husband had planned a dinner party and ended up cancelling it at the last minute due to a family emergency, the reason was that Tia's husband did not want any black people in his house, which was ridiculous since he was married to a black woman. Daria was convinced that he had married Tia only for business reasons in order to gain favor at his diverse company.

Daria made me sick. The fact that two people could honestly love each other and desire to commit their lives to each other regardless of race was absurd to her. There always had to be a motive. My sister was caught up in her own beliefs. She had a deluded viewpoint for every jaded thought that crossed her mind. Yet for the one occasion that she should have questioned—my very own wedding—instead of trying to understand my discomfort, she discounted my feelings, never once asking me how I felt or how the father of my children felt about it. Every waking moment was dedicated to the wedding that Daria had always envisioned for herself.

Daria made sure that one of the top chefs in Seattle catered the food with her favorite dishes. She allowed Astrid to provide the dessert, which was very gracious of her. Astrid made my cake, which was a gorgeous five-tier cocoa-flavored cake iced in white chocolate. *Oh yeah, baby, I'm looking forward to that.*

My sister had invited all of her friends and some family from Alabama. Everyone was surprised that Diamond and I were set to wed. Folks back in my hometown had never given up on my marrying eventually, yet many believed that I would reunite with my old flame. However, my close friends tried desperately to talk me out of it up until the actual wedding date. All I could tell Astrid and Serenity was that I had my reasons.

Daria and Diamond's mother were elated that Diamond and I were getting married. Diamond's mother was a lot like my older sister, controlling and manipulating, so to say the least, I did not like her, either. She expected a lot from Diamond, and when

Diamond failed to meet her expectations, she could be harsh and downright cynical.

Diamond's mom was a heavyset, light-skinned woman with hazel eyes immersed in pride. Mrs. Franklin dressed rather nicely, I suppose. Even though her clothes were expensive, they were too small and hugged awkwardly around the rolls of her body, making her appear overly stuffed and exhausted as she walked. Mrs. Franklin wobbled around town as if her feet hurt, almost limping from side to side in her expensive tight-fitting shoes that the top of her foot fat overlapped. Her last husband had left her a large sum of money, which only added to her ego problem.

She and Daria had teamed up together to work out the details of my marriage. Diamond's mother even purchased a ticket to Maui to join us on our honeymoon. The way Mrs. Franklin viewed our situation was to benefit her own selfish nature. All of her husbands in the past had promised to take her to Maui, but the plans never worked out. So she decided to join Diamond and me without our consent. After all, Diamond and I should have felt privileged to have such a caring woman as Mrs. Franklin join us on our honeymoon.

Of course, I was still a bit bitter over the whole underhanded scheme that had cost me the relationship with the father of my twins. Brandon hadn't left the picture. He'd hired one of the best lawyers in Seattle to legally sustain joint custody. Brandon was set to fly back into town the day of my wedding to pick up the twins from Tia. Brandon had bought a beautiful house located in a prime community that catered to children. The twins were set to spend two weeks with their dad while I enjoyed a nice vacation with my new husband and my evil mother-in-law.

Chocolate Burnout

CHAPTER 34

Chantel

The wedding was set to start in thirty minutes, and I was nervous. My sister was making matters worse as she kept picking on me.

"Chantel, did you gain weight?" she asked angrily.

"I don't think so, Mom," I voiced through gritted teeth.

"I think you did!" She began poking around my stomach area and tugging at the sides of the dress. "Oh, girl, you have definitely put on some weight! Why did you do that?"

"I did not do it on purpose! I had twins, remember?"

"Girl, those twins are almost a year old. You should have been able to take that extra weight off by now. You should want things to be perfect on your wedding day, Chantel!" She fussed while tugging on the train of my dress from behind.

"Things are far from perfect, Daria. I'm about to marry Diamond, not the father of my children...not to mention that I got pregnant before marriage."

"There you go calling me Daria again! I have cared for you like a mother! I deserve that respect! Your younger sister, Lamina, and Robert call me by my first name because they lack respect, Chantel. You are better than those two," she huffed.

"Is that why you did not invite them to the wedding...because they lack respect for you? This is my wedding, Dar—...Mom. I would have liked them to be here. They are family."

Daria sighed in frustration. "None of that matters. The important factor is that you found a suitable man within your own race to help you raise your kids."

"You know, Brandon is still a part of my children's life. He has a beautiful culture as well. I want my children to know their background on their father's side, too. I want them to be well rounded."

"Chantel, drop it!" she yelled. "Don't get yourself all worked up. That relationship did not work out!"

"That's because you did not want it to work out! So you did everything in your power to sabotage our relationship." No sooner had those words left my lips than Daria slapped my face. The sting startled me. As I rubbed my cheek, I turned to look into the mirror and studied the mark left behind.

Daria reprimanded me. "There is nothing that you can do about that situation. You are getting married to Diamond now, and that is all that matters. I have taken care of you just as if you were my own child, Chantel. Your constant complaining has worn me out. Not once have you thanked me. I deserve respect. And another thing, this wedding has cost me a fortune. Everything I do is for you, so I'm going to need some help from you and Diamond after the honeymoon so that I can build my savings back up." Looking into the mirror, Daria fixed her makeup and began studying her image rather vainly. "I hated to do that Chantel, especially on your wedding day, but you have been ungrateful and needed to be knocked down a notch or two. I will always be your mother. You should be grateful that you have someone to look after you, Chantel. Not every woman has a forgiving sister who they can look up to like me, to help them out of their mess. Most women have to grin and bear it, honey."

She turned to me. "Now, get that scowl off your face, girl. You're about to get married today!"

CHAPTER 35

Chantel

I was nervous as some strange man I had met only the night before at the rehearsal banquet marched me slowly down the aisle. He smelled of beer and cheap cigars. As I looked around nervously from underneath my veil, all eyes were on me. Daria was right; I had put on some extra weight. Every night I had indulged in my favorite chocolate desserts while in front of the television. Most brides would be at the gym, religiously trying to get in shape for one of the most important events of their lives, and there I was, stuffing my face with chocolate cake, ice cream, M&Ms...and the list went on for days. I had eaten so much chocolate leading up to this wedding that I was truly suffering from a different kind of chocolate burnout—I craved the day that I would truly hate chocolate and eliminate it from my life for good.

I was slowly approaching Diamond. Even though he was dressed sharply and cleaned up well, he still looked like a sneaky, deceitful jerk all decked out in a suit. Sitting in the front row was my evil future mother-in-law. Wearing an ivory-colored, tight-fitting, two-piece ensemble with a matching hat, she resembled an overstuffed turkey. The hat she was wearing had tall, white feathers sticking out from behind. The skin on her neck slightly hung, which made the perfect turkey wattle.

Before the wedding, as I was preparing to change into my dress, she just sat there in the dressing room eating from a jar of pickled pigs' feet. The smell stunk up the entire room. Mrs. Franklin did not offer to help me or ask if I was OK. I tell ya, you can take the girl out of the country, but you can't take the country out of the girl. Sitting next to Mrs. Franklin was her evil twin! Daria was only slightly younger, looking as arrogant as they come.

Astrid and Serenity looked beautiful in their maroon gowns, yet Serenity looked worried as usual, and Astrid looked as if she'd rather be anywhere but here. Against my friends' better judgment, they had agreed to support me. Sure, I had to agree to attend one of Serenity's expos in Phoenix, but it was worth it.

Once I finally reached Diamond, the foul-smelling man instructed to give me away lifted my veil and gave me a sloppy wet kiss on the cheek in the same area that Daria had slapped. I could still feel the sting. There Diamond and I stood in front of a pastor and a room full of onlookers. I was so nervous. The thought of my spending the rest of my life with a man who had trouble standing up to his mom and could be easily swayed into deceiving me turned my stomach. As the pastor spoke, my mind took off in different directions. I reminisced about the events that had led up to this moment. I was so deep in thought that I barely could hear the pastor's words meant to attach me and Diamond together for life.

I snapped out of it just in time to hear the pastor say, "Do you, Diamond, take this woman, Chantel, to be your lawfully wedded wife, to have and to hold, in sickness and in health, in good times and in bad, for better, for worse, for richer, for poorer, keeping yourself solely unto her for as long as you both shall live?"

Diamond smiled proudly and said, "I do."

The pastor then turned his attention to me.

"And do you, Chantel, take this man, Diamond, to be your lawfully wedded husband, to have and to hold, in sickness and in health, in good times and in bad, for better, for worse, for richer, for poorer, keeping yourself solely unto him for as long as you both shall live?"

I could feel my throat closing up. I'd been waiting for this moment, my chance to fully express how I felt, and now it was my turn.

"I *don't!*"

My heart began to pound deeply as I heard the guests gasp.

"I don't want to marry this trifling man!" I yelled.

The look on Diamond's face was mortified, and the pastor seemed confused. Before I knew it, Daria had raced forward to confront me. Grabbing my arm, she whispered into my ear, "Chantel, what are you doing?"

Looking at the pastor, she apologized. "I am so sorry for this little snag. My sister must be nervous and a bit tired from all the excitement. If you could just give us a moment, I'm going to escort her outside for some fresh air and get her a glass of water. I can assure you, it's just a little jitter. All brides go through this, you know..."

"Shut up, Daria!" I screamed, yanking my arm out of her grasp. "I don't want to marry him! He is trifling, and you are one of the most selfish people I have ever encountered. You don't care about me! You just want to use me. Well, I have had enough."

Daria was infuriated. Before the pastor and every witness in that church, my sister slapped me once again in the exact same area! This time, the impact echoed throughout the hall. My cheek was now throbbing with pain. "You ungrateful little brat! Do you know how much I have sacrificed for you to have the finer things in life? I put my dreams on hold to help raise you after Mom passed away, and this is how you repay me? Do you know how much money I invested in this wedding? Do you?" she screamed.

The pastor tried to calm us down, but it was too late. Before I knew it, I had experienced an out-of-body occurrence, causing me to hurl my bouquet across the room. It was as if my body had been overtaken by a spirit of rage as I grabbed hold of my sister's stiff neck, and both of us went tumbling to the ground. We rolled around like two rivals, my sister fighting to maintain control over my life and me fighting for the liberty to be myself, free from her judgment and expectations.

We were wrapped up in our own world of chaos. I heard screaming and clamor throughout the church. The scuffle lasted for a while before two groomsmen tore us apart. Only then did I notice a room filled with terrified family members and friends. I felt bad that it had boiled down to this. My plan was to tell my sister off and then leave, but I guess my anger had gotten the best of me. I felt ashamed of my actions. I truly felt sorry for a couple of people I grew up with back home; they had genuinely wanted to see me happy. I didn't feel sorry for Daria and Mrs. Franklin, even though she apparently had a heart attack and had to be rushed to the ER. Personally, I think the cause of her discomfort was eating that entire jar of pickled pigs' feet. I could not have cared less, to tell you the truth.

The only person who knew about my true plan was Astrid, who did her part by not telling Serenity and by securing the wedding cake. Eventually, I was escorted out of my own wedding by a couple of security guards who watched over the venue. I should have been humiliated for a lifetime, but those feelings of inadequacy seemed to slip away as the limo driver who was initially hired to escort Diamond and me to the airport drove me home. My embarrassment eased as I thought about how long my sister had been deviously manipulating my life. By the time I reached my condo, Serenity and Astrid had already arrived. Astrid's face was red. I could tell she had been laughing by the gleam in her eyes. And Serenity? Yeah, Serenity was pretty upset with me.

"Why didn't you tell me?" she asked as soon as I walked in. "Astrid knew! She had the key to your place! I had to help her carry your wedding cake up a flight of stairs because your elevator is being repaired."

I should have been concerned about Serenity's feelings, but I could not find that place of empathy. I was happy to end that chapter in my life. I know it seemed reckless, but at the time, it all seemed logical to me. I was a ticking bomb, and unlike my younger siblings, who had dealt with Daria up front and then moved away, I chose to stay and allow her to control my life. I could not bring my kids into such a controlling environment. As far as I was concerned, Daria's reign was over, and the best part of that whole event was knowing that Astrid had secured the safety of my delicious chocolate wedding cake. I'm not sure what my sister was going to do about all of that food, but all I truly cared about was my delicious chocolaty cake. It looked beautiful sitting on the marble countertop. I wanted to dive right into it. But I knew that I had to apologize to Serenity first if I wanted to indulge in my chocolate paradise in peace.

"Serenity, I didn't tell you because I knew you would try to talk me out of it."

"You hurt a lot of people back there."

"That was not my intention. I just wanted my sister to realize how deeply hurt *I* was. She never took time to truly consider my feelings. I've felt trapped ever since I was a kid. I felt as if I had to make up for my mother passing away. I felt as if I had to make my sister proud. I think she took me for granted. And I allowed her to become comfortable doing so."

"Chantel, you could have handled things differently. You know, there is peace in the power of forgiveness. Chantel, I know it's easier said than done, but you should not have looked for your peace through such a vengeful act."

"But my sister betrayed me! Scheming and plotting is the only form of communication that she acknowledges! I hated to stoop to her level, Serenity. I really did! But she left me no choice."

"Please don't make Chantel feel bad," Astrid chimed in. "I'm sure that this was a tough decision to make.
I don't think she planned to fight her sister. Look, can we change the subject? I'm dying to try a piece of that cake!"

"Me too!" I agreed. I headed to the kitchen and washed my hands, which felt so rough and tense due to all the drama. I then prepared myself for the best part of my failed wedding. Oh yes, I should have pulled off my tattered wedding dress, but I didn't. Instead, I handed my girls a fork each, and we proceeded to dig into the best part of this unsuccessful union, the chocolate cake. Serenity was still a bit upset with me, but regardless, she stuck around and helped me and Astrid put a dent in that oversized enchanting chocolate wedding cake.

CHAPTER 36

Serenity

Weeks had passed by since Chantel's circus wedding. I did not agree with Chantel's revenge plot, and she was right: if I had known that she was planning such a vengeful act, I would have tried to talk her out of it.

In spite of it all, my new take on life was working out rather well. I'd been focusing on the event that Alison really wanted to make happen. Going over the final preparations for the big women's gathering in Phoenix was my main goal. I'd learned not to allow situations to stress me out so much, especially things that I had no control over, which had softened the hearts of my close friends by allowing them to be able to confide in me. Everything was running smoothly as far as I was concerned, that is, until I received a peculiar phone call from Brandon.

Brandon had asked to meet up with me at a nearby bistro for coffee. He shared briefly over the phone that he was contemplating trying to get back with Chantel. Of course, I always tried to encourage couples to genuinely reunite for the sake of the children, so without contemplation, I agreed to meet up with him.

As we sat across from each other, I couldn't help but notice how unkempt Brandon appeared. He had never looked this bad before. His eyes seemed cold, to the point that I began to feel a bit uneasy. As he muddled over the thought of reconciling with Chantel, he mentioned that he had met another woman during his stay in London while visiting his ailing dad, a therapist to be exact, who had captured his attention. From the sounds of it, this other woman had given him second thoughts concerning reconciling with Chantel. Just as Brandon was about to share why he had been seeing the female therapist in London, a woman—the manager, to be exact—approached our table. Tall and a bit plain, the woman asked Brandon if she could meet with him in her office to discuss some kind of business opportunity. Brandon told me he would only be a second as he briefly expressed his interest in taking over the bistro. Part of me wished that he would do business on his own time because I had a lot of things to take care of back at the office, yet he assured me that he would not be long.

Two large chai teas and one blueberry muffin later, I became jittery and restless and went looking for Brandon. Following the path that Brandon and the plain manager had taken led past the bathrooms and around the corner. My journey led me to a door marked, *Restricted Area, Authorized Employees Only.* Looking behind me to make sure no one was watching, I slipped inside the room.

There were rows of shelves and boxes everywhere. In the dimly lit storage room, I heard panting sounds coming from around the corner. I quietly weaved throughout the boxes and shelves. My curiosity led me straight to Brandon and the female manger. They both were going at it, hot and heavy. Brandon had the woman pinned against the wall, his back facing me. The lustful vision caught me off guard, so much so that it caused me to trip over my own two clumsy feet in a backward motion. My attempt to exit quietly was unsuccessful. As I maneuvered in a clumsy motion out of the maze of cluttered to-go boxes and plastic cups, I bumped into an unsteady shelf stocked with silverware that went crashing to the ground. The two were startled. Brandon immediately tried to regain his composure as the two fumbled around, the woman desperately trying to pull up her underwear and then button her shirt, and Brandon reaching down for his pants.

He called my name. "Serenity! Wait!" he yelled.

Running out of the back room, I moved quickly down the hall and out into the restaurant. Pushing past mingling patrons, I made my way outside. Surprised to find Brandon close behind, still fumbling with his zipper as I proceeded to run to the car, I realized that I had parked far away, and to make it worse, my stupid heels hindered my progress. It felt as if I were wearing circus stilts. I finally reached the car, but by then, Brandon had forcefully grabbed hold of me.

"Let go!" I screamed.

I attempted to fight my way out of his grasp. He yelled, fighting for my undivided attention. "Serenity! Please! Just hear me out!" he screamed. "I can't let you go until you hear me out! Please, Serenity!"

I looked around the secluded parking area surrounded by hovering oak trees. No one would be able to hear my scream. I should have parked closer to the restaurant. I always parked far away so that I could get my exercise, which was usually a great regimen. Now, looking at Brandon's adamant face and seeing that he was not going to let me go until I agreed to hear him out, I had no other choice but to calm down and listen. "Say what you have to say, Brandon, and then please let me go."

Brandon released his strong grip. His face showed deep remorse. His eyes were red and dark. Rays of sunlight shone upon his unshaven face. His hair was messy. He was panting and perspiring, I didn't know what to think.

"I'm sick. I...I need help, and I'm seeking help." He sighed. "I'm a sex addict." His eyes looked tired. Brandon no longer represented the business-savvy man I had first met. "What you saw back there meant nothing. It was an act of weakness. I called you here to tell you that I had been seeing a therapist in London. I...I've been trying to get help."

Moving closer toward me, he placed his head onto my shoulder and began to sob. I could feel his weakness, and even though I could not take away the pain that his addiction provoked, I gave him a consoling embrace. It was then that I could smell alcohol and cigarettes on his clothing. I couldn't stand the smell. Backing away, I said, "Wow! Brandon! Dude, you smell like the inside of a rundown casino!"

Trying to compose himself, he asked, "Are you going to tell Chantel?"

"No. That's your job, Brandon, not mine. You don't look well.... I suggest that you get help wherever you can find it. And just be up front with Chantel. She's been lied to enough in her life. The truth would be a refreshing change. Is there anything else you want to talk about?" I asked as I removed a tissue from my purse to wipe the perspiration from his forehead. "Are you on drugs?" I asked.

"No.... I mean, I smoke every now and then, and I had a drink today just to keep my mind off sex, but what good did that do? And...well...yeah, sometimes I...I take a sex enhancement drug, and I—"

"Wait, what?!" I yelled. "Why are you taking sex enhancement drugs if you have a sex problem, Brandon?"

"It's too difficult to explain, Serenity. Please, could you just...?" Brandon moved in once more for consolation, and I noticed that his pants zipper was still down.

"No, Brandon, I can't comfort you, not like this." I knew that he desired to be consoled, but I was not the one to provide him with that crucial need. Backing further away, I neared the car door. "Brandon, please, get help, and...zip your pants up, man."

Sadly, these were my final words to Brandon. Upon entering the car, I fumbled with my car keys. My mind went back to an interview I had had with an Uber driver a while back while I was out of town on a summer getaway. The driver had shared that he was a sex addict. He explained that eventually his craving for sex disappeared. He said that he had prayed to God to get rid of the addiction. He shared that it was a humbling experience, in such a way that he chose to stay Serenityful to the woman he had married. I thought that perhaps the urge for sex ultimately disappears, but for some addicts, the absence may be so unbearable that they turn to sex enhancements to hang onto the dark thrill of addiction. Going through life with the craving could be torment within itself.

I finally focused enough to calmly place the keys into the ignition. As I drove away, I watched Brandon from my rearview mirror. He looked lost and helpless as he wandered aimlessly through the parking lot, running his fingers through his matted hair. Part of me hoped that Brandon would not tell Chantel what happened, just for the sake of peace. Eventually, every dark force comes out into the light, including all of our addictions.

CHAPTER 37

Serenity

My relationship with Astrid had gotten better. Astrid had taken time out to be at peace with herself. We had all been very busy lately, wrapped up in our own lives. We had not seen one another since we had torn into Chantel's reject wedding cake. So you can imagine my surprise at meeting up with Astrid one rainy Seattle morning. We sat near the bay window inside my high-rise office overlooking the busy streets. Sitting there across from Astrid was now a peaceful situation void of tension and discomfort.

I sat contentedly listening to Astrid's new voyage in life. Her face shone vibrantly as she filled me in.

"I had a lot of soul-searching to do," Astrid revealed. Her cobalt eyes sparkled as she reflected on her ongoing journey toward inner healing and acceptance. "I suffered from a chocolate burnout situation of my own as I lost interest in my business for a while. Unable to create new recipes, I lost the desire to create. I noticed that I was gaining a lot of weight, so I stepped back from the business and tried weaning myself off chocolate. I started taking a variety of exercise classes at a nearby gym. I even joined an online dating site, which was a joke!" She laughed. "Most of those guys had more problems than me! I met up with this one guy who resembled George Costanza from *Seinfeld*. I was trying to keep an open mind, but we had nothing in common. He liked bowling, rock collecting, and organ music, and he played the banjo. By the way, none of this weird stuff was listed in his bio. Not only that, he also seemed to have more hair on his profile picture than in person. The picture he posted must have been of his son or something because he looked nothing like his picture. This guy even had the nerve to tell me that I looked nothing like my profile pic. I had just taken that picture! Anyway..." She paused, taking a sip of warm tea. "My dating experience seemed to reflect this reoccurring dream of my having a choice of men. In reality, the men were not as good-looking. I was an equal opportunity dater, too. Race was not an issue for me. I was searching for compatibility."

"Are you getting discouraged?" I asked.

"Not at all." Astrid smiled confidently. "I had a peaceful dream that put all of my anxiety to rest."

"Really?"

"Yes! I dreamed that I was on a game show. I had two doors to choose from, and this time, I chose the door with the room full of men, examining the demeanor of each man closely. I finally came across one guy who seemed to stand out from the rest. I chose this man, and in return, he handed me a ring made of chocolate." She laughed. "As crazy as it seems, Serenity, that dream was confirmation that I will find my true love one day, and he will be sweeter than chocolate. In the meantime, I have to get myself together, too, so that I will have the right kind of love to offer this man in return." She smiled.

CHAPTER 38

Serenity

I wanted to confide in Astrid about the incident
Brandon had caused. But I knew there was no way that
Astrid would let it slide. I knew that Brandon was not
the right person for my friend. But there was no way
that I could tell her because her hope depended on him.
Instead, I drowned myself in the event ahead and flew
out for a well-anticipated event.

My girlfriends and I were finally in Phoenix
attending one of the most uplifting expos to date. I
decided to call it the Chocolate Burnout Expo, which
was an odd name, but I thought that the title truly
covered the theme.

According to Harvard Health Publications,
"chocoholics" have three essential components of
addiction: intense craving, loss of control over the
object of that craving, and continued use or engagement
despite bad consequences. Yet as I have observed,
women who have struggled with severe chocolate
cravings are unable to control their own lives. They
may have hang-ups that stem from their pasts. Sweet
food or food in general is an escape that instantly fills
the void. Food does demand effort, as do relationships.
It is there to consume without rejection. However, the
danger of overindulging can lead to health issues such
as obesity.

The real cause is to get to the root of the problem,
to confront the underlying issue, and to address the
situation with forgiveness. Of course, there was humor
at the expo. What would a chocolate convention for
women be without the existence of healthy, guilt-free

chocolate? Astrid had created guilt-free chocolate: dark chocolate mixed with fruit and other alternatives that tasted divine. There were booths that celebrated the diversity of women.

Yes! This enriched expo fed women in every way. My dear friend Camila displayed her latest work, and her illustration of the woman with the full lips deep in thought appeared on well-made women's tees. There was also a fashion show. Models of all shapes and sizes confidently walked down the runway. There was also food for the soul as young up-and-coming poets and singers expressed themselves through their art.

I was blessed to see this harvest of women from all walks of life and cultures, women who held important positions in the business world and women who made a difference as homemakers.

The women who have spoken understanding into my life such as Joyce Meyers lift up others through their personal tragedies by leaning on the kind of faith that moves mountains. This encouraged me to move forward in assurance that life gets better through perseverance and forgiveness and grace.

Speakers informed us about the missing relationship that is needed in every woman's life, a strong father–daughter bond. This bond is rarely acknowledged here on earth. The longing for a woman to be accepted by her biological dad or any sincere male bond that represents the meaning of unconditional love is vital. The void of such understanding sets forth insecurities that bind her in unstable relationships revolving around abusive men or men who put forth a false perception of love. How would a woman know what true love is if she had never known the honest love from her earthly father? This journey of acceptance will either lead a woman to hunger for love in a broken man who can offer nothing in return, or to an all-knowing and loving Father who reigns beyond human comprehension. This fatherly bond is hard to conceive because it comes from the inside abyss that man cannot see.

CHAPTER 39

Chantel

I arrived back at Seattle from Serenity's Chocolate Burnout Expo early in the morning. That gave me enough time to unpack and unwind before facing my most difficult challenges to date. The children were with Brandon for the remainder of the week, which allowed me to contemplate the drama ahead. There were people whom I had to confront and people who had issues with me as well, and first up to bat was Diamond.

I met up with Diamond at a nearby park. Diamond was still very much in shape and enjoyed running, so I agreed that I would meet with him after his run. I couldn't deny it. Diamond still looked good. His running attire made him look like an Olympic athlete. I had to give the brother credit for keeping himself up. I wished our meeting had been on different terms.

As we began walking around the park laced with dark evergreen trees, Diamond was the first to speak. "I still don't know why you did it, Chantel. I really cared for you. Do you know I had to still take our honeymoon trip to Maui with my mother? Do you know how awkward and humiliating that was?" I could see the pain and frustration still in his eyes.

"I'm sure Mother secretly preferred it that way, Diamond. She never really liked me in the first place. You know no one was ever good enough for her boy, anyway."

"That's not the point, Chantel. That wedding was about us! I don't understand why you did that in front of all of our guests!"

"You are a good-looking guy, Diamond. You can find someone else."

"Chantel, I'm sterile! I can't have children! Our being married was a way to fulfill my dreams of becoming a dad!"

After hearing Diamond's pain, I truly felt bad that I had handled things the way I had. And still I tried to make him understand my position. "Is it really that hard to understand?" I replied. "You betrayed me, set me up. Because of you, I missed out on the chance to have a relationship with the father of my children."

"That mess wasn't going to work, and you know it."

"No, I don't know that, Diamond!"

"Look, Chantel, I know you still have feelings for me. I could feel your desire when we almost hooked up back at my place that night. You still have feelings for me, right?"

Diamond was right. I did have feelings for him. After all, Diamond was handsome, and he reminded me of my first love, Martin. I knew every curve of his body. I was the first to see his Kappa branding. I used to rub my fingers over the symbol as we lay in bed together. His body and his ways were familiar to me. And the thought of our past love affair played in my mind on that night. But those thoughts were a part of the past, and as far as I was concerned, my future was with Brandon.

"Yes! I had feelings for you, Diamond, but that was only temporary. Life goes on."

"Chantel, I still want be with you. I am willing to change my life for you. I may have gone about the whole thing wrong, and looking back, I wish I could have been up front with you." He sighed, contemplating with regret.

"But no!" I snapped. "Instead, you let my sister and Brandon talk you into betraying me."

"I'm a grown man, Chantel! At the end of the day, it was my choice."

"Stupid choice, Diamond."

"Yeah, I guess so."

"Look, I'm sorry about your mother, and I'm sorry about the way things turned out. And I'm sorry that you can't have kids. But to be honest, I want to be with my children's father. I grew up without a mom and a dad. I don't want that for my kids. I'm going to try to make things right with Brandon."

Diamond was hurt. But deep down inside, I knew that he would keep trying to win me over. I could have never guessed that his real intent was to get back at Brandon for an incident that had occurred in the past, a betrayal that ran deep within the depths of his heart. Most important, I could have never guessed that I'd be stupid enough to fall for it, but that was a whole different story.

CHAPTER 40

Chantel

The next meeting was with my two sisters. Lamina had just returned from a long excursion and was running late as usual. The three of us met up at Daria's favorite restaurant, which overlooked a secluded lake just outside of Everett.

Once Lamina arrived, we sat still, staring at one another until finally I decided to break the ice. "So, how was your trip, Lamina?"

"It was all right. I enjoyed myself, I guess." She shrugged.

"Why haven't you returned my phone calls, Lamina?" Daria snapped. "You know I've been trying to contact you."

"Usually when you call me, you ask for money. I'm not your local credit union, Daria."

"Don't disrespect me, child, after all I've done for you," Daria snapped.

"Don't you throw that guilt trip on me, Daria," Lamina snapped back.

The two began to go back and forth.

"Yeah, let you tell it," Lamina huffed. "You always got to bring up what you did for us! You did what you had to do, Daria! Any decent human being would have taken it upon herself to try to step up after such a tragedy in life. You act like you pulled us out of a burning building!"

Daria began her woe-is-me speech. "You are so ungrateful! The both of you! I have not heard from you in years, Lamina. All I ask is that you keep in touch. And you, Chantel"—she glared at me—"you still owe

me money for turning that expensive wedding into a circus."

Lamina burst out laughing. "Yeah, I heard about that. Way to go, sis. Dang, I wish I could have been there to see that!" She shook her head. Grabbing a piece of bread, she dipped it into a bowl of olive oil and began feasting.

"How dare you act so insensitive, Lamina! Diamond's mother had a heart attack."

Lamina gasped. "No, she didn't! Chantel told me that she ate a whole jar of pickled pigs' feet. That's what caused her heart palpitations: trapped gas. Ha, ha, ha."

I wanted to join Lamina in laugher, but I couldn't. Part of me felt bad for spending so much of Daria's savings on that hoax of a wedding. Even though a large sum of that money had come from my lending her money constantly, at the end she chose to reinvest in my wedding.

"Mom, I'm sorry. I was hurt at the time. I'm going to work on paying you back."

"Mom?" Lamina shook her head. "She's not our mom! Chantel! And you don't pay her back!" Lamina shouted in disapproval. "As many times as you have given Daria money, she owes you."

"She does not owe me anything," I said.

"Stay out of this, Lamina!" Daria shouted. "You don't have any say in this matter. You abandoned this family long ago. You are nothing but a disrespectful hood rat!"

"Oh yeah?!" Lamina shouted. "You are the reason why Robert and I left, Daria. You are a control freak! You have to control everyone and everything around you. We left to get away from you! Robert never calls,

and he never visits. He can't stand you! And Chantel has finally broken down. Pretty soon she will move away from you too. You'll be stuck with Frank,
the village idiot for the rest of your life."

Lamina's words hurt Daria. "Do you feel the same way, Chantel?" she asked, her eyes flooded with tears.

"The truth is...you can come off a bit controlling, Daria." I confessed. "And even though I know that you mean well, it can be frustrating and a bit stifling."

My words did not help ease Daria's pain. She leaped up. "Well, you all don't have to worry about me anymore. I won't bother you two, my own flesh and blood, ever again."

She left in tears. To be honest, I had no desire to run after her, and neither did Lamina. Both of us knew that she would be calling in a week or so, begging for money or asking us to stop by for dinner.

So I sat there with my younger sister as she reminisced about her trip. Lamina had met a nice guy in Germany named Janez. From the picture that she showed me on her phone, Janez appeared calm and fun loving. He was tall with dishwater-blonde hair and deep-blue eyes. It was hard to decipher if my sister had a case of chocolate burnout or if she was just switching things up a little by indulging in a bowl of vanilla Häagen-Dazs. Only time would tell.

CHAPTER 41

Chantel

"But Astrid—"

"I'm not taking no for an answer, Chantel." Click. She hung up.

Astrid had turned over a new leaf. She used to be the friend all cooped up at home, and now the tables had turned. Last week, she made me meet up with her at a new health club. Astrid had become so outgoing, it was almost as if she had zapped all of the energy that I used to have. Now she was forcing me to go out dancing with her. Astrid and I had not gone out dancing in years.

As I sat on the side of the bed thinking about what to wear, I could not get over Astrid's newfound zest for life. There was something more going on with her. Astrid's enthusiasm almost seemed contagious as I began to get a little excited about that night. Brandon and I had not been communicating as much as I had hoped. My goal was to get our family under the same roof. I wanted him in my life. But lately, he had been avoiding me.

Don't get me wrong; Brandon was a great father to our children. But his attentiveness toward me was a whole different story. He treated me as if I were the nanny. I was contemplating how I could get us back on the right track. I was devastated when Brandon told me of his plans to go back to London for good. He did not threaten to take the kids—he said we would work things out—but I did not understand why he would want to leave his children for months on end to stay in London. Part of me believed that he might have met someone else. Nonetheless, I knew that for now, I was going to have to look on the bright side of life vicariously through Astrid. Astrid was actually a joy to be around lately. I was going out with a confident single woman.

Yet on the flip side, I must admit there was something about Astrid that made me sick in some ways. The twins were now a handful—they were in their terrible-everything stage, running around whining and crying, bumping into furniture, and wrecking everything. My once-beautiful decorated home now resembled a war zone. There were sippy cups everywhere and tiny fish-shaped crackers lodged between the couch cushions. I was exhausted half of the time. Even though I loved my kids, at times I felt trapped. I just wanted to sleep.

Seeing Astrid with her happy-go-lucky demeanor made no sense. It seemed like a crime to walk around happy all the time. There were days that I actually dreaded being around her, though not today. I would think, *I'll tell her I'm sick. I won't answer the door.* But no, the new, persistent Astrid was worse than our friend Serenity. She insisted on ringing the doorbell until I answered.

Astrid always made good on her promise, arriving shortly after I dropped the twins off at day care. I quickly changed back into pajamas and a comfy terry-cloth robe, eager to get some sleep. And here came Astrid, ringing my doorbell. I'd open the door and watch as she'd skip through like a giddy five-year-old. I can recall one sad day when Brandon had told me that he was thinking about moving back to London, I was feeling really down. Astrid had come over to coax me out my robe and go jogging.

"Hey, girl. You can't go jogging like that." She pointed at my robe.

"I'm not going, Astrid. I just can't, not today."

"Why?"

"I can't talk about this right now." I struggled to keep from bursting into tears.

She pulled me over to the couch and patted the space next to her. I reluctantly sat.

"Please, Chantel. What's going on?"

I swallowed, forcing the tears to stay back. "I think Brandon's maybe contemplating moving to London for good. He said that we would figure out a reasonable schedule for the kids, but...I want to be in his life. I wish I hadn't been so focused on trying to get back at my sister. I know that confused him. He couldn't understand my logic, and now that I look back, that was a stupid thing to do."

"Cocoa, don't beat yourself up."

"It's OK. I'll be OK."

"You don't look OK. It looks like you need a break."

"No, I'm so sick and tired of crying over men! What's wrong with me?"

"You need to let it out."

"I want to scream from the top of my voice, but I can't. I refuse to give Brandon the satisfaction."

"Do you think there is someone else in the picture?"

"I believe so."

"Do you know who?"

"No, but I'm determined to find out."

"How?"

"I don't know. A man's steps are never too hard to trace."

"Maybe you should leave it alone for now, Chantel."

"If I don't do something to let him know that I'm interested in holding our family together, I may lose him for good."

Ever since that day, Astrid had been trying to get me out to get my mind off of Brandon. That evening, she showed up promptly at nine, wearing a leather tube top and matching skirt with a high slit on the side. Astrid had fluffed out her golden-blonde locks and accented her look with sapphire hoop earrings. Astrid had lost a lot of weight. It was clear that this woman was no longer dependent on the Serenity of chocolate as an escape.

"Wow, Astrid," I commented. "You look amazing, diva!"

"Well, I try!" She laughed. "Let's go!"

Of course, I felt a little insecure about my outfit. I loved my curves back in the day, but now, nothing wanted to hug correctly to my body.

Astrid took me to a place called Dexterity. It was an older crowd with a few young people in the mix. I appreciated the peaceful surroundings and the soft jazz music that flowed throughout the venue. Astrid led me across the room, over to a reserved table located in a spacious area that showcased the distinct layout of the setting.

"So, what do you think?" Astrid asked as she snapped her fingers to the music.

"It beats sitting at home." The truth was that I felt completely out of place—lost, to be exact. My hair was in a too-tight twist; I could barely close my eyes! My head was throbbing. I waited for a waitress to stop by so I could order a drink to calm my nerves. As I sat there trying to look as if I were having a swell time, I was surprised to see a tall, dark, and handsome older man approaching the table. He was downright fine. I tried to maintain my composure. *Wow, he's just what I need to get my mind off of me. Um, um, um, oh yes, I believe in miracles.*

Once he arrived, I was utterly surprised as I watched Astrid leap out of her seat and give the tall, dark stranger a heartfelt hug and a warm kiss on his sinuous lips.

"You made it!" She smiled with sheer excitement. I'd never seen Astrid so overjoyed. "Chantel, the main reason why I wanted you to meet me here tonight is so that you could meet the new man in my life—my love, Evan!" She glowed. "Evan, this is my best friend, Chantel."

"The pleasure is all mine." Gracefully, he greeted me with a gentle peck on the cheek. *Um...he smells dreamy*, I thought, knowing I had to grab hold of my thoughts as I cleared my throat and tried to stay focused on Astrid's happiness, which was very hard for a selfish person such as me to do. "Nice to meet you, Evan. I wish I could say that Astrid had told me a lot about you; however, this is all new to me."

"Well, Astrid thinks the world of you, Chantel." He gave a charming smile. "Did you all order drinks yet?"

"No," Astrid answered. "I would love one of their signature cocktails. What about you, Chantel?"

I was in a daze. When did Astrid start dating black men? He was tall and handsome, yet I detected an accent of some sort. I knew that she was doing some online dating, but... . *Dang*, I thought, *if this is what they are serving up online, I need to be part of it.*

"Chantel! Are you OK?" Astrid asked, snapping me out of my bewildered thoughts.

"Oh...I'm sorry. Yes, I'll take a drink. I'll have what you're having."

"They serve food here, too. Did you want something to eat? Their menu is amazing. They hired a chef right out of one of the most well--respected culinary schools in Seattle. Did you want to take a look at the menu?" she asked.

"What, are you the waitress of this place now, Astrid?" I asked.

Astrid laughed. "No. Ironically, Evan is part owner of this fine establishment. We met at a chocolate festival in Dallas."

"In Dallas?" I asked, not having remembered Astrid taking off for any convention.

"Yes! Remember? It was a while back. I asked you to come with me, but the twins were sick."

"Ah! Yes, I remember. Well, if I knew they were serving up chocolate men, I would have made an exception!" I laughed.

Astrid and Evan stared awkwardly, and they broth broke into a slight laughter, almost as if they could sense my off-balance nature. To shake off the ill-at-ease moment, I stuck to my drink order. "Um, yeah, so, I'll have whatever you are having, Astrid."

"OK! Do you mind if I go with Evan to pick up our drinks? He just flew in from France. We did not get a chance to talk much while he was gone."

"Were you in France on business?" I asked.

"No, I was visiting relatives."

"Oh, I see. Um, sure. You both go on and catch up. I'll just wait here."

I watched the vibrant couple as they disappeared through the crowd hand in hand. Astrid appeared to be very happy. As the live band began to play, I couldn't help but feel detached from the surroundings. Reaching for my purse, I retrieved my phone and began to check my social media page. As I sat there scrolling down countless posts and pictures, I couldn't help but feel a little jealous. Astrid had never told me about Evan. I wondered, *Is her relationship getting serious?*

As I sat there in a trance, someone else approached.

"Chantel Reed! Well, I never thought I would find you here."

I looked up to find the familiar face attached to the memorable voice but was having a hard time remembering the name and the place. I studied the buff man up and down. He was wearing a Giorgio Brutini cream suit with a black weave shirt underneath. He sported a clean-shaven head and a well-trimmed goatee. I simply could not place his name.

"Have you forgotten about me that fast? It's me, Eugene."

I almost fell out of my chair. *Eugene!* He looked good. He had lost weight, and his face appeared well defined! Who would have known that under those chubby cheeks of his were chiseled cheekbones, and underneath all of that body flab was a healthy physique? In fact, he looked like a million bucks! Eugene had ended up putting in for a transfer shortly after our departure. Honestly, there was not a day that had gone by when I did not wonder about his well-being.

"Oh, my heavens! Eugene!" Jumping up, I gave him an immense embrace. I could tell he was overwhelmed by my response. "Please, have a seat. What have you been up to?" I asked, pulling my chair a tad bit closer to his.

"Well," he chuckled, "after you shamelessly broke my heart, I relocated to Northern California. Started a business out there."

"What kind of business?" I was *very* intrigued.

Eugene laughed. "I opened a boutique selling designer clothes."

That sounded too bizarre. Eugene had been a successful engineer. *Why would he throw it all away to run a boutique?* I wondered silently. "You sell clothes?

I have to be honest, that sounds very odd, but whatever makes you happy. You look great, Eugene. You took off a lot of weight!"

"I'm very happy. The clothes that we sell stem from an exclusive line. It's one of a kind. We should have our website up and running soon. And you're right!" I gave a broad grin. "I got serious about dropping some weight. My health was a major factor as well. The change was good for me. Anyway, enough about me, Chantel. What about you? How are the twins? I bet they're getting big now."

"Yes, they're getting so big!" I pulled up a picture on my phone of my wild handfuls at the beach, Isabella wearing her bright swimsuit with ruffles around the waist, and Isaiah sporting his swim trunks bare-chested and wearing a sunhat that practically covered his entire head, as the two intensely dug holes in the damp sand.

"Wow! They are beautiful, Chantel."

"As for me, I'm getting big, too. As you can see, I think I found your extra weight." I laughed. "But I'm hitting the gym first chance I get. I took some time off to raise the kids. When they get a little older, I'll probably head back to work. I feel that they really need a stay-at-home mother since Brandon and I are living apart. Our relationship did not work out, and, um...well, yep, I'm still single."

As I sat there looking at Eugene, I realized that I had made a big mistake. Maybe his being here was a sign that I should give him another chance. Looking back, I realize that my thoughts were both narcissistic and inconsiderate, being that none of my concerns had to do with Eugene's purpose in life. All I cared about at the time was my own happiness and how everyone around me could add to it. It would be through the difficult inherited and selfish nature of having raised my own children, Isabella and Isaiah that I would come to realize, that life does not work that way. Nonetheless, I was blindly in the moment. "You know, Eugene, I never got to apologize for the way that I treated you. I'm—"

"Chantel, don't apologize." Shaking his head in a disapproving motion, he said, "Letting me go was one of the best things that could have ever happened to me. I wouldn't have met Frances."

"Who?"

Eugene reached inside his jacket and pulled out his phone. He retrieved an image and shared the picture of a fair-skinned woman with thick, black, curly, long hair. She appeared to be in her late thirties, and apparently she had an attitude. Her persona displayed her nicely manicured hands placed on her slim waist. She had features comparable to a porcelain doll.

"My wife, Frances, is the love of my life." Eugene stared down at her picture ever so lovingly, as if she were before him in person.

"Yeah, she's cute!" I forced myself to smile, knowing that I probably resembled someone who had just gotten smacked in the stomach with a baseball bat. I had no idea why I was feeling jealous. Of course, Eugene used to worship the ground that I walked on, and now, now he's affectionate toward some other woman. Nonetheless, I knew that I could not allow my insecure moment to take center stage. "So, what brings you back to Seattle?" I asked, trying to shake off the envious vibe.

"We flew in for Cameron's wedding."

"Wait...what? You mean to tell me that my worthless, shiftless, lazy, thoughtless, freeloading ex-boyfriend Cameron is getting married?" I asked in shock.

Eugene chuckled. "Yeah. Actually, Cameron's doing pretty well for himself. He got his act together, found himself a good job at an automobile manufacturing company, met a nice woman. He really made a change for the best."

What the heck! I thought. *What was I? Some kind of shelter for misfit men until they can get their act together, run off, and marry some other woman? That's not right. Some other woman is reaping the benefits of my hard work.*

Just then, Eugene's phone went off. He viewed the text for a moment and shoved the phone back inside his jacket. He responded in haste, "Chantel, I was just stopping by to say hi. My wife just walked in. It was good seeing you again." Eugene patted my shoulder. "You take care of yourself, OK? I'm wishing you the best."

I watched as he made his way over toward the entrance and embrace his new love, Frances. The two looked perfect together as they held each other. I started feeling sick and a bit angry—not at Eugene; I was frustrated with myself for taking Eugene for granted. I knew that Eugene deserved the best after all that I had put him through, yet that night should have been a joyous occasion. I should have been happy that Eugene was able to pick up the pieces and move on. But deep down inside of my dark heart, I longed for him to still have feelings for me, and for unknown reasons that only deep therapy and endless soul-searching would be able to reveal, as time moved on, I would replay this event. Anytime I was in a club environment, I would replay the unexpected meeting between Eugene and me, and with every imaginary delusion, the outcome would be different. Sometimes our meeting would end in a hateful manner, and sometimes it would end in a sorrowful manner, but the one thing that I noticed is that it would take years for me to find peace with Eugene moving on, for the reason that I myself had yet to find the kind of happiness that would allow me to move forward without any regrets.

Astrid and Evan eventually came back with colorful cocktails and fabulously prepared appetizers. As we ate and sipped on, the two lovebirds filled me in on

how they had met, which was nauseating. My behavior toward Astrid was also annoying. I had no right to feel this way. After all, Astrid had stood by my side through thick and thin. My good friend had attended a counseling session with me. She had gone to meet Brandon's cuckoo family, and she had stood by my side through a phony-jackass wedding and had still managed to smuggle out my gigantic chocolate wedding cake. Astrid had tried to comfort me during the most helpless and dysfunctional times in my life. *I should be happy for my friend. She finally found a guy she trusts with her fragile heart, and I'm sitting over here sulking, acting like a castaway stuck on the island of forbidden love,* I thought. *Shame on you, Chantel Reed.*

Even though I wanted to go home, I made myself stay. I watched as Astrid and her new man slow danced. Astrid and Eugene had finally moved on. Yep...they had found completeness. As for me, I was far from it. The only happiness I had that night was the illusion of happiness in a martini glass. Yep, I had plenty to drink, courtesy of Evan. But the more I drank, the more depressed I became. Ironically, sitting in a club called Dexterity, which stood for so many positive elements such as skill, harmonization, adroitness, and direction, I felt the exact opposite—ineffective, stupid, unmotivated. I felt ugly inside and out. I had not been able to get rid of the baby weight from the twins; if anything, I was gaining even more weight. The twins were not helping. I was their human garbage disposal.

Whatever they did not finish on their plates, I did the honors. I was sluggish half of the time. All I did was sit home watching game shows, talk shows, and the news—none of those programs did anything for me!

Here I am, blotted, discontent, and suffering from a bad case of the 'don't gots'! That's right! I don't got patience, I don't got goals, I don't got energy, and I don't got a man. I hated everything about my life. Come to think of it, the best part of my life was my friends. I had just received a text from Serenity, who was working on an interview with an inspirational speaker out of Israel. Serenity was amazing. She clung to her own Serenity like a surfer who clings to his board, riding out the most challenging waves in life. In some ways, I admired Serenity's need to provide her viewers as well as her inner hunger with motivation, and yet there was a part of me that wanted to tell Serenity to stuff it. I had to be real with my feelings. I found it hard to be happy all of the time, especially when I was caught up in hating myself at that very moment! That's right; I hated myself right then. I hated the way-too-tight dress that I was wearing. It was supposed to be a little black dress, but I was fat, which made it the little black bloated dress. The off-the-shoulder strap was hanging on for dear life. I could barely find anything to wear half of the time. I used to wear my clothes with pride. But now, the once simple task of getting dressed was like some kind of cruel, awkward dance aerobic workout. I literally broke out in a mad sweat trying to get my pants or skirt to go over my thighs. I couldn't even pull off the dress I was wearing.

As I sat there negatively complaining my life away, fate decided to taunt me further. My dress strap broke, and my pitiful-looking breast flung out! Of course, the revealing body part was covered with bra tape since I could clearly visualize the wardrobe malfunction ahead of time. Sadly enough, numerous wardrobe malfunctions would continue to haunt me, and it would take episodes such as these to eventually convince me to make some life-changing commitments. But for now, it was definitely time to call it a night.

CHAPTER 42

Chantel

Well, here I was again, plopped in front of the big screen. Flicking through the channels, I came across *The Psychic Gal Hotline.*

Maybe this psychic can tell me if Brandon has a new woman in his life, I pondered for a few minutes, and then thought, *Chantel Reed, what are you doing?* As I sat there feeling lost and agitated, the phone rang. It was Brandon. I guess I didn't need any psychic to tell me anything. I knew that Brandon cared for me and could never be separated from me or our twins. I was finally going to live happily ever after.

Brandon asked me to meet him for a late lunch at Dakota's Bistro. He wanted to talk about our future! Brandon said he had a big announcement to share with me!

Everything had to be perfect. I wore a two-toned black and white form-fitting dress so I would appear thinner, and I put my hair in a sleek updo. I topped off the look with studded gold earrings and sleek high heels.

I arrived at two, as we had planned. I took two deep breaths, then made my way inside the brightly colored eatery. Brandon was standing near the entrance.

"Chantel, it's good to see you." He gave me a generous hug, which I desperately needed. It had been a while since I had talked to Brandon face to face. He picked up the kids every other week but stayed in the car.

The hostess sat us at a small corner table. Sitting across from Brandon brought back cherished memories of when we were dating, when he used to take me to his restaurant after hours.

"How have you been doing?" he asked with genuine interest.

"Fine." My voice was shaking. I took a sip of water and cleared my throat.

"Are you sure? I mean, you look great, but..."

"But what?"

"Chantel, I'm not sure why you went so far as to seek revenge in the first place. I still feel that was an unnecessary move."

"And I don't see why you went so far as to deceive me. You brought your best friend into the picture, Brandon!"

"Chantel, I'm sorry. I did a lot of stupid things, but now it's time for me to get myself back on track for the sake of our children.

"I'm sorry too, Brandon. I did some stupid things also! I was out of my head, confused, but now I can see clearly. I know that you care for me."

"I do care for you, Chantel, and the kids. That's why I decided not to move to London."

My heart skipped a beat. I knew Brandon could never leave me and the children.

The waitress came over and took our order, but my stomach was doing cartwheels. I was anxious to hear Brandon pop the question. Of course, we would probably need counseling before we married. But this time, my wedding would be something that I truly consented to and I would prepare.

"Are you sure you don't want to eat?"

"I'm sure."

Brandon fidgeted with his silverware and took a deep breath, brushing his fingers through his wavy, sable hair. "Chantel..."

"Yes?" I responded eagerly.

"Well, through the years, I have been searching for completion. I...I often wondered if I'd ever find it. And once I did, it frightened me, but in a good way. I could no longer fight the feeling. I'm in love, Chantel."

"Yes?" I was on the edge of my seat. I must have looked like a contestant on *The Price Is Right* waiting for my name to be called.

"Her name is Kara. We met in a layover in San Francisco. Um..." There was an awkward silence. The hesitance in his voice and the tensed look upon his face seemed to dread my reaction. "She's a great woman. Well...we're getting engaged. Kara also has family in London. She grew up there; however, business opportunities landed her here in the US."

Kara who? I thought. I felt like a child who runs to the tree on Christmas morning only to find a pair of ugly socks. This would be one of many instances in which I would have to step down and watch another woman take my place. I despised this woman! I silently yelled in pain.

"Chantel, are you OK?"

"What?"

"Are you OK? You spaced out on me."

"You're marrying someone else?"

"Yes. Haven't you heard a word I said?"

"What about the kids?"

"The kids will always be a part of my life; you know that. I'm hoping that I can persuade Kara to move out here. She's a marketing director, passionate about her job; however, I sense that she's looking for change. I'm sure she can start a successful career out here as well."

I had to ask. I don't know why, and not that it should've mattered, but it mattered to me. "Is she white?"

"Does it matter, Chantel? I found someone who I believe I can make a life with."

"That someone, Brandon, should have been me!"

"Chantel, stop. Don't do this to yourself." Looking around, Brandon tried to maintain his composure and mine. "Look, if we need to go somewhere private to have this conversation, then—"

"How long have you two been dating?" I asked in a sharp tone.

"For two years now."

"Why didn't you tell me?"

"I didn't think it was that serious."

"Is she pregnant?"

"Chantel, that's none of your business, but to answer your question, no, she is not."

"If my children are going to be interacting with this woman, I need to meet her."

"Kara is wonderful with kids. She's a doting aunt and spends a great deal of her time with her nieces and nephews."

"I see that you are quite fond of her, Brandon. Good for you! That's just great. I'm glad you found yourself a woman. Now maybe you two can live happily ever after with our children."

"Chantel, what are you talking about?"

"What about us, Brandon?"

"Chantel, I had to move on. I wasn't going to wait around for you!"

I was upset. Brandon's life mattered to me more than my own life, and it bothered me that some other woman was going to take my place, and in the midst of it all, the color of her skin concerned me. "Fine, you're engaged. What color is she?"

Rolling his eyes, he said, "Are you really this shallow?"

"Brandon, we have two biracial children. And when you marry this woman, they will automatically become a part of her life and will mix in her world."

"She's black, Chantel. Does this ease your mind?" His handsome face tensed as my jilted heart sank into the pit of my stomach. I instantly realized that the color of this woman's skin was not the issue; it was the fact this woman had something that once belonged to me, and I wanted him back.

"I have to go."

Brandon grabbed my hand. "Don't go, Chantel. Wait."

"No, I can't discuss this anymore."

"You can meet her if you want. She's coming into town next weekend. We can have dinner. You can bring the kids."

"No. It's too soon." Yanking my hand away, I hurried out of the restaurant and went directly home.

That evening, I turned on my favorite Jill Scott tune and baked an old-fashioned Hershey's chocolate fudge cake. I ate the whole thing, and I loved every minute of it.

CHAPTER 43

Chantel

Remaining in this house was torture. The walls seemed to close in on me. Astrid announced that she and Evan were engaged. I wanted to be happy for her, I really did, but deep down inside, I was envious, which I had no right to be. Astrid had waited a long time for Mr. Right. Astrid had left a message letting me know that this evening she was going to pick me up to have dinner together with Evan, Serenity, and Serenity's husband, Ray. But guess who did not have a mate? Me.

Yep, I'm a loser. I thought about my children having to call me Mother. I was not worthy of that title. I had messed up my life and theirs. It was their bedtime, and the twins were exhausted by the events of the day. I rarely hung out with the kids. I had hired a part-time nanny, who did most of the work. I know that's shameful, and I needed help. I know that I should have used my savings more productively. Instead of hiring a nanny, I should have joined a gym, yet having a nanny provided help on my tired days, which was most of the time. And it was a shame I was depending on the nanny, Carla, way too much. I felt so useless, so insignificant. I wanted a run-of-the-mill life, but apparently that was too much to ask for. My spirit was crying for peace, for love. I was uncomfortable in my own flesh, and I hated myself. I was in desperate need of affection.

Brandon made me feel special and adored. I reminisced about the beautiful moments we had once shared. He made me feel sheltered and was erotically appealing. The color of his ivory skin was never a factor once I became imprisoned by his love. My heart ached for his touch, his jubilant chuckle. I desired his deeply dimpled grin. I longed for the way his rich emerald eyes would place me in a trance with just one glance. Most of all, I missed his presence—his being a part of me and making me whole. I longed for him, the father of my children, but now he was to be engaged. A new woman had found pleasure in him. She would cherish moments that should have been mine. I desperately wanted him back. I needed to glue my family together again. Maybe if he knew just how much I cared for him, he would call this engagement off. I had been too silent in the past. I hadn't pursued Brandon the way that I should have. It was time for me to make my intentions crystal clear.

Even though I should have contacted Astrid to let her know that I would meet her at the restaurant, my mind was controlled by my addictive desire to have Brandon back into my life. And who knew? Maybe if I could win him over, he could join me tonight. I envisioned all of us sitting together toasting one another. And even better, maybe Astrid and I could have a double wedding! As ridiculous and far-fetched as this all may have sounded, I was encouraged through the betrayal of false hope, nonetheless. I devised a plan to get Brandon back into my life.

It was now nine o'clock. I called the restaurant, and the hostess verified that Brandon had left for the evening. I was on a new mission now: I was going to get my man back. I searched my closet for the sexiest outfit I owned: a form-fitting leopard-print satin gown. It was cut low to bare the curve of my back. The dress had always been a bit loose on me; now it fit perfectly, actually complementing my extra pounds. I topped off the look with my leopard-print ankle-wrap stilettos, slicked my hair back in a sophisticated bun, slipped on my leather trench coat, and grabbed a bottle of Brandon's favorite wine from behind the wet bar—a vintage bottle of Cabernet Sauvignon Fay Estate out of Napa Valley. Of two wines when Brandon and I reunited, one was a bottle of *Dom Pérignon,* which still lay cradled in its green designer box, and the Cabernet Sauvignon. For some reason, I'd hoped that cab would be the celebratory wine that would help christen our reunification.

As I headed out the door, a silver Mercedes pulled up. It was Astrid.

CHAPTER 44

Astrid

I had been trying to get hold of Chantel all day. That girl had been acting strange lately. When I told her that Evan and I were engaged, I expected more enthusiasm from her. Instead, I got some lame "good for you" response, as if I had told her that I had just got back from the dentist and I was cavity free. Chantel's response was insincere. I didn't know what was going on with my best friend. I had invited her to spend time with us, to celebrate our engagement. I had left a message to let her know that I was going to pick her up for our gathering, and still there was no response. So I did what any good friend would do; once I got dressed, I decided to check in on her. Lately, she had been cooped up in that house, stressing over Brandon moving back to London. I took it upon myself to drive over and try to get her dressed so that she could attend my engagement dinner. It was not a big gathering, just my close friends. Camila was on an art tour, and Isidora was travelling again, so that left just Serenity, her husband, and Chantel. I really wanted Chantel to be there.

I was surprised to see Chantel dressed and leaving the house as I pulled into her driveway. I parked, leaving the car running. "Chantel, I've been leaving messages and trying to call you all day. I got worried."

"Oh yeah, I know. I just got distracted. Sorry."

"You look ready to go. I thought we'd head over together." Looking at the wine bottle in her hand, I smiled. "Is that for us?"

"This..." She looked at the bottle as if she'd forgotten that she was carrying it. "Oh, this! I...no. It's not. Actually, Astrid, I have to make a quick stop first before I head over."

"Oh? Where?" I asked.

I could tell that Chantel did not want to share that information with me, but reluctantly she did.

"I'm heading over to Brandon's place."

"Seriously? Come on, Chantel, don't do that."

"Look, Astrid, if I don't express my feelings for Brandon to him, I may lose him. He's engaged to be married to some woman. Kara is her name. I need to fight for my family."

"I understand that, but this is desperate. Don't lose your self-respect over a man."

"This is not just any man. This is the father of my children, Astrid. I don't want them to grow up without a mother and father like I had to. I'm looking out for my family, Astrid."

"Yeah, but—"

"'Yeah, but' nothing. I have tried everything! I prayed like Serenity instructed me to do. I've prayed so much, I don't even think God is listing to me anymore. I'm pretty sure He's got that button on mute. I'm not even paying attention to myself anymore when I pray because I'm so tired of all of my babbling. I sound like a broken record. I need to take action."

"Seems like you tried everything except patience. Girl, I know all about a lack of patience. Been there, done that."

"Oh, so now you're a patience expert?"

"I've struggled in the area of relationships, too. I don't have all the answers, but sometimes, Chantel, you have to let go and allow the outcome to take place."

"Look, Astrid, I'm happy for you. I'm glad that you finally found someone you can relate to. I really am.

But I have to fix this. It's gone on too long. I'll meet up with you all in a bit, I promise."

"Yeah, but Chantel—"

"I have to do this for me and my children. I have to try, Astrid."

I watched Chantel as she raced into her car. She was so caught up in her own world. Her mission was to bring her family together, and at that moment, I realized that I was unable to reason with this woman. I had to allow my friend to make her own mistakes. In the midst of it all, I had to be strong enough to console her after her failed attempts and patient enough to see her through the pain that rejection carried.

CHAPTER 45

Chantel

When I finally reached Brandon's place, I became nervous making my way up to the thick oak doors. I had to ask myself, *Am I doing the right thing?* I hesitated for a moment. Then I rationalized that I was doing this for my children. They adored Brandon. I couldn't let their father run off and marry some other woman who would monopolize all of his attention. What if they were to have children? Isabella and Isaiah would lose their father's attention. With that painful thought in mind, I rang the doorbell.

After the third ring, Brandon answered. His muscular chest was uncovered, and he was wearing black midlength cotton briefs that he filled out quite nicely.

"Surprise!" Raising the Dom Pérignon in front of my face as if it were some kind of peace offering, I pushed my way past him.

"Chantel? What on earth are you doing here?"

"I brought some Dom." I placed the box carefully down on top of the glass dining-room table and then pulled off my trench, letting the coat fall to the floor. Brandon's face turned brick red.

"Chantel," he sighed, covering his face. "I wish you would have called. I..."

Just then, a woman's voice sounded from behind me. "Brandon? What's going on? Who's at the door?"

Not one but two slender women—one Asian and the other a redhead wearing a silky bob wig—appeared behind me. Both women wore black lace, off-the-shoulder nightdresses. Their bodies glowed with sensuality.

"Is everything OK?" one of them asked.

Brandon ran his fingers through his hair. "I'm sorry, but I think you'd both better go."

Without a word, they disappeared around the corner. I wanted to crawl into the nearest hole and die. I retrieved my coat from the floor and quickly covered myself.

"What's going on, Brandon? Those women are not black! You got chocolate burnout? You tired of black women now? You seem to have a wide variety!"

"Chantel, that's not it."

Grabbing my wine off the table, I headed outside. Brandon followed closely behind.

"Chantel, will you listen to me?" he pleaded.

"What?"

"I'm going through some things right now. It has nothing to do with black women or white women or any one race. I have issues with all women right now. I thought being married would make me take control of this addiction. I still feel that marrying Kara is the right thing to do. Getting married is not the only action I am taking to turn my life around. I've been seeing a therapist as well in London and right here in Seattle. That's why I've been avoiding you and the kids lately. I need to get myself together." He began to perspire.

"What is it, Brandon?" I asked, not sure if I could take another surprise. I could feel my body tense. "Is she pregnant?"

"No." He shook his head, looking more guilty and ashamed than I'd ever seen him look before. He confessed, "I...have been seeing a woman who works at a local restaurant, and...I initially called Serenity for advice, but while I was at the restaurant trying to seek help from her, this woman, the one at the restaurant, sidetracked me. She asked to speak to me about some things having to do with business, so I left Serenity sitting there. We went to her office, and before I knew it, one thing led to another. I confessed my problem to Serenity that day."

"Wait...what?" My mind tried to grasp what Brandon was trying to convey.

"Chantel, I was not in my right mind when I did it. I can't even explain why. I was out of it. I'm embarrassed, and I..." Brandon stood there looking confused and helpless, a vulnerable trait that I had never seen in him until now as he stood there trying to make sense of his reckless addiction. He continued, "At first my mission was to try to reconcile with you. I wanted to get Serenity's feedback, so I asked her to meet up with me. I needed some advice, but it was as if this out-of-control compulsion made the decision for me. I'm not in a good place right now, Chantel. I'm sorry."

At this point, I couldn't comprehend a word that Brandon was saying. I was confused, hurt, and angry. Complete and utter rage took over. Removing my high-heeled shoes, I threw them at him. Both shoes barely missed his face. He ducked, and the shoes hit the towering oak door. Running to my car, I screeched out of the driveway. As I headed recklessly to the restaurant, my thoughts weaved throughout the corners of my clouded mind. This scene between Brandon and me would be one of many played out having to do with his addiction and having to deal with my being held captive by the desire to gain power over his addiction.

Once I arrived in the parking lot outside of the venue covered in twinkling lights, I sat there, drifting deep in thought. Opening the glove compartment, I pulled out a wine opener. Call me crazy, but I never leave home without one. A woman never knows when she might find herself heartbroken in a parking lot clenching to a bottle of wine. To be honest, I had acquired a new bad habit of driving down to a nearby lake some nights and drinking a bottle of wine near the dock. I'd like to say that this ritual eased my mind, but it didn't; it just left me confused and hung over.

Nonetheless, I opened the wine and swigged the whole bottle down, stopping every so often in fear of choking. The wine had drizzled everywhere. I tried to clean my face and wipe the wine off my nightgown. I was too out of it, too mentally disturbed to notice that I was not wearing an outfit suitable for dining out. I was wearing a leopard nightgown. Yet in my semi-drunken world, this attire could pass as an evening gown. But then a hazed reality took over, which caused me to become paranoid. I should not walk into an establishment wearing a nightgown. I covered myself up, tying the trench coat up securely. I pulled out a compact mirror to check out my complexion. My eyes were tired and glossed over, and my makeup appeared smeared on. I tried to fix my face and hair. My lipstick was a bit grubby as well; I tried my best to even it out. And last of all, what should have concerned me the most was the fact that I was not wearing shoes. There seemed to be a simple fix as I decided that my trench was long enough to somewhat cover my feet.

Trying to pull myself together, I entered the restaurant. The slightly balding, stiff, and prudish host dressed in his stuffy black and white penguin suit gave me a strange look as I asked to be seated with Astrid's party. Yet, being the professional that he was, he led me to their table. Astrid and Serenity looked happy to see me. Astrid jumped up and gave me a hug, and she obviously caught a whiff of the wine on my attire. Astrid could tell by my glazed-over eyes that things had not gone well between me and Brandon.

"Chantel, do you need me to take you home?" she whispered.

"Nope." Pulling away from her embrace, I found an empty chair across from Serenity and her ever-so-charming husband, Ray. It took me awhile to position my oversized behind just right on that tiny chair, and the fact that I was a wee bit tipsy didn't help. But in the end, I worked things out. Once I was comfortably seated, the unimpressed host handed me a heavy black menu.

"Your server will be with you in a moment. Enjoy your dinner." Giving a stale grin, he quickly made his way back to his station.

The guests of honor, Evan and Astrid, who sat across from each other, looked like the ideal celebrity couple as the twinkling lights laced around the well-known eatery shone down on their beaming faces. Serenity and her husband resembled a powerhouse couple fit for royalty as they complemented each other quite well. And then...there was me, the woman without shoes and the woman without a man. I thought, *How lovely it could've have been if Brandon could only have gotten his act together. We could have been sitting right here, being just as happy. Everything could have been perfect if only Alison were still around. She could be sitting here, too, with her charming husband, Mr. Alono Marquez. But no, she's never coming back. And as for me, well, I was too dysfunctional to hold a relationship together.*

Just then, the waiter came over and asked me for my order. I passed on the food yet had the audacity to ask for a Long Island iced tea.

It was then that Serenity asked, "Chantel, are you OK? You seem a little sick."

"I'm just fine, thank you, Serenity." I smiled. I felt as if my head were in the clouds. Everything around me seemed like a dream. Everyone at the table looked so lovely in my hazy dream. And yet I felt out of place, just floating there, detached from everyone around me.

For some reason, my attention focused upon Evan. He sat there with his appealing movie-star good looks, Astrid's knight in shining armor. And I sat there wondering what it was that he was hiding. I noticed a tiny wooden cross around his neck and wondered if it was just a symbol for him. Was he trying to pretend that he was all into his Serenity? But underneath his façade, I knew that he could be just like the rest, a jackass of a man. I figured that this deceptive man had made his way into Astrid's life to deceive her, just like the man before him. I had to save Astrid. I was going to expose his plan right here and now. I began to bombard the master of deceit with questions. In spite of their conversation about the weather that was taking place, I decided that my questions were more important.

"So, Evan, what's up with the cross around your neck?" I blurted out.

Evan stared at me for a second, then glanced over at Astrid, who looked as if she wanted to tell me to hush up. Evan didn't miss a beat. Kissing Astrid tenderly on the hand, he answered, "It was a gift."

"From who?" I asked.

Evan looked around for a moment as if he were trying to read the faces of those at the table to verify whether I was sane or not. He answered, "It was a gift from my son."

"Oh! Are you still married?"

"No, I'm not. I'm divorced."

"So you have kids from your first marriage?"

"Yes, my ex-wife and I, we have a son together. His name is Kyle, and I love my son very much."

The waitress set down the cocktail. Even though I should have passed on the drink, I took a long swig and continued to ask Evan questions in spite of Astrid's and Serenity's disapproving facial expressions.

"Did you even try to hold your marriage together?" I asked.

"It was a bit more complicated than that."

"How so?" I asked. "Did you even try?"

"Chantel, that's enough!" Astrid voiced sternly.

"No, it's OK, Astrid. I want to be up front. Chantel is one of your best friends. She cares about you. That's what this gathering was for, to get to know me better. I don't mind."

Taking another swig from my strong drink, I now felt like Clint Eastwood. I was facing down my opponent.

"Chantel, when I married my wife, she was pregnant with our son. Looking back, I should not have done that. We were young," Evan said. "I tried to stay in the marriage for our son, Kyle. However, we grew apart. We tried to keep the romance alive in our marriage. We tried everything: counseling, seminars. Nothing really seemed to work. To be honest, I take most of the blame. I checked out, and sometimes I would take Ivory, my ex-wife, for granted. Finally Ivory gave up on me. She met some guy I did not approve of. He ended up taking advantage of her, she ended up getting involved in drugs, and then she began neglecting Kyle. So I had to fight for custody.

"During the summer, my son stays with my mother. He loves his grandma dearly, who is a heavy churchgoer. One summer, Kyle returned home from his vacation with a gift. He was so excited." He smiled as he recalled his son's delight. "Kyle handed me a small colorful envelope. Inside there was a tiny wooden cross that he had made for me in Sunday school.

"My son is very important to me. Everywhere I go, I take a little piece of him with me." He pointed to the cross. "It's not much, just a small wooden cross with no worldly value. However, it means the world to me."

"How sweet." I smiled. "The only thing my children made me was a macaroni necklace. I can't wear that anywhere." I laughed. I noticed that Serenity and Astrid were not laughing, and out of kindness perhaps, Ray and Evan chuckled a bit.

My head began to spin in such a way that I could not continue to interrogate Evan. Even if I were to point out Evan's flaws, I knew Astrid would ignore them, as I had done with Brandon. Love is blind. If anything, right then and there, I became a bit irritated as I thought about my situation and Brandon. Of course, I was happy to see Astrid with a man she loved and someone who seemed to love her equally. And I was happy that Serenity had found a long-lasting relationship. Yet still, I felt that both Serenity and Astrid were judging me for my failed relationship, which made me both paranoid and angry. They had no right to judge, I thought. We all make mistakes, and just because I was having a difficult time finding Mr. Right did not give them the right to look down on me. Looking over at Serenity, I despised her face, sitting up here trying to appear innocent. Looking over at Astrid, I realized that she made me sick as well, sitting up there as if she had found the last good man on earth. It was sickening to watch.

Finally, I decided to give these two women a piece of my mind. Yep, I felt that I was brave enough, enlightened enough, and most important drunk enough to express my feelings. "Could you gentlemen excuse us ladies for a second, please?" I asked, trying to stay calm. "I would like to talk to my girls in private for a sec...if you don't mind."

Ray announced to Evan, "Yeah, man, why don't we head over to the bar area? I think we can catch the end of the game."

"Sounds good," Evan agreed. I watched as he lovingly planted a soft kiss on Astrid's cheek. His seemingly charming nature made me sick.

Once the men made their way over to the bar, I decided to let Serenity have it. "So Serenity, what happened between you and Brandon?"

"What?" Serenity looked shocked. I couldn't help but notice that Serenity was dressed in a rather revealing red dress with deep red lipstick to match. She looked stunning, to tell the truth, but through the eyes of an angry, inebriated woman who had just found out that her ex had confided in one of her best friends, her appearance made me despise her.

Astrid intervened. "Wait...what? Chantel, are you trying to say that there is something going on between Serenity and Brandon?"

"Stay out of this, Astrid. This is between me and Serenity." I cautioned Astrid with the point of my wavering finger. "Why didn't you tell me that you met up with Brandon and that he confided in you about his addiction? I'm your friend! I would have told you if it were Ray!"

Astrid shook her head in disbelief. Looking over at Serenity, she could sense her discomfort. "Look, Chantel, I'm sure Serenity was only looking out for your best interests. I agree that you two should address this situation, but not now. It's not the right place or time to settle this issue," she firmly stated.

Not at all willing to change the subject, I was up front with Astrid. "I disagree. I can't sit though dinner putting on a front like everything is OK, because it's not! I want answers, and I want them now."

Astrid rolled her eyes. Sitting back, she shook her head, utterly appalled.

"I'm going to make this brief since today is supposed to be Astrid's night, Chantel," Serenity reminded me through her stern motherly stare. "I'm relieved that Brandon told you, Chantel." Serenity gave a sigh of liberation. "It was not my place to discuss your ex's addiction. That had to come from him, not me."

Serenity always had to be right about her actions. I don't think she took into consideration how Brandon confiding in her made me feel, so I lashed out. "I bet you liked the fact that Brandon reached out to you, didn't you, Serenity?! I bet it made you feel important and special! Are you going to write a book about it? Or perhaps you will blog about it! What do you plan on doing with your newfound information?"

Serenity's face turned bitter. I had never seen her look so enraged. Serenity sat there for a moment, becoming angrier as she grabbed a nearby cocktail napkin. She began to crumple it up in front of my face. Afterward, she ripped the napkin into tiny pieces. Speaking through clenched teeth, she said, "This is what I want to do to your face, Chantel," she shared as she continued to shred the pieces. Throwing the fragments in my face, she went off into a rant. "You are one of the most selfish people I have ever met! You walk around whimpering about your love life and pondering about Brandon. 'Is Brandon in love with me? Am I in love with Brandon?' And the most irritating question that you harp on the most...drum roll, please!" Serenity began to beat on the table in a drumlike motion and then stopped. "'Does Brandon have chocolate burnout?' And the answer is no, Chantel, because there is no such thing! The guy you are in love with is a sex addict. But you are too caught up in your own world of self-consumption to realize this. You keep walking around playing the wounded woman. And for your information," she added, "no, I'm not going to write a book or blog about Brandon's addiction. But perhaps you should write a book, Chantel! You can call it *Chocolate Burnout!*" Serenity raised her hands in the air, forming an invisible sign for all to see. "Yeah, that's what you should call it! Yep, *Chocolate Burnout*, a story about a self-centered woman who desperately seeks a man, but due to her own insecurity and narrow-minded ways, she is convinced that she is being treated poorly by a certain race of men, failing to realize that men and people in general should be judged by their character and not their skin. And eventually she finds out that all men and women have problems that have nothing to do with race. Their problems are a part of life. But being the selfish person that you are, let's not openly discuss the heart of the matter. Why don't you share your one-sided story with readers? Never mind your friends who have tried to reason with you. Don't even tell our side of the story. Just stick to your own self-centered story. Because your side of the story is the only side that matters! Who cares about other people?! We don't count!" she yelled.

The environment seemed quiet, and all of a sudden, I didn't feel so great. I became nauseated. Leaping up from the chair and practically knocking it over, I screamed, "Maybe I'll do that, Serenity! Maybe I will write a book!" Running outside as quickly as possible, I headed to the back of the building with Astrid following close behind.

Stopping near the Dumpster, I cautioned, "Look, Astrid, I'm going to need some time. I don't feel too good!"

"Serenity is right, you know, Chantel. You are selfish!"

My head was spinning. "Astrid, please, not now."

"There you go again, Chantel! Wanting everything to happen on your own terms! Tonight was supposed to be *my* night." Astrid's shrill voice echoed in the back lot. "We care about you, Chantel! Enough to waste our time with your trifling failed weddings, your relationships. We even went to counseling for you! Why can't you show up for anyone else? Why do you have behave like such an idiot?"

"Astrid, I...I... . "

And then just like that, right there near the

Dumpster that smelled of tainted fish and raw sewage, wearing a trench coat with a nightgown underneath and in my bare feet, I threw up all over the place.

CHAPTER 46

Chantel

I knew that sitting in my house hiding from my friends was not the answer. Weeks had passed, and I had yet to apologize. So I reached out to Imari to help me mend my broken friendships. Serenity and Astrid agreed to meet at Imari's office. And of course this session opened with all eyes on me.

Astrid looked great! She had lost a lot of weight. Serenity looked tense as usual. Nevertheless, she was dressed for success in her bossy dress suit. As for me, I was dressed exactly how I felt, miserable. I would have worn my bathrobe if that were acceptable, but instead I settled for a gray sweat suit. My hair was a mess, and I didn't care. All I cared about was releasing the pain in my heart.

"I'm sorry. Both of you are right. I'm selfish. I should have been there for you both. I should have been there for Alison. Alison was always there for me, and the one night that she called, I was caught up in my own drama!" My eyes began to water as I reached for a tissue off Imari's desk.

"Chantel," Serenity said, moving over to comfort me, as she comforted everyone in distress, "you can't blame yourself for Alison's death."

"Serenity's right, Chantel," said Astrid. "Alison had her own demons to deal with."

"Chantel, do you feel like sharing?" Imari asked. "What happened to Alison?"

I took a deep breath as I looked back on that unforeseen night. "Things were actually going well. I had just received a raise from work. Things were going well with me and my live-in lover at the time. I was content. Alison called me that night, but I ignored her call. My boyfriend had promised to take me out that night to celebrate my raise. Things were going so well for once, I wanted to seize the moment. Alison never called with any issue, so I figured it could wait. The next call I got was from Serenity. She had left a message. Alison had been rushed to the ER. When I got there, she was pronounced dead. She had wrapped her car around a tree. The cause was drunk driving. I had no idea that Alison struggled with alcoholism. I learned from her housekeeper that Alison's husband had filed for divorce prior to the accident. But Alison never confided in anyone! She suffered alone. How could I not see her private pain?"

"Alison was good at hiding her pain, Chantel. We all knew this," Astrid whispered.

"None of you are to blame, and the more you keep holding onto regret, the more control Alison's death has over your life. Would Alison want any of you to suffer in this way?"

"I know that Alison is at peace now!" Serenity stated. "I can feel her peace at times."

"Serenity is right!" Imari answered. "Choose to celebrate the good that Alison brought into your lives. And I have the perfect way for you all to express your love for her by letting go. You all feel that you did not get the chance to say goodbye, yet there is a way to obtain closure even after a loved one is gone."

Imari shared a way of letting Alison go through the light of celebration. The only problem was that I wasn't ready to let go of Alison. I felt abandoned, and Alison's memory was the only thing I had left in this world to hold onto.

"I'm not ready," I said.

"What?" Serenity and Astrid responded in unison.

"I'm not ready to let go. I think I'm going to marry Diamond."

"Yeah, right! Ha! Wait...seriously, Chantel?" Astrid yelled.

"Yes! Seriously! Everyone has someone or something that defines their purpose in life. Everyone is moving on! Eventually I have to meet Kara, Brandon's new wife to be. She's taking my place! Brandon has his faults. He's a sex addict, and Kara is still willing to marry him. Astrid, you have finally moved on and you met Evan. Serenity, you have a successful talk show, and now you are writing books and reaching out to women all over the world! You are spreading Alison's great cause to women who are in need of inspiration in this dark and lonely world. Where does that leave me?"

"Do you think that marrying Diamond is the answer, Chantel?" Imari asked.

"I don't know, but I'm about to find out. The guy can't have kids. I have twins. Maybe things were meant to work out this way."

"No way, Chantel! I'm not going through this with you again! It's not about you! I'm trying to prepare my own wedding. No one has time for your ridiculous schemes." Astrid spoke out of sheer frustration.

"Hold on now. Listen," Imari intervened. "You don't have to agree with each other. Friendships are not based on doing what the other desires. Friendships are based on being there for each other through thick and thin. Chantel, if you wish to marry Diamond this time around, do so. If you feel that this marriage will make both you and Diamond better people, go through with it. But I warn you, don't jump into a marriage just to make someone else happy. Happiness is a choice that must be found within yourself before you dive into any relationship."

Imari raised a good point. I desperately did not want to drag Serenity or Astrid into my relationship with Diamond this time around. I desired to be there for my girlfriends wholeheartedly. I did not want to suck as a friend. Mental note to self: I was determined to be the most sincere friend in the world.

CHAPTER 47

Astrid

Chantel Reed was the suckiest friend ever. It was as if all the good advice Imari gave her went in one ear and out the other. She was late to the fitting. She didn't bother to show up to help me bake my own wedding cake. Of course, Evan offered to buy a cake for our wedding, but I wanted to bake it. After all, no one could bake a triple-decker fudge cake as good as I could. Chantel was supposed to stand by my side as I did through her fiasco wedding. I understood that she was nervous about meeting Brandon's new fiancée. And against my better judgment, she and Diamond decided to elope. It was almost as if she wanted to be the first to marry before me or Brandon. How selfish is that? Nonetheless, I could not allow Chantel's drama to ruin my special day.

Evan and I had a small wedding near a signature lake amidst a beautiful backdrop of mountains. All of my close friends were there. Evan's son, Kyle, was there. It was beautiful. What more could a girl ask for? And even though I should have been happy to move forward with my life, I was still perplexed about Chantel's life. I spent so many years wrapped up in Chantel's spectacle of a life that it took Evan to point out the fact that I needed to move on for the sake of our own marriage. But moving forward was hard for me to do. Even though Chantel had her selfish ways, she was honest with her emotions. All she ever wanted was what every woman wanted: a man to call her own, a committed relationship, and peace. I felt sad for my friend. Sure, she had gone on to marry Diamond, and she pretended as if everything was OK, but deep down inside, I could tell that she could not stand being married to him.

As for Evan and I, our marriage was the perfect union. We rarely fought, and when we did, we resolved things quickly. There were times when his son would try to pit us against each other, but most children do that regardless in quest of their own desires. Evan and I worked things out. We traveled, we baked together, and most importantly, we loved each other. The only thing that could heighten our love for each other was a baby of our own, and just when I thought life couldn't possibly be any more alluring after all I had been through, I found out that Evan and I were expecting. I began gaining weight quickly, which scared me; however, the extra weight pleased Evan. He liked a lady with meat on her bones. Surprisingly, no one was happier than Evan's son, Kyle. He couldn't wait to become a big brother.

The only other person whom I was sure would be just as thrilled about my news was Chantel. However, our communication level had dwindled down to e-mail conversations, which were vague. Long before the world of texting emerged, we had the miscommunication of e-mails to add distance to our friendship. However, I knew my friend. When Chantel distanced herself from friends, she did so not out of anger but depression. I knew that Chantel was unhappy with her life, and rather than continue to complain about her misery, she chose to go into hiding.

CHAPTER 48

Chantel

I was in hiding. My life was not at all what I had planned. I tried my best to hold my friendships together. However, everyone had ventured off into lives of their own. And I was not feeling good at all about my decision in life. I had taken up with some other friends who were just as screwed up as I was and seemed to look the other way while I continued to make my ill-fated mistakes! As much as I wanted to be there for my uplifting friends, my mistakes would only make them upset. I was really happy to hear that Astrid was finally having a baby. I could only imagine that her thoughts on having a baby after her past sorrows brought about mixed emotions, yet I did not know how to reach out to her.

Besides, I had other things to worry about. Today was the day that I dreaded the most. I was set to meet the infamous Ms. Kara! And to make matters worse, I looked like crap. My misfit season had been consuming my life ever since the twins were born. Don't get me wrong; my children, Isabella and Isaiah, were the best part of my life. They were helping me get my mind off myself. That's the humbling part of parenthood; it turns me into we and mine into ours. I needed the twins' presence in my life to save me from a world of selfishness.

As I sifted through my closet of clothes, some covered in spit-up that I had yet to take to the cleaners and others that I should have donated but hoped that someday I would be able to wear again once, I became motivated enough to either join a gym or jog my fat behind around a track somewhere. So far, that day never presented itself. I finally decided on a pant suit that was way too tight around the stomach area, but if I sucked in just right, I figured I could make it work.

As I entered the quaint café, I suddenly became fearful. I was about to meet a woman who had captured my ex's attention. My kids would now look to her for advice. They would probably even resort to calling her Mother. In that case, I would have to take her out. After all, I was protective of the word *mother*. I provided for my children the love and care they needed. Even though I was used to calling my oldest sister Mom, Daria had stepped in because she had to. Kara was in the picture because she was destined to become Brandon's wife.

As I stood there feeling apprehensive, I was approached by a well-groomed host.

"Do you have reservations, miss?" he asked.

"I'm here to meet up with someone."

"May I have her name, please?"

"Kara."

I did not know her last name, but the thought that also plagued my mind was that if she were to marry Brandon, her last name would be Fabes. However, I did not need to know her last name. The host nodded and led me to a secluded table.

She stood to greet me, and what could I say? She was young, striking, and shapely. It looked as if she had her life together. Her hair was glossy and her skin golden, blazing with an undertone of vitality. Just when I thought she couldn't possibly be any more youthful and perfect, she spoke. Her British accent, the one that I was not going even to bother to imitate, had a striking and very polite tone.

"It's such a pleasure to finally meet you, Chantel." She pronounced my name with such care and respect.

"Please have a seat." She pointed to the chair across from her. "Can I get you something to drink?" she asked.

I noticed that she had a pitcher of water with lemon at the table. "I can help myself, thanks." Nervously, I proceeded to pour myself a glass of water. My hands began to tremble. My insecurities began to whisper that I was nowhere in her league. Putting the pitcher down, I took a sip of water, hoping that some way, somehow I would be able to calm my nerves.

As if Kara could read my very thoughts, she said, "Chantel, please don't be nervous. I was just as terrified to meet you as well." She smiled timidly. "I changed twice."

Well, she probably didn't have a problem finding an outfit to cover her rear end, I thought.

"I think we both want the same thing—a peaceful relationship," she said.

I knew that I had to be up front and honest with Kara. Clearing my throat, I said, "Look, Kara, even though I'm married, I'm not happy. I'm still very much in love with Brandon."

Kara did not seem the least bit surprised by my rather bold statement.

"I can imagine how hard it must be to try and move forward, especially when there are children involved," said Kara. "I understand that this can be a tremendously painful process, Chantel, but I care for Brandon."

"Why?" I asked.

"Excuse me?" She appeared baffled.

"You..." Stopping myself, I pondered if I should share what I was about to reveal. Brandon would probably be furious if he found out that I had shared this information with his fiancée. However, I felt that I needed to be up front. Kara seemed like a wonderful young lady who I felt needed to know the truth.

"Well...Kara, you are aware that the man you are looking to marry is a sex addict, right?"

Kara stared at me for a moment. Rubbing her hands together, I couldn't help but notice the beautiful sapphire ring that I had seen years ago. The ring that Brandon had once planned on giving to me sat glowing on the finger of another woman. "I'm fully aware that Brandon struggles with sex addiction and is in need of help when it comes to his ability to love. In fact, that's how we met, Chantel. I was his therapist through a brief stage in his life. Once we discovered that we had feelings for each other, I could not go on seeing him as a patient."

"That's not how Brandon told me that you two met. Well..." I thought for a moment. "Obviously, he lied to me. How long have you two been seeing each other?" I asked.

"Before he met you, Brandon was seeing me regarding some issues that he had concerning his parents, some reoccurring issues from his past that he struggled with."

"What kind of issues?"

"I'm not at liberty to say. I will say that when Brandon told me he had met you, our relationship ended. Then once his father took ill, he reached out to me in London, and that's when our relationship picked up again."

"He came back to you after he had broken up with me? I'm sorry, Kara, I'm afraid that Brandon has not been up front with me. For starters, how old are you? It looks like you just graduated from high school."

"Chantel, he had planned on reconciling with you. However, when he returned, he said that you had become perplexed concerning relationships with other men. And yes, most people consider me to be young, but I call it driven. I graduated from high school when I was sixteen and went on to obtain a degree in the medical field. I took quite the interest in psychology. I ended up opening my practice in London."

"Well, I commend you on your accomplishments. I too consider myself to be a driven person; however, as time moved on, drama got in the way. I wish I could've dodged that bullet. But most important, Kara, I don't want to come across as some kind of easy woman who jumps from man to man. Brandon and I have a very complex relationship. It was hard to read him, and at the time I did not know if his intentions were true or not. And I'm still not sure, but I am certain of my feelings toward him."

"Look, Chantel, let's stick to the point at hand, which is the children. There is nothing that I can do about your feelings toward Brandon. I just wanted to assure you that even though I just met Isabella and Isaiah, I want you to know that they are dear children and that they mean the world to me."

"That's nice to know, Kara, but they already have a mother."

"Chantel, I would never try to take your place."

"What do you know about children, Kara? Do you have any kids of your own?"

"No. However, I have nieces and nephews."

"That's not the same."

"My sister traveled a lot, and I would watch my nieces and nephews. I love children. I also plan on opening a practice to help children overcome their childhood hardships"

"Kara, I don't doubt that you love children. It's just that, well, you're so young."

"Chantel, please, let's not make my age a factor. I have an old soul." She smiled. "I've always been a mother hen sort. I was the one who took really great care of my baby dolls growing up. I was the one who stayed in on weekends babysitting while my friends took off on dates, and I preferred it that way. I couldn't wait to make a life with Brandon."

"Kara, you are young. Do you know what you are getting mixed up in? Brandon is a sex addict. Aren't you afraid that he will hurt you? How do you know that he will stay committed to you?"

Kara looked down for a moment. "I don't know, Chantel. I just have to give love a chance."

I liked Kara, but I knew what she failed to see. Brandon was untrustworthy. And yet regardless of what I knew about Brandon, I still wanted him back. Even though I had begun a life with Diamond, I was comfortable with Brandon. I knew all of his secrets, but Diamond was a mystery that I had yet to uncover.

CHAPTER 49

Chantel

My marriage to Diamond was as jaded as when we had first met. We eloped in Vegas. We spent our honeymoon at the Palazzo Resort and Hotel Casino. Our intimate life was not as I had imagined. In my mind, just because the guy was sterile did not mean that he had to move like a stiff between the sheets. I'm not a hungry sex-craved woman. In my opinion, sex is overrated and oversaturated on television and over the Internet; however, if I am going to tangle in the sheets, it had better be worth my time. I'm just saying. To be honest, I would be lying if I did not express my discomfort with Diamond's performance in the bedroom. He had a gorgeous body. He just didn't know how to work it. It was like looking at a stunning restaurant from the outside, but once you entered, the whole place was broken down and the food tasted horrible. Brandon and I had had a passionate relationship. I enjoyed the way he made me feel intimately and in almost every area of my life. It was sad that one crucial mistake had cost us our relationship.

I still clung to the hope that one day we would be together.

Despondently, another problem that I had with Diamond was that he lacked parental skills. Plainly said, the twins did not take to him. As soon as he came home, he expected me to have dinner on the table and the house to be spotless, which was impossible with two toddlers running around. He never greeted the kids.

In some ways, he seemed resentful that Brandon was the father of my children. The kids seemed much happier coming from Brandon and Kara's house. It made me sad when they would cry having to leave him. But when I would drop Isaiah and Isabella off at their house, they ran inside. They were elated to be around Kara, who was great with the children. I could not help but wish that I could step into Kara's place. After all, she was living my life.

Of course, I had no one to blame but myself. Serenity and Astrid warned me not to marry Diamond, but once I plunged in, there was no escape. I was stuck. The only means of escape was through reckless behavior. And eventually it all caught up with me. Diamond was just as miserable in the marriage as I was. His mother barely came over to see the children because she was ill the majority of the time. For Diamond, becoming a father was not all it was cracked up to be. Eventually Diamond ended up having an affair with a so-called "friend" of mine, who acted as if she had my back, but instead she stabbed me in the back. The tell-version of that division was a story in itself that could only be told in the ongoing unraveling of my life, which was an ongoing mystery to me.

Needless to say, my behavior after our divorce was inexcusable. But what more could I do? It was like watching a war movie. The scene was complete chaos left and right. And it was not as if I did not want the war to end; it just seemed to be what it was designed to be, a war. Even though I hated it, there was one thing I could count on—another explosion and a giant smoky mess. Eventually I came to accept it for what it was. I became immune to the destruction, the noise, the hazy smoke that was my life. Some say I was in denial. Others tried to pull me out. But I realized that the war was going to end when it was meant to, and until then, I stood still waiting for peace. I encountered a set of friends who would add to my war and other inspiring friends who examined the mass destruction, shook their heads, and then moved on, always in such a way to let me know that I was always welcome in their lives if I was willing to move forward in peace.

Isabella and Isaiah were in grade school now, and I still could not get myself together.

My inspiring friends who had moved on consisted of Astrid, who now had a son named Jonathan. And Serenity was writing novels and touring the country. She had taken Alison's cause to the next level. As for me, my turning point occurred when I was driving home one night as drunk as skunk. Yep, alcohol was my new boyfriend. It filled the void. It did not cheat on me. However, it could be a little delusional at times. Sometimes I'd wake in the middle of nowhere, and sometimes, I'm ashamed to say, I woke up next to men for whom I wished that I would've had a built-in mechanism to remind me how ugly they were after I got drunk. I was indeed one hot mess!

And on this Serenityful night, I learned a lesson that would haunt me for the rest of my life. Prior to this costly warning, the flashing police lights tailing me as I weaved down the long, narrow dark road leading home was apparently not enough to catch my attention. It took the announcement over the policeman's loudspeaker to grasp my awareness. After I pulled over to the best of my ability, the officer approached the car.

Letting the window down, I gave the policeman one of my best lines. "What seems to be the problem, officer?" I asked.

"Ma'am, do you have any idea why I pulled you over?"

"Umm...not really."

The officer looked a little closer as if he knew me. "Chantel?" he asked.

Well, I guess he did know me. Taking a closer look at the officer, I examined his features. Due to an extraordinary amount of alcohol, my vision was a bit impaired.

"It's me, Anthony. We met on an online dating service."

After my divorce, I had tried my luck on the online dating scene, and so far I realized that most of the guys I met were even more screwed up than I was. Trying hard to refocus on Officer Anthony, I asked, "So we met online you say?"

"Yes, we did. We went out to the jazz club that your ex owned."

"Oh...well, how did that go? Because I can't remember." I gave an embarrassed smirk.

"Not well. You seemed inebriated, and you kept talking about how much you despised your ex...and his new wife."

"Oh, sorry.... . Can we do a do-over?"

"I don't think so, Chantel. I'm going to have to ask you to step out of the car, please."

I reeked of alcohol, and I was definitely a danger to myself and anyone else on the road that night. Looking back, I wish I had been a better date for Officer Anthony. Maybe I wouldn't have gotten a penalty with a DUI. Yep...I had to serve time in jail, and I had to pay a hefty fine, which sucked because I had ended up quitting my job to be a stay-at-home mother at Diamond's request. I realized that he really wanted to be in control; otherwise, he would not have had me quit my job. But that was an issue in itself. The major issue that I had was having my license suspended.

I was no longer the successful businesswoman that Mom/Daria had molded me to be. I had hit rock bottom.

Daria was no longer talking to me because when I hit rock bottom, she hit rock bottom as well. Daria had to move out of her luxury condo that I had funded for years and move into a low-income neighborhood. My half-brother, Frank, ended up moving back to Alabama to stay with in-laws. My sister Lamina ended up selling her place and moving to New York to be closer to work and the new guy that she had met. I had a little savings left, but I needed a roof over my head.

What concerned me the most was my children, of course. Brandon and Kara obtained full custody of the twins until I could get back on my feet. I had planned on reaching out to Astrid, but she was starting a new family, and Serenity traveled a lot and was really dedicated to her writing and ministry, for which she also traveled. It would be an unlikely source that reached out to me during these hard times. To my surprise, Kara and Brandon offered me a place to say in their guest house. Of course, I declined the offer at first. I couldn't possibly live off my ex and his new wife, or so I thought. My ego was too big for that. It was Kara who convinced me to move into their guest house to be close to the children. Not having any other logical offers, I moved in.

The arrangement was nice for a time. I got to see the kids more often. Even though Astrid invited me to work at her restaurant as a manager, I was used to having my own office and working behind the scenes rather than dealing with people. Even though my old company said the door was always open, once they found out that I had a DUI, they hurried up and closed that door. I had nothing to fall back on, and for once, I began to understand my sister Daria's concerns about my being an independent woman. For the first time, I understood her fears. I only wish that living in my ex's guest house had been enough to motivate me to get my act together, but it would take something more reprobate to make me change my ways.

CHAPTER 50

Chantel

I had a throbbing migraine. Lying on the bed, I waited for the pain meds to kick in. To make matters worse, I stayed cooped up in the house, feeling somewhat ashamed to leave the place. I had no leads on a job. The only beautiful part about my life did not belong to me. The safe haven that I retreated to belonged to Brandon and his wife, Kara, who allowed me to stay in their Hamptons-inspired two-bedroom guest home equipped with beautiful bay windows and spacious frost-colored, beach-enthused furniture. It was peaceful.

Any down and out, self-respecting human being could have found the inspiration to get off her backside and conquer her calling in life, but this was me, and seemingly I had lost all hope. I was too busy focusing on the things that I did not have, things that I thought would make me feel whole. In time, I would come to realize that it never took things or a person to make one complete. The hope that one must uncover in themselves must be fed to the point of completion in order to reflect the proficiency solidity.

Night fell instantly, and my young daughter was skilled enough to demand a lot of things but not yet old enough to serve herself. She entered my room and asked if I could get her a glass of water and tuck her into bed. A bit tired and hindered by depression, I asked Isabella to go back up to the main house and ask her dad or Kara for a glass of water. Isabella reminded me that Kara was out of town on a business trip, and her dad was in his office on a call. I tried everything to refrain from leaving the house. I even offered Isabella a drink there and tried to talk her into lying down with me for the night, yet my demanding young daughter wanted me to go back up to the main house with her. She wanted a drink out of her special pink cup with the blue flowers around the trim. She wanted me to tuck her into her own bed fashioned with her favorite quilted blanket and to read her one of her favorite bedtime stories, "Peter Rabbit."

All of this sounded simple to a young child, but to a mother who was buried deep in the abyss of despair and self-loathing, it sounded tiresome and life altering. Being that I had not left the house all day, I agreed to what mothers were built to do and took care of my child. Quickly washing up, I threw on a t-shirt and silk pajama bottoms. At least my daughter had inspired me to clean up and comb my hair.

Once we headed back to the main house, I met my daughter's demands. She drank her water. We went upstairs. I tucked her in. I read her a story, kissed her on the forehead, and turned on her nightlight before leaving. While upstairs, I looked in on my son, Isaiah, who was sound asleep. I loved my son. I thought he was very low maintenance. I loved my daughter as well, but unlike my son, everything was a big production with Isabella.

As I proceeded to head back down the spiral staircase to the garden trail leading to my safe haven, I couldn't help but notice the family picture that I despised—a huge portrait of Brandon, Kara, and the kids. The only thing that was missing was me in Kara's place. This picture always made feel like a complete failure. I had never stopped to look around their house. Either Kara or the housekeeper was usually there, and I did not want to seem as if I were snooping around. Yet tonight the place seemed empty of the intimidation of piercing eyes since Kara was out of town and their housekeeper was off duty.

I noticed the double doors leading to the master bedroom were wide open. Even though I knew that I should've headed back home, curiosity got the best of me as I made my way down the hall and into their master bedroom. I was greeted by the huge California king-size bed fitted with Egyptian cotton sheets. The surroundings reminded me of a model home. Everything was neatly established. The double doors leading to the balcony gave the room a romantic ambience as the moonbeams filtered through the glass. I know that I should've headed back home, but I just had to check out the closet. And just as I had planned to enter the colossal room filled with clothes and shoes, I heard Brandon's voice from behind.

"Curious, are we?"

Wearing pajama bottoms and a tank top, Brandon appeared rugged holding a glass of cognac. It looked as if he had not slept in days. His eyes were red.

"I...I..." I was unable to find the word that described *nosy* in a positive manner. "I'm sorry, Brandon. Yes, I guess...I...Isabella asked me to tuck her in, and I guess..."

"No need to explain, Chantel." Taking a swig from his glass, he then placed it on a nearby end table. "I guess I would be curious if I were you, too. Why are you here?"

"I told you, Isabella asked me to."

"No, Chantel, why are you here living in the guest house? When Kara told me that you had accepted her offer to live in the guest house, I thought she was joking."

"I had nowhere else to go. It was a very generous offer."

"You have Astrid and Serenity, your sister—why would you choose here?"

"To be near the kids."

"I see. You've really hit rock bottom this time. What a shocker that your marriage to Diamond failed."

"Look, Brandon, I don't want to talk about mistakes. I'm trying to piece my life back together."

"Is that why you're standing here in my bedroom? What answers could you possible find here?"

"I guess a great deal of me wants to know what I'm missing out on. This is natural considering that—" I stopped myself. Even though Brandon had seemed to have changed and his addictions were a major drawback for me, I still harbored feelings for the man. And I knew that he could sense my longing. Realizing that I had nothing left to hang onto except the truth, I disclosed, "I still have feelings for you!"

"I think you're like most women, Chantel. You want what you can't have."

"Or maybe, Brandon, I want what always belonged to me! I want my family to be a family! Is this so difficult to understand? I come from a broken home. Is it so wrong for me to want my children to grow up with their biological parents?"

"So that's what you want?"

"Yes!" Hoping that the sincerity of my plea seemed heartfelt, I yearned to find familiarity within Brandon's core, the recognizable person I had once fallen in love with. "I'm being truthful with you, Brandon."

"I thought you wanted revenge, Chantel. Why else would you marry one of my best friends and rivals?"

"I made a mistake. We all make them, Brandon, and since you are so curious trying to figure out what I want, why don't you tell me what it is that you want, Brandon? Because you don't seem happy in this marriage."

Brandon gazed at me for a moment. I was unable to discern his feelings. He seemed so shielded and on guard, and still, in spite of his cold demeanor, I stood there searching for what once was.

"I don't know what I want, Chantel." He turned and closed the double doors behind him. Removing his shirt, he responded, "But I'm willing to find out."

Brandon approached me, and without hesitance, he kissed me. Sadly, I felt nothing. My heart was beating rapidly. This was the moment that I'd been waiting for, the chance to feel his touch and his love, but his carnal touch no longer felt the same. I did not know if I was incapable of feeling due to the migraine pills that I had taken, but the sensation felt wrong, and even though my heart and body desired his affection, deep within the back of my mind I felt a void, an emptiness, that I chose to ignore. I wish I could depict a feeling of warmth and affection, but there was nothing there. His breath smelled of alcohol and cigarettes. I'd never known Brandon to smoke. Our physical reunion was uneventful as we went through the motions. My body desired to be loved; instead, the feeling of recklessness and coarseness played out. I wanted his love, but instead I was subjected to irrelevant sex. Finally my body went numb due to the medication I had taken, and I was happy that I could no longer feel his insensible display of affection. After his harsh show of reckless craving was complete, drowsiness took over my body, and Brandon and I both fell asleep, too numb to feel any lucidity of moral significance.

The following morning, a light voice coaxed me out of my dead sleep. It was our daughter Isabella.

"Mommy," she whispered, "did you have a sleepover with Daddy?"

Jolting up, I wiped the sleep from my eyes and found Brandon lying next to me. I was at a loss for words, as I had not expected to stay overnight.

"Um...no, honey, this was not a sleepover."

"Then why are you in the same bed as Daddy?" Isabella's soft brown eyes took on a confused appearance.

As I searched for a proficient way to tell my young daughter that Mommy had screwed up big time, Brandon awoke. Once he had adjusted himself into a sitting position, he responded to Isabella, controlling the damage that had taken place. Diversion was his go-to approach.

"Hey, princess!"

"Hi, Daddy! Did you and Mommy have a sleepover?" she asked again.

"Isabella, why don't you go down to the kitchen and find the big green bowl? Daddy is going to make chocolate chip pancakes for you and your brother."

"Yeah!!! That's my favorite! Can I help you make it?"

"Of course!" Brandon smiled faintly.

"Can I pour in the chocolate chips by myself this time?"

"Yes, you can, Isabella," he responded. "Now, go get your brother, and head down to the kitchen. Daddy will be there in a minute."

"Can Mommy stay for breakfast, too?"

Brandon looked over at me as if Isabella had asked to bring a stray dog to breakfast. "Yeah, Mommy can stay for breakfast." He smiled half-heartedly.

"Yes! This is the best day ever!" she screamed as she raced out the door full speed ahead.

Brandon and I quickly leaped out of bed and began getting dressed.

"So what now?" I asked as I threw on my shirt.

"What do you mean?" he asked.

"After last night, Brandon, what now?"

Brandon chuckled in an exhausted manner. "What are you expecting to happen, Chantel?" he asked.

"Should we talk about what happened last night?"

"What is there to talk about, Chantel? We had sex."

I still had hope. Even though last night felt empty, we could have been nervous. Perhaps with time, I felt that we could rekindle what we had both had and reconcile for the sake of our children, and I let him know. "What are we going to do about our relationship, Brandon? How are we going to fix this?"

"The only relationship we have, Chantel, evolves around our children."

"How can you be so cold, Brandon?"

He stated firmly, "Chantel, I'm being real! Both of us are in no condition to function as a family. You're a mess, and I'm a mess. I guess you didn't notice I was a mess when you met me!"

"No, you weren't, Brandon. When we met, you had just opened a successful jazz establishment! You were positive and charming. What happened to that guy, Brandon?"

"Chantel that guy never existed. It was an illusion that I projected in order to hide my insecurities and my addictions! You met me on the Metro, Chantel! A bus! We met on a bus! Did you ever stop to think about that?" Tapping his temple in an animated thinking motion, he continued on with his rant. "Did you ever stop to ask yourself why I was taking the bus? I had to take the bus because my license had been revoked! I had a DUI! I was hooked on sex, drugs, and alcohol. My dad offered to jump-start the club for me if I got help, so I did what I had to do to stay clean. I completed my twelve-step program and went from there. I was not supposed to be in a relationship, Chantel."

"Why didn't you tell me?"

"Why didn't I tell you?" He seemed surprised by the question. "We all have our addictions, Chantel. Let's not forget you were on that bus, too," he recalled. "So tell me, Chantel, what's your addiction?" he asked irately. "What is it that you don't want society to know about you? Tell me, Chantel! I want to know, what are you addicted to?"

Sharply, I responded, "I'm addicted to the wrong men!"

"You got that right!" he shot back. "You let the wrong kind of men drag you down. That's why you're living in our guest house. You can barely get out of bed to take care of your own children. You can't even drive them to school because you lost your driving privileges just like I did. Do you know who is picking up your slack, Chantel?" he asked. "Kara! She's the one taking our kids to school, helping them with their homework, attending parent–teacher conferences, cooking for them, and tucking them in bed the majority of the time. And what are we doing, Chantel, while Kara is standing in? We are allowing our addictions to reign over our lives." He paused. "I don't want to be with you, Chantel. I want to be married to a better version of myself. I want a relationship with someone who can see the best in me even when I can't see it in myself. That's not you, Chantel. It never was."

"Why are you so angry, Brandon?" I asked.

"Because, Chantel, I may have just messed up the best part of my life, and that is my marriage to Kara." With those words, he stormed out of the room.

Chocolate Burnout

CHAPTER 51

Chantel

If I hadn't promised my daughter that I would stay for breakfast, I would have been gone instantly. But I stayed. As Isaiah sat on my lap at the kitchen table while humming and playing with his favorite action figure hero, I watched as Isabella helped her dad fix breakfast. It was not the ideal family as Brandon stood there stirring the mix with a cigarette hanging out of his mouth.

"You're not supposed to be smoking in the house, Daddy," Isabella warned like a mother hen while she poured the chocolate chips into the bowl, standing on a footstool in her bare feet and wearing a colorful full-length cotton nightgown. She continued to scold her dad. "You know smoking is bad for you."

"She's right, Brandon," I intervened. "Especially secondhand smoke around your children."

Not letting up, he responded coldly toward me, "Please, Chantel, you are the last one who should be giving parental advice." Glancing over at me, his eyes squinted as he puffed streams of smoke into the air.

Isabella continued, "Besides, Kara hates when you smoke in the house. That yucky smell gets in our clothes and hair, Daddy."

Brandon walked over to the sink and threw the cigarette down the garbage disposal. He turned on the disposal briefly and turned on the faucet, wanting the cigarette dissolved. He went back to preparing breakfast.

"Thank you, Daddy!" Isabella smiled.

"You're welcome, princess." Brandon smiled. "Oh, and Isabella?" He smiled lovingly at our daughter.

"Yes, Daddy?" she responded as she busily used the giant wooden spoon to stir the batter.

"Please don't tell Kara about me and Mommy, OK?" Brandon gave Isabella a cautionary look.

"You mean you don't want me to tell Kara about your and Mommy's sleepover, right?"

"Right," he confirmed.

"I know why." Isabella reckoned, "Because it would make Kara sad because she wasn't invited, right?!"

Brandon glanced over at me. There was a shameful look in his eyes. "Yep," he responded dejectedly. "That's the reason, princess."

"Don't worry. I won't tell her, Daddy. Your secret is safe with me." She gave a playful wink.

After breakfast, I made my way back home, determined to move out as soon as possible. Kara returned home early from her trip later that day. I followed up on a couple of leads for jobs that did not pay much, but at a least it was a start.

A couple of weeks went by. I had never felt so lost. Serenity had reached out to me a couple of times to attend one of her women's gatherings, but I wasn't feeling up to it, to be honest. I did not feel worthy enough to sit around a group of women and share my sins. I felt ashamed. I was void of all hope as I had lost my ability to function confidently in society. I had lost everything—my driving privileges, my enthusiasm to even land a successful occupation. I had nothing of worldly value. I even managed to lose my earrings that my sister had given me. I turned practically the entire guest house upside down looking for those earrings. My beloved earrings made me feel special. I wore them all of the time, never stopping to take them off. They served as a reminder that I once mattered to someone and had accomplished something great. I'd been so out of it lately, I couldn't tell you where I had misplaced them. Of course, I had unconditional love for my children, but I felt unworthy of their love. I had not heard from Astrid, either. Motherhood consumed her life after she gave birth to her son, Jonathan. I visited once or twice see her little son, yet our friendship had turned awkward as time moved on.

Finally, there seemed be a glimmer of hope as I received a call for a job interview for an emerging technology company in their HR department. On Monday morning, as I prepared myself for the interview, I received a call from Kara. She asked if she could meet me. She did not want me to stop by the house, so we decided to convene at a coffee house not far from my hoped-for place of employment.

It never failed. I was running late once again, and as usual, Kara was on time and seated in the back of the café, true to form in a secluded area. Unlike our first meeting, Kara appeared serious and concerned, to say the least.

"Kara, sorry I'm late. I have this interview coming up that I was trying to prepare for, and then I was trying to find the earrings that my sister gave me. I thought they would go great with this outfit. I'm a bit nervous. This is my first interview in years. I'm afraid I'm a bit rusty, but I'm trying to stay positive, if you know what I mean."

As I sat across from Kara, I could not help but notice the discomfort written all over her face. Kara always seemed undisturbed, but this time, she appeared a bit worn and weary. Her youthful disposition seemed exasperated.

"Is...everything OK, Kara?"

Getting straight to the point, she said, "Chantel, I have a question to ask you, and I want the truth." Her deep brown eyes stayed fixated on me. "I had an interesting chat with your daughter, Isabella, a few days ago, and I thought that I'd come to you with my concern rather than Brandon. All I'm asking is that you tell me the truth." Her gaze intensified as she asked the question. "Isabella told me that she found you and Brandon in my bed together. She explained that she was not supposed to tell anyone. It was supposed to be a secret. But you know as well as I that secrets are not a child's strong suit. So I will ask you, did you sleep with my husband while I was out of town?"

My heart began pounding. It felt as if it were going to explode right out of my chest. I knew I should have told the truth, but to be honest, her questioning caught me off guard in such a way that my first response was to lie. "Isabella has quite the imagination. I spent some time over at the house to help out with the kids, but sleeping with Brandon was not part of the plan. You'll have to excuse Isabella for her outlandish thoughts." I tried to force a convincing grin, yet I was nervous. My eyes took on an expression of fear, which I was sure she could perceive.

"Chantel, I'm going to ask you again. While I was out of town, did you sleep with my husband?" I could hear the pain and frustration in her quivering voice, and yet, having only concern for the welfare of my own being, I stood by my dissolute lie. "No, Kara, I did not."

"I see." Shaking her head in disbelief, Kara reached inside her handbag and retrieved the earrings that my sister had given me. She dangled them in front of my face and placed them carefully upon the table. She responded, "Then why did I find your beautiful earrings in my bed?"

Staring down at the shiny convicting jewels, I instantly became sick. No longer did the beautiful pair of earrings hold a sense of accomplishment. Instead,

they would hold the memory of adulterous shame. I was at a loss for words.

Drawing in deeply, Kara responded, "Chantel, Brandon and I will be leaving for London for a couple of weeks to visit his brother and my family. We will be taking the children with us. Hopefully this will give you plenty of time to dedicate your energy to finding a job and suitable living arrangements." Shaking her head and still holding a look of mistrust and antipathy within the core of her eyes, she went on to say, "Chantel, I know you have some issues that you need to work out, and Brandon does as well. We all do. But you see..." She paused, looking away momentarily. "I relied on your integrity to overshadow deceit. I now see that I was wrong for doing so," she expressed bitterly. "I'm uncertain as to how things will turn out between Brandon and me. However, there is one thing that I'm certain of—I want you out of our guest house when we return. I don't ever want to cross paths with you again, not even for the sake of your children. Do you understand, Chantel?" she asked sternly.

Shame took over my thoughts. I responded, "Yes, I understand." I felt extremely low, and the only thing that I knew to do was to apologize, even though I was sorely aware that there were no words and there was no excuse for what I had done. Through boundless conviction, I strived to express a sincere apology. "Kara, for what it's worth, I am truly sorry for my actions. If I could erase what happened, I would. Please know that I am truly sorry."

In an unsympathetic tone, Kara responded in her British accent that could transfer between such distinct beauty one minute and a dialect of such sheer and utter hate the next. "Yes, you most certainly are sorry—a sorry excuse for a mother, a sorry excuse for woman, a sorry excuse for a human being, Chantel Reed."

And with those words, she left.

CHAPTER 52

Chantel

I had anticipated a day of change. But after my meeting with Kara, things seemed to take a turn for the worse. My interview was awful as my thoughts were intertwined with regret and shame. I was unable to answer many of the questions thoughtfully and professionally. I got the "we'll put your application on file for six months, and if we find a job that will suit your needs, we'll notify you" response.

I headed to a nearby tavern and did what I should not have done—I drank heavily. And yet the strongest drink did not seem to lighten my load. There were only a few people at the saloon-inspired venue as it was still early in the day and perhaps people who worked night shift jobs stopped by.

As I sat there walled in a gloom of self-pity, one of the patrons asked the waitress to sing a song. The bar was set up for karaoke on the weekends, but the waitress decided to fulfill the request. Taking center stage, she song a famous tune by Cristy Lane, "One Day at a Time." The words comforted me at the moment. As I sat, I pondered if I was patient enough to truly live one day at time. My world seemed to crumble all around me because of mistakes I had brought upon myself. I wondered, had I buried myself so deep that not even my sins could be expunged on a repetitious basis? The song the waitress poured her heart into reassured my restless heart through the influence of hope.

I headed straight to the guest house. I packed my bags. Under such crucial circumstances, I couldn't continue to stay there. Because Kara's car was parked in the driveway, I refrained from going to the house to say goodbye to the twins. Instead, I left several messages on Brandon's phone to call me and to allow me time to say goodbye to the kids. However, Brandon was nowhere to be found.

CHAPTER 53

Serenity

I was nervous, to say the least. I had not spoken to Alono Marquez, Alison's husband, in years. He had left so fast after the funeral, not allowing any of us to speak to him or ask questions. I can imagine the grief that he had to be going through. I had left numerous messages on his voice mail, and just as I was finally ready to give up on ever speaking to him again, he returned my call out of the blue. I was determined to complete my upcoming book, and I really hated to leave the office. Alono agreed to meet me at my place of work and bring lunch.

My mind was spinning. I was anxious to ask him so many questions about Alison. When Winnie, the workplace secretary, escorted Alono into my office, I became overwhelmed with excitement, yet in the same breath, I was angry. Winnie seemed starstruck as she stood there in a trance staring at Alono, who was a noticeably eye-catching male.

He was born in Cuba, and his family had migrated to Florida when his was a young child. His mother had dedicated her time to raising a fine young man rich in their Cuban roots and business-savvy in the American way. Alono became a successful businessman overseeing several well-known corporations in Florida, Dallas, and Seattle. Alono had been on several covers of influential magazines. Always dressed to the nines in the finest suits, Alono was a ladies' man. Alono and Alison met in Seattle when he was closing a deal. Alison was working at a well-known dessert shop at the time. Alono often tells the story that he had the most delicious buñuelos in the world. He shared that the last time he had had such a tasty treat was when his grandmother was alive. He had to meet the pastry chef. It was then that he'd met Alison, and he says that she was the sweetest dessert that he had ever laid his eyes upon. Charming he was, and the two got married in Florida. Alison tried to adjust to Florida, but her roots were here in Seattle, so she talked Alono into moving to Seattle with her, and I'm glad he agreed to move back. I would have never met her if she hadn't moved back here, but on the other hand, I would have never known such pain when she passed.

I had to know, was he suffering like the rest of us? Every time I turned to the business channel, I'd see him in an interview discussing the next big business deal. I even saw him on the cover an upscale magazine with a beautiful new business partner. Things seemed to be business as usual. Ever since Alison had died, he didn't even have time to return a phone call to one of her closest friends. This bothered me.

Once I snapped the secretary, Winnie, out of her trance, I asked her to hold all my calls, and absolutely no interruptions unless it was my husband or one of the kids.

Alono was holding a huge bag with *Charleston's Café* scrolled across the front. That was one of our favorite restaurants. Alono, Alison, Ray, and I used to get together to have a couples date night. Alono seemed nervous as he walked over to the small dining table that I used to host some clients for a hospitable meeting. Pulling out my favorite Cobb salad, he set it down. Pointing to it, he smiled. Alono had a thick accent that many women found alluring. "You see? I remembered." He flashed his flawless media smile as he pulled out a stir-fry entrée for himself. Lastly, he drew out my favorite bottle of wine that Alison had introduced me to, a sweet red that complemented the colorful salad.

"Wow!" I smiled, walking over to the table. "What's the occasion?"

Alono moved over, giving me a custom cheek kiss. He smiled. "Please, Serenity, sit and eat. I went to a lot of trouble to get this meal prepared just as you like."

Feeling relaxed, Alono removed his jacket and placed it on the back of the chair. Being the gentleman that he was, he pulled out my chair, and reluctantly, I sat. Sitting across from me, Alono gave a quick Catholic hand ritual prayer across his broad chest in a cross motion. He kissed his forefinger and pointed into the air. Immoderately afterward, he dove into his food as if he had not eaten in years. I was amazed at the way men could just eat at any awkward moment. My stomach was in knots. I was sitting across from my deceased friend's husband, whom I had not seen in years. The fact that he could just eat as if everything was the same, as if Alison were seated at the table with us, disgusted me.

Looking up, he noticed that I was not indulging. "Oh, please forgive me. I just flew in from a business meeting, and I have not eaten all day. Yet I have not forgotten about you, the special friendship that you and my wife shared. I have something just for you." Reaching into the bag, he pulled out a velvet maroon bracelet box. Inside was the golden tennis bracelet that Alison had worn all the time. I often joked that if she ever died, she'd better leave that bracelet to me in her will.

"Allow me," said Alono. He took the bracelet out and fastened it around my arm. Memories of Alison instantly flooded my mind—her engaging eyes, her vibrant smile, her infectious laugh. I tried to hold back tears as Alono continued to make things worse.

He smiled. He pulled out a wine bottle opener from the bag and opened the wine. Pouring a glass for me and himself, he lifted his glass. "To new beginnings." He smiled, still chewing on his food.

"Seriously, Alono?" I asked in a frustrated tone. "How do you expect me to eat or drink wine when you have failed to acknowledge the death of your wife and my best friend?"

"What are you talking about? Can't you see that I'm trying to make this a special memory in honor of Alison?!"

"Where have you been all of this time, Alono?"

"What do you mean?" He appeared confused.

"I have left several messages. You just left after my Alison died."

Still dumbfounded by my behavior, he answered, "I had to work, Serenity."

"Did you even take time to grieve?" I asked.

"I'm still grieving, Serenity! Everything about Seattle reminds me of Alison. Our house, even the dog reminds me of Alison! Do you know how difficult it has been to watch her dog sit by the door, waiting and yelping for her to come home? I had to get out of here. I had to leave Seattle."

"Why didn't you call me or my husband, Ray? You two were good friends. Why didn't you call to talk?"

"I did not want to talk about it, Serenity. I still don't want to talk about it!" he screamed. His accent was no longer sensual as I reflected back on brief conversations Alison and I would have about Alono. Alison shared that when Alono became angry, he sounded less like Ricardo Montalbán from the TV series *Fantasy Island* and more similar to Ricky Ricardo from the sitcom *I Love Lucy*.

"What is it that you want from me, Serenity? I called your husband. We talked briefly before I arrived here. Ray told me that you may be a little upset, but this is crazy."

"I lost my one of my best friends, Alono. What were you expecting?"

"And I lost my wife, Serenity."

Shaking my head, I said, "I feel like you are hiding something from us!"

"Who is 'us,' Serenity? What are you talking about?" he asked. "You sound loco!" He pointed to his head in a crazy motion.

"Astrid, Chantel, and I, we were her friends. We deserve to know the truth. I feel like you are hiding secrets from us!"

"What?!" He became furious. Springing from his chair, he pounded his fist upon the table, causing the light fixture to rattle. "Do you think I killed my wife, Serenity?" His eyes glinted in sheer pain. "I loved Alison, Serenity! Alison was the cause of her own suffering. I couldn't take it anymore. She was depressed all the time. She drank every night!"

"Oh, and I suppose you were just perfect throughout the entire marriage, right, Alono?" I huffed.

"I will admit I have a good appetite for beautiful women. I flirted here and there, but I never slept with another woman, not while I was with Alison. Serenity, can't you see"—he ran his fingers in annoyance through his glossy black hair—"Alison was her own worst enemy. I could never make her happy, and in return, she was making me miserable. The night of her death, she was out of control. I asked for a divorce, and she lost it. She started yelling and throwing things at me. This was not the beautiful woman I had met once upon a time. Don't you see, Serenity? The woman I had once loved was no longer there. That night, she must have had way too much to drink, as usual, and got behind the wheel. I carry that pain that maybe I could have stopped her, but no one, Serenity, no one could protect Alison from herself. I have no secrets, Chantel. The only secret I carried in my corazón"—he pointed to his heart—"was wanting to leave sooner."

As I sat there trying to comprehend all that Alono had said, the door flew open. It was Brandon, and he was clearly upset. He blurted out, "Serenity, I have to talk to you. It's urgent. I'm in a lot of trouble, and I need help!"

A distraught Winnie was standing close behind the disheveled-looking Brandon. "I tried to stop him, but he rushed right by me before I could stop him," she gasped, out of breath."

Rising from the table, I yelled, "Brandon! Now is not a good time."

"I have to talk to you. It's urgent."

Offended in every way, Alono Marquez grabbed up his jacket. "I was just leaving." Looking at me, he said, "It looks like you have some secrets of your own, sweetheart. Look, don't bother to call me, ever. I'm heading back to Florida. I've had enough of you and Alison's bad memories. I don't deserve this. Give my regards to Ray." And just like that, he left as inexplicably as he had appeared.

"Look, I'm sorry to disturb your meeting," said Brandon.

Winnie interrupted, "Do you want me to call security, Serenity?"

"No, I'm fine."

Winnie left, hesitantly closing the door slowly behind her.

"What is it now, Brandon?" I asked, moving from the table behind my desk just in case I had to call security. Brandon looked rough. His hair was a mess. He had dark circles underneath his eyes. A shabby beard was growing in as well. I did not know what to think.

"I'm going to get straight to the point, he said. "I made a mistake. I...slept with Chantel, and Kara found out."

My ears began to ring. I could not believe what I was hearing. "You did what?"

"Serenity, please don't judge me. I know what I did was wrong. Kara kicked Chantel out, and I don't know where she will go next. Could she stay with you?" Looking around the office helplessly, he revealed, "I don't think Kara will forgive me for this one. She wants to go back to London for a while, but I don't think she will return back to Seattle with me. In the meantime, I need to know that Chantel has a place to stay."

I was angry, and even though I had no room to judge, judgment spurted out of my mouth. "What in the world were you two thinking?" I asked, not really desiring an answer to the action of stupidity. "You can't toy with the emotions of others. You both are reckless. It's time to grow up. You have kids who depend on you both to guide them in the right direction."

Humiliated, Brandon responded, "I know, and yet I continue to carry on in such a dishonorable manner. I want to change. You've got to believe this. It's just that it's going to take time, Serenity."

"How much time?" I asked. "How many people have to suffer before you decide to change, Brandon?"

Brandon held his head down. Looking back up, his eyes were watery. "Will you help Chantel?'

"She's my friend," I responded. "Of course I will. But she's going to have to make some changes. I can't allow Chantel to drag me down with her. That's not how it works at all."

Chocolate Burnout

CHAPTER 54

Serenity

I tried several times to get a hold of Chantel, but there was no answer. On the route home, my mind began
to wonder about everything that needed to be done. Once I arrived home, I tried to leave work and my worries at the door. However, my contemplations took over my mind as I entered a house that I had spent years to turn into the perfect sanctuary of peace. The warmth of plants and water fountains livened up the foyer; however, once I entered, the kids ran up to me with complaints.

The middle daughter was complaining about the younger boy child, who had taken it upon himself to try to bake a cake for the bake sale at his school. The spacious chef-inspired kitchen was covered in flour, my son was covered in flour, and the place was mess. "I'm trying to be helpful!" he smiled, with his two front teeth missing.

"Look at this mess!" my daughter screamed.

"Help him clean it up," I told her.

"Why? I didn't make this mess," she huffed.

"You are going to help him clean this mess, Violet, and then you are going to show him the correct way to bake a cake."

"Why?" she asked.

"Because that's how older sisters are supposed to behave."

"But Mom!" she whined.

"Violet, please just do it. If you want to receive your allowance, you need to watch your brother. That's a part of the deal."

"OK," she muttered.

Any other time, I would have been livid to find my kitchen in such a wreck. But I was emotionally drained thanks to the events that had taken place earlier, and I was thrown off by everything that needed to be done. As I removed my shoes, I leaned against the staircase. Thinking about how I was going to meet the deadline for my upcoming book was taking a different kind of toll on my life. In the midst of it all, attempting to master the patience of motherhood was a task in itself. I found it somewhat difficult to get any work done back at the office due to all of the client meetings and random interruptions. I tried relentlessly to work on the book in the spare bedroom that was within earshot of my family distractions. I needed space, inspiration, and isolation to finish this project.

And just when I thought my life couldn't possibly become more strained and cluttered, the doorbell rang. It was Chantel.

CHAPTER 55

Chantel

There I stood, bloodshot eyes, messy hair, holding onto two suitcases and a manifestation of drama and guilt. Indeed, I was ashamed to find myself on Serenity's doorstep in need of a place to stay. Knowing that Serenity was my last resort terrified me. Of course, I craved to stay with Astrid, but I had not talked to her in months. It would be so wrong of me to show up out of the blue like this. And yet even though Serenity preached too much, I knew that I could reach out to her no matter how much time had passed.

"Let me guess," Serenity said. "From the looks of it, you need a place to stay. Am I right?"

"Yes. That and some money to pay the cab driver," I responded shamefully.

Serenity had known me for a long time, and it seemed as if it pained her to see me in such distress, financially, physically, and emotionally. I had seemingly fallen apart overnight. After she took care of the cab driver, Serenity led me up to the spare bedroom, which also happened to be her office. I was tired, and Serenity could sense that I did not want to talk. She allowed me time to rest, which was comforting to my soul. However, just like life expectancy, a time to rest also has its own expiration date.

Days seemed to run into one another. I slept without any acknowledgment of time, waking up only to eat the meals that Serenity left by my door. I'd get up late at night to use the restroom to avoid having to speak anyone. There would be many times when I felt as if depression ran in my family, but just because this dark curse ran through my family line did not mean that I had to give into it. I just didn't know how to break it. But apparently Serenity did.

Marching into the room one early morning, she began relentlessly banging on a bell often found at the front desk of a hotel. "Get up, Sleeping Beauty!!!" she screamed while ringing the bell. *Bring, bring, bring, bring, bring!* The bell chimed throughout the room in a rather disturbing manner.

"OK, Serenity. Please stop it already," I pleaded. "And please don't call me Sleeping Beauty. Sleeping Ugly is more like it," I moaned, kicking the covers off.

"You are having a moment. It happens. Get up! We are going to Audrey's Vineyard."

"Audrey's Vineyard? That's far out on the outskirts of the city."

"I know that. I have to get away for a while and work on my book. A good friend is allowing me to stay at her villa."

"What about your kids?"

"It's spring break. Ray is off as well, so he agreed to watch the kids. He is working on a trip to Disneyland."

"Wow, Disneyland sounds fun. I have not taken my kids to Disneyland yet, but I guess that won't happen since they are heading to London over the break." My head began to spin as I thought about all of the trouble that I'd caused that had separated me from my own children. "You know, if Ray is taking the kids to Disneyland over the break, why don't I just stay here? I can house-sit while you're away."

"No, Chantel."

"Why not?"

"Because I want to make this a girls' retreat. Astrid is meeting us out there."

"What? Chantel, I haven't spoken to Astrid in months. I can't. I'm in no position to..."

"If you don't change now, Chantel, you will never be in a position to do anything! Get moving! Pack up! We're leaving in one hour."

Serenity was serious about finishing her book and making me her new project. Looking around the room, I noticed pictures of Serenity with a woman I had never seen before. Most of Serenity's friends I knew, but this woman, a cheerful-looking woman appearing to be in her early forties, was different in an exotic way. She had long, light-brown curly hair. There were pictures of her hanging out at Serenity's pajama gatherings that I never attended and even at secluded restaurants with her select circle of friends, Isidora, Rebeca, and women I felt I knew because Serenity had talked about them so often. Yet within the mix of pictures, Serenity and the woman I had never heard of were always by themselves. Of course, there were pictures of us with Alison, pictures that I had forgotten we had taken of happier days when all of us seemed to have our stuff together. Either that or we became very good at faking it. There were pictures of her designer friend Camila holding up the designer cover of one of Serenity's latest novels.

I guess it was not too bizarre that I did not know of Serenity's mystery friend. There were friends of mine I would never think to introduce Serenity or Astrid to, such as Janeva, Tatum, and Tas. These three women would clash with Serenity's well-being. Some women think that Serenity is a bit of a know-it-all, too insightful for her own good, perhaps, and a bit pushy. However, there were times in a friendship that Serenity's so-called "flaws" could be helpful for someone such as me, who had fallen on hard times. I realized that it was easy for my own sister to give me advice and instruction when I was a successful businesswoman, but when I was down and out, she had no guidance to give.

CHAPTER 56

Chantel

Part of me wanted to open the door and jump out of the car. I was not ready to face Astrid. I knew Astrid and I would reunite someday, yet I was hoping, that it would be during a time when I felt more secure about myself as a human being. I knew that Astrid was going to ask me questions that I still had no answers to. After all, Astrid had moved on, and I was standing still in the same wishy-washy relationship. I had yet to break free. Trying not to stay trapped within the desolate walls of my own head, I decided to take the focus off myself and put it onto something else.

Serenity had her eyes on the road as we moved slowly around the paved road enclosed by rugged mountains.

"So, Serenity," I said, "who is the woman with long, brown, curly hair in the picture, the one in your office?"

"Huh?"

"I was looking at your pictures in the spare bedroom. There's a woman with long, brown, curly hair. I feel as if I know all of your friends because you talk about them often, but I don't think you ever spoke of this particular woman."

"Ah yes, the woman with the long, curly brown hair. Her name is Tessa."

"Why don't you ever talk about her?"

"Let's just say that there are some friends you meet who make a positive impact on your life, friends you speak of often and continue to form a friendship with, and then there are those who teach you negative aspects of life, yet the pessimistic attributes of life can still serve as reminders of what not to do. Let's just say that Tessa was one of those friendships in life that served as an episode of how not to behave."

"What did she do? And if it was so bad, why do you still have her picture up?" I asked.

Serenity weaved around the curves carefully as she searched cautiously for the right words to say. "Tessa was strong willed, and her views on woman friendships were not the kind of vision that God had marked out for my life. She was very structured and controlled by her own anxieties, which made it extremely difficult for me to build an authentic friendship with her. Now, don't get me wrong, Chantel; Tessa had some great qualities. I could use much structure in my life, but when it comes to friendships, I'd rather be genuine and not an imitation."

"So she was a fake friend?"

"Not purposefully. I believe Tessa was just wired that way. She had yet to understand how to be a friend outside of her own controlled outlook of what a true friendship should be."

Shifting conversation to the levels of relationship between man and woman, I had to ask, "Do you think that's what happened with my relationship with Brandon? Do you think that I had an illusion of how things were supposed to be instead of allowing him to be himself? Do you think that I was too controlling?"

"Honestly, Chantel, I believe that most relationships are different from friendships because relationships are intimate, in which structure is very important. Two people must join as one to create the kind of union that will secure the value of family for generations to come. Friendships change, and you can outgrow each other. Some friendships are just for a season, and there are some friendships that last forever due to certain circumstances that evolve in the same direction until the end of time."

"Is your relationship with God different from the rest?" I asked, not really wanting to get on the subject of God and all that, but something inside of me was curious.

"Now my relationship with God is different, Chantel. Even though I am supposed to have an honest and loyal union with my creator, He knows that I will fall short, so He gives me grace on a daily basis. Even though I desire to be perfect, I fall short. I don't have to perform for God the way I do for man. All I have to do is allow Him to love me and build me up from the inside so that I have enough to give on the outside, if that make sense."

In a way it did, being that I had nothing left to give, not anymore. I felt as if all the love had been sucked out of me. I desired to be a better friend to Astrid and Serenity, which made me feel guilty. After all, I didn't want to suck the life out of them the way others had done to me, so I asked, "You spend so much time with different women, Serenity. Am I your only jacked-up friend? Am I the only one who does not have her stuff together?"

"Chantel, you're just going through a learning process. I invite you over to join me at one of my pajama parties. Sometimes we bake, which does not turn out great all the time, but it's fun. The last time Isidora and Rebeca watched a classic flick that still has great meaning, *When Harry Met Sally*, and before that we watched *Something's Gotta Give*. It was great! We girls sit around and talk about relationships. Our last topic on the matter came from Isidora, having to do with some article she read online about her empathic way and lethal attraction to a narcissist. Isidora believes that she is attracted to a man who seeks attention through past pain and hurt. She wants to fix him, yet it is hard to repair anyone from the inside without that person truly desiring the change from within for themselves. Slowly, Isidora has found herself becoming a part of his pain instead of the solution, desperately trying not to lose her Serenityful value... . And then there is Rebeca, who is fully aware that men by nature are the hunter and that women should let the man pursue his mate. Yet even so, some men can flip the table and become the victim in a relationship, leaving the woman, who is structured to nurture and feel guilty and responsible for their happiness. Now that Rebeca is in a new relationship, she is cautious to maintain the boundaries of respect on both sides of the coin/relationship."

I understood what Serenity was saying, but sadly, I was in too deep, past the hunter stage, and probably deeply in love with a narcissist. Indeed, Brandon was a sex addict, yet he was one of the best lovers I had ever had. I had tried dating other men, but no other man could satisfy my needs the way Brandon could. I didn't want to share him with any other woman, but the more I held on, the more the challenge of having Brandon all to myself consumed me, and the more he seemed to drift into the hands of other women. Kara would not be the first woman to challenge my womanhood and status as a mother. I would encounter other women who would awake my insecurities, no matter how. And as timed moved on, I attempted to lose myself in retreats. For one, Brandon escorted me to visit a wise family member who lived deep in the mountains. I'd hoped that astuteness would reveal itself. Perception clung to me as long as I stayed around those who bore righteous intellect, yet once I fell away from their fruitful guidance, I seemed to lack significant wisdom of my own, which left me weak regarding my inner craving, leading to self-destruction. I often wondered how much was enough? Would Brandon's straying ways cause me to hit rock bottom? Due to his frequent infidelities, would catching an STD finally awaken my need for inner change? I wondered what this desire was within me that craved to be good enough for one man but was not good enough for me. This was a hunger to please a desirable man not even the most beautiful woman in the world or most talented woman could achieve.

And now I was on my way to a secluded place, another retreat organized to help me. Astrid would be there, a friend I had pushed away in my blind pursuit of Brandon. I felt so ashamed. I was not prepared to face Astrid. As with everyone else in my life, I was sure that I had let her down.

As soon as we drove up, I prepared myself for the straightforward scolding I fully deserved. Yet once I arrived, the unthinkable happened. Astrid ran out the door. She looked like an excited schoolchild. Her hair had grown; it was straight. She looked different, more mature, and naturally contented, and surprisingly she looked delighted to see me, of all people. Astrid ran over to me and gave me the most heartfelt hug. I felt...loved.

CHAPTER 57

Astrid

I arrived early to prepare the villa for the girls. I did not know how to conduct myself. I had been trapped in the world of motherhood, and part of me was relieved to take a break. Of course, I was reluctant to leave my son, but my husband persuaded me to take a break, and once I arrived to the villa, I was glad that he had talked me into doing so. We were lucky to find reliable renters who took great care of the house. The fireplace was tidy, the custom Spanish tile throughout the space was suitably treated, the floor rugs had been dry cleaned, and the wood décor was polished, leaving behind an orange blossom aroma throughout. The stunning spacious windows gave a clear overview of the breathtaking scenery lined in bike trails and emerald green trees.

I did not know how much I needed this mini-vacation until I arrived. I decided to throw on a pot of coffee and start lunch. I was sure the girls would be starving once they got here. As I headed over to prepare the coffee, I heard a car pull up in the driveway. Excitement took over me. Rushing out the door, I watched as Serenity and Chantel struggled to get out of the car after their long journey. Serenity waved. Popping the trunk, she took off to retrieve their luggage. I could not help but notice Chantel, who looked tired and broken, nothing like the strong, confident, and optimistic woman I had known. She was a lost little girl trying to survive in her perplexed world. I had not seen my friend in months. Running over to her, I gave her a hug. Chantel seemed surprised by my greeting as she began to cry.

"What's wrong, Chantel?"

"I can't believe that you..." She paused, overwhelmed by her emotions, then tried to express her thoughts once again. "I thought you would be..."

"Angry?" I asked.

"Yes!" She nodded.

"Life is way too short for anger, Chantel."

We embraced once again, but our reunion was interrupted by Serenity's frazzled voice. "I hate to break up your hug fest, but could you guys help me with these bags, please?" Each of us grabbed an overstuffed bag and made our way into the house.

We each did our part developing a delicious meal. With great zeal, we ate and talked about the latest trending events. The conversation was light, and as much as Serenity talked about her crucial need to work on her book, we were able to entice her to go for a little bike ride.

It was a wobbly start for us girls in the beginning, yet once we got into the groove of things, our bike-riding skills flourished. The light breeze was refreshing as we rode down the trail taking in the breathtaking scenery. Before winding back to the villa, we decided to rest at a nearby lake. And it did not take long for Alison's name to come up.

"Alison would have loved this," Chantel said.

"Yes, she would've," I agreed.

"I can't help but feel guilty about everything. I wish I was a better friend to you and to Alison." Chantel shook her head.

"Chantel." I intervened on her attempt to beat herself up over the past. "I'm not going to allow guilt to take over this trip. We came here to have a peaceful retreat."

"Astrid is right, Chantel. This trip is about reconciliation."

"Come on, guys. You have to admit I'm selfish. I don't even know how your baby is, Astrid, and I'm supposed to be his godmother."

"The baby is just fine, Chantel. I will admit, raising a baby was not easy. I went through a very trying time when my hormones were all out of control. I suffered from anxiety attacks once the baby was born. Having lost a child in the past, I was scared. I feared for the life of my child. There were some parts of me that did not feel worthy to be a mom, and there were some parts of me that feared for my child due to this harsh world. I wanted to protect him from all the pain that I had endured, yet the thought of my not being able to save my child from pain terrified me. I fell into a world of depression, and even though my husband was understanding, I needed more help than he could offer. I went in for therapy, and I can now say with time, I'm just now learning to move on with my life with confidence and excitement about a future and purpose that my own relationship with God has granted me." She smiled.

Looking at Serenity, I caught an elated smile as I realized that she truly wanted me to secure my own spiritual walk that would strengthen my own testimony in life. I continued, "I'm not saying that I have motherhood, life, or my own Serenity all figured out. I'm learning as I move forward, but this is my life, and I'm not going to hold anyone accountable for fixing my world. I'm going to conquer each day one day at a time without set expectations from anyone, not even myself."

CHAPTER 58

Chantel

Standing near the lake listening to Astrid share her insecurities sparked a desire within me to live again. I loved these women. Serenity, striving to be as strong as her name, had bared her own uncertainties that I will never know anything about, having been ensnared in my own world.

I shared, "I wish I could reach that point of solitude. My world is still a big mess." I confessed, "But now I'm determined to make it better, at least for the sake of my kids." Drawing in deeply, I exhaled. "I'm ready to let go." Shaking my head sternly, I said, "I can no longer afford to hold onto pain, regret, and anger. It really is way too much of a burden to bear. I have to start off by letting go of Alison. I realize that it is OK to hold onto the good parts of Alison, but the dark parts, the guilt and nagging thoughts of what if and why, I can't afford to hold onto any longer. I'm ready to let go, and I want to honor her memory in the way that Imari had suggested," I shared adamantly.

It was there near the lake that three women on separate journeys joined together in one embrace to honor Alison's short yet significant life that had ended so tragically, yet in the midst of sorrow, strength sparked the burning will to move forward in victory.

Our stay at the villa flew by. As we baked and talked of things in the past and promising future to come, we were all committed to taking time off once a year to meet up at the villa to recharge are batteries.

On the way back home, we stopped by a gift store. After we made our way inside, we purchased four helium balloons, one white and three red. Afterward, we made our way to Endless Journey Mortuary. After making our way to Alison's grave, we all took a moment to study her headstone. Alison Marquez 1970–1996.

It seemed so surreal that someone as vibrant as Alison was no longer with us. Her fearless personality and outgoing nature had seemingly vanished like mist into the air, making our world as we knew it feel disillusioned and empty. As it was, we all knew that we had to cling to the power of infinity, passing her hope and her legacy on to generations to come for a greater purpose.

I for once was the first to lead us onto that path. Holding onto the white balloon, I revealed,"This balloon represents peace. Our sister, Alison, was strong enough to move forward in a way that comforted those around her. In this world, vulnerability and weakness are mocked, and those who reach out to others who are hurting, oppressed, or struggling can be considered a burden. In this world, one must learn how to roll with the punches or deal with it, so to speak, yet everyone has their moment of weakness. Alison was not afraid to embrace those and lift others up during times of rejection and lowliness." I hung my head down for a moment. My heart felt heavy as I searched for the right words that would not open a floodgate of tears. Looking at the picture etched onto her headstone, I shared, "I...we only wish...that we were attentive enough to know when you needed someone to lean on. Alison, we wish that you did not have to hide your pain from us." Tying my white balloon onto the red balloon, I breathed in deeply. Trying to conceal my tears, I continued, "You have taught me peace in a form of awareness and the power to reach out to others who may need help, not from a standpoint of pity but in a form of strength, the kind of courage that encourages others to press on."

Once I finished tying my red balloon onto Alison's white balloon, I handed them both over to Astrid. She sighed as she stared down at Alison's headstone. "Alison, you taught me how to embrace the hardships in life through the value of lessons, having the courage to look back and learn from our mistakes. You gave me peace in knowing that even when I mess up in life, I have the power needed to make a difference through grace. Thank you."

Tying her red balloon onto the set of balloons, Astrid then handed them over to Serenity, who took a deep breath and then exhaled. "Well, Alison, sister, I always thought we'd have more time," she said. "Your courage has brought me a sense of peace in knowing that love conquers all, and that even though we may feel we may never transpire the kind of love that we feel

we deserve in this world, let us know in confidence that the power of love that is inside us is the greatest love and the only adoration that is needed to move forward in victory."

With those words, Serenity let go of all four balloons. We watched as they soared up into the sky, heading north. We watched as the three red balloons trailed behind Alison's as if it were leading the way to a mysterious world of peace. In no time, the balloons sailed into the deep-blue-sea sky and finally disappeared into a heaven of wonder.

Serenity moved on to run one of the most exciting reliance-based expos that reached out to women all around the world, which attracted artists of all backgrounds. She also became a best-selling author, releasing books based on countless interviews with men and women of all ages and backgrounds.

As for Astrid and Evan, the two flowed together like an endless stream of loyalty. Their union surpassed the color barrier, and what remained was the kind of compatibility that defeated all doubt and insecurities. Their secret supplication bridged the gap against all odds. Their relationship was safe. It was the kind of connection many seek but fail to find.

Even though my friends forgave me for my transgressions, I could not forgive myself. And even though I had children who needed me, I searched for closure through meanings, relationships, and dangerous addictions. All I can say is that I lived. I had my days. Brandon and I would go back and forth throughout the years, but our relationship seemed to worsen as Brandon struggled with dark emotions dating back to his childhood. These buried secrets were never dealt with, and like many men who deal with similar issues, Brandon struggled with sex addiction, caused by his tormented childhood.

As for me, I constantly made mistakes throughout my life as well. I went back and forth through different relationships. I rekindled old romances that should have never been reignited.

There were times when I exasperated myself and others with my search for completion. There was a time in my life when I had three men fighting for my affection, and now I couldn't even find a frog to commit.

I was so wrapped up in the fear of being alone for the rest of my life. There were girlfriends such as Serenity and Astrid who gave me hope, and then there were mutual friends who didn't care to hear about my toxic love life. I even had one so-called friend tell me to sit my ass down because I was disturbing the public with my problems.

I am now turning forty, and yes, there are those who hate me and very few who love me. "You are too needy," some women say. "Chantel, you depend too much on men. Why do they have to complete your life? You are so desperate! You are supposed to be an independent woman!" Yeah, but I'm not. I yearn to be in love. I get lonely. I want someone to laugh with, to hold me when I cry. I want someone to snuggle on the couch with me and watch classic movies with me.

Some people say the reason I'm so needy is that I never had a good relationship with my dad. Maybe they are right. But there is nothing I can do about the past.

Now my children are nearing their teens. Sure, they have endured some pain. And yes, they have inherited some of the toxic struggles of their parents. Brandon and I had made plenty of mistakes in front of them. We all had a lot of forgiving to do.

I had to learn how to forgive my mom for passing away and leaving me with Daria. Yes! I was angry that she had left me with my oldest sister, who seemed like a kid herself. I know my mom had no control over death, yet I felt abandoned. Every girl I knew growing up had her mother to rely on, and Daria was so busy working and trying to make ends meet.

I was mad at my dad for leaving, too. I wanted to have a relationship with him. I wanted him to walk me down the aisle on my wedding day, not some old drunk dude. I may never get married, so I guess that desire was and is insignificant.

I had to forgive my younger sister, Lamina, for leaving me with Daria. There were times when I wanted her to take me away with her on one of her trips to a different country. I wanted to escape the madness that had somehow become my life. But deep down inside, I knew Lamina had her own demons to battle, just like everyone else.

And yet there was a part of me that did not want to take the time needed to get to know a significant other. A lasting relationship takes time, and a satisfying, intimate bond takes years of discovering what pleases your mate as well as what turns him off. A relationship is an investment that goes beyond the color barrier. What we all are looking for is safety, the ability to be ourselves around someone without judgment, and the security in knowing that he will always be there for us through thick and thin.

Sadly enough, I'm still trying to define my own relationships and purpose in life. But I have come to realize that one of the best unions one can ever have through this process is learning to love yourself.

I continued to date men from all backgrounds in search of Mr. Right. Chocolate burnout was no longer an issue. And yes, I still had sweet cravings for chocolate treats every once in a while.

Finding the right man who was loyal and committed and safe was my problem at hand.

So what I learned in the process was simple: a man is a man no matter what flavor, yet a committed man has a distinguished flavor of his own.

THE END

Brandon's Story
Chocolate Burnout Part: 2
Nonchcocophobia
Brandon Fabes has his challenges in life. He has a
psychopathic ex-girlfriend. He is now being charged by
Glenview police over the disappearance of Astrid Issa.
There Are Four Sides To Every Story.
Indulge in this sweet addictive 7 part series.

Emunah La-Paz c/o Little Ant Productions

Website: www.eumunahlapaz.com

Emunah La-Paz researches and covers realistic
events through countless interviews featuring men and
women who deal with real-life issues in their
relationships.

Made in the USA
Coppell, TX
07 May 2022

77535174R00184